The
LEAP
YEAR
Proposal

Also by Susan Buchanan

Sign of the Times

The Dating Game

The Christmas Spirit

Return of the Christmas Spirit

Just One Day – Winter

Just One Day – Spring

Just One Day – Summer

Just One Day – Autumn

A Little Christmas Spirit

The LEAP YEAR Proposal

SUSAN BUCHANAN

Copyright

First published in 2025 by Susan Buchanan

Copyright © 2025 Susan Buchanan
Print Edition

Susan Buchanan has asserted her right to be identified as the author of this Work in accordance with the Copyright, Designs and Patents Act 1988.

This novel is a work of fiction. Names and characters are the product of the author's imagination and any resemblance to actual persons, living or dead, is entirely coincidental.

All rights reserved. No part of this publication may be reproduced, stored in a retrieval system, or transmitted in any form or by any means, electronic, mechanical, photocopying, recording or otherwise, without the prior permission of the copyright owner.

A CIEP catalogue record of this title is available from the British Library.

Paperback 978-1-915589-03-3

Dedication

For Tony
Well, you did give me the germ of the idea for the story,
albeit unwittingly.

About the Author

Susan Buchanan lives in Scotland with her husband, their two young children and a crazy Labrador called Benji. She has been reading since the age of four and had to get an adult library card early as she had read the entire children's section by the age of ten. As a freelance book editor, she has books for breakfast, lunch and dinner and in her personal reading always has several books on the go at any one time.

If she's not reading, editing or writing, she's thinking about it. She loves romantic fiction, psychological thrillers, crime fiction and legal thrillers, but her favourite books feature books themselves.

In her past life she worked in International Sales as she speaks five languages. She has travelled to 51 countries and her travel knowledge tends to pop up in her writing. Collecting books on her travels, even in languages she doesn't speak, became a bit of a hobby.

Susan writes contemporary romantic fiction, partly set in Scotland, usually featuring travel, food or Christmas, but always with large dollops of friendship, family and community. When not working, writing or caring for her two delightful cherubs, Susan loves reading (obviously), the theatre, quiz shows and eating out – not necessarily in that order!

You can connect with Susan via her website www.susanbuchananauthor.com or on Facebook www.facebook.com/susancbuchananauthor and on Twitter @susan_buchanan or Instagram authorsusanbuchanan.

Acknowledgements

Huge thanks to

Claire at Jaboof Design Studio for my gorgeous cover. I know this one was a stretch and we had to pivot a great deal, but you managed admirably!

Perfect Prose Services for proofreading www.perfectproseservices.com

Paul Salvette and his team at BB Ebooks for book formatting www.bbebooksthailand.com

Wendy Janes, Catherine Ferguson, Katy Ferguson, Heather Harkin, Babs Wilkie, Fiona Graham, Susan Allan and Anne Pack for doing such an incredible job of beta reading for me.

Suzanne Cowen for naming Zach's cat, Gypsy

Jodi Wresh for naming the breed of cat – Nebelung

The Procrastination Begone WhatsApp group

The Scottish chapter of the Romantic Novelists' Association

The Romantic Novelists' Association

My Advance Review team whose reviews and sharing info on my books on social media helps greatly

Susan Buchanan's Bookworms Facebook group

Rachel from Rachel's Random Resources for filling up my blog tour to maximum capacity and to all the amazing bloggers taking part.

Sue Baker of the Riveting Reads and Vintage Vibes Facebook group for my launch day celebration and general all-round support.

Thanks to the following Facebook groups:

Lizzie's Book Group, run by the amazing Lizzie Chantree, for constant support.

The Friendly Book Community and its wonderful admins

Chick Lit and Prosecco, run by the fabulous Anita Faulkner

To all of my super-supportive fellow authors – your support is much appreciated.

Most important of all – my family. To my children for putting up with me and my deadlines, and to my husband, for feeding me and doing the laundry.

And to you, my dear readers. Thank you for continuing to invest your time and energy in my books. It means everything to me, as do your lovely comments. If you want to connect with me about my books, feel free to email me at susan@susanbuchananauthor.com

Chapter One

Anouska

Friday 20 December

Oh shit! I can't be. What am I going to do?

Anouska glanced down at the white stick in her hand – two distinct blue lines and then *2–4 weeks pregnant* appeared.

No, no, no!

Anouska needed a couple of minutes to compose herself. Pregnant. But how? She was on the pill. She didn't recall any accidents.

Her stomach churned as she considered the ramifications. How would she run her business with a baby? She wouldn't be able to jet off to the States or Asia whenever she felt like it.

In eight months she would be a mother. What the hell was she going to do? Her lifestyle would have to completely change. More importantly, what would Zach say? They hadn't wanted children – they were too busy with their careers and happy as a couple. They'd both thought children would only dilute that.

Her head was a whirl of thoughts. She'd have to delegate even more work to her staff, train up new people.

Who would replace her whilst she was on maternity leave? How much maternity leave could she reasonably take?

Her heartbeat sped up. Never mind the work stuff. She was going to be a mum. She and Zach were going to be parents. Dear, sweet Zach who had spent the last few years working fourteen-hour shifts, opening his travel bookshop and bistro and turning it into the success it now was. They barely had time for a relationship, let alone a baby – babies took up a lot of time. A crazy amount of time. Nothing would ever be the same again.

What a mess. With a final thought to the imminent upheaval to her life, Anouska unlocked the bathroom door and returned to her office.

'You OK?' her assistant, Leigh-Ann, asked. 'You're looking a bit peaky.'

Anouska made a face. 'Bit of a dicky tummy. The joys of jet lag.'

Leigh-Ann gave a wry smile. 'I guess I've that to look forward to, what with my trip to the Maldives.'

'Let's hope not. I need you firing on all cylinders.' Anouska grinned and Leigh-Ann smiled at her.

As Leigh-Ann ran through the messages that had come in and discussed the matters she considered most pressing, Anouska's primary thought was that she'd have to be ultra-careful. She couldn't have Leigh-Ann finding out before Zach.

Anouska was pretty sure she'd managed to get through the day without Leigh-Ann twigging something was wrong. She felt a bit guilty about duping Leigh-Ann into thinking she was tired from her flight back from Singapore, or even suffering from the aeroplane food, but needs must. No, now she had another problem. Zach. She was dreading him coming home. He knew her too well and she was afraid he would guess something was up before she had mentally prepared herself. She needed time to regroup after seeing him and before delivering the news of her pregnancy.

Her life was about to be put in a spin-dryer and put on fast spin, yet no matter how difficult life became, she was having this baby. She just hoped Zach wanted it, too, as she loved Zach more than she'd ever loved anyone, and she couldn't imagine her life without him, but if it came to a choice between Zach and the baby, the baby would win. Anouska exhaled heavily and sat down on the sofa, her hand gripping the armrest. Wow, where had that come from? The baby was barely a collection of cells at the moment. Clearly the maternal instinct to protect was strong. Anouska placed her hand on her abdomen, a twinge of excitement pulsing through her as she spoke her first words to her unborn child. 'I'm here for you, baby. Whatever happens.'

Anouska had paced the flat a hundred times, waiting for Zach to come home so she could get this over with. Her thoughts boinged around in her head like the fast balls in a game of squash. Gypsy, Zach's cat, eyed her from the single armchair.

Anouska only hoped Zach understood why she had to keep the baby, and even more importantly, she hoped she could count on his support; otherwise, where would that leave them? A baby hadn't figured in their plans, but ultimately it was a part of them, so there was no way she could ever contemplate getting rid of it, and that was without even considering the moral implications.

Exhaustion swept over her and she reclined on the bed, the revelation and the subsequent self-analysis too much for her. Within minutes she was yawning.

She woke around midnight. Alone. She vaguely recalled flopping onto the bed around half past ten. Where was Zach? Her hand landed on her phone. She switched on the bedside lamp to find she'd received a text from Zach telling her not to wait up as they had some late diners scheduled and he wouldn't be home until around two. Normally, Anouska would have felt aggrieved at the situation, but despite wanting to relay the news to Zach earlier, now she was grateful for the reprieve.

Saturday 21 December

The next morning Anouska woke at ten o'clock. This time Zach's side of the bed had been slept in, but he was still notable by his absence.

'*You must have been shattered,*' said Zach's note. '*I didn't want to wake you, or rather I did, and wanted to do some unmentionable things to you, but you were sound asleep. See you around nine tonight. I've left you some* kofte *in the fridge. Have a good day, Zach x.*'

How long had she slept?

She had been truly out of it. But she couldn't wait until tonight to see him. And it was just as well she had woken up when she did as she needed to crack on with work, because the items on her to-do list were stacking up. At least it was the weekend and she didn't need to go into the office. Leigh-Ann knew her better than she knew herself, so there would be no hiding the difference in her behaviour from her. She'd already eyed her suspiciously yesterday, albeit she hadn't cottoned on to the enormity of the situation, just called her on being out of sorts.

Today she'd work from home, bury herself in her emails and projects, something familiar, to stop her from overanalysing every detail of her impending motherhood.

And on Monday, she needed to call the doctor or nurse or midwife about what to do next and who she was supposed to see. With a yawn, she sat up on the edge of the bed, allowed her brain to catch up, then headed for the shower.

As the welcome jets of water cascaded over her body, taking away the aches in her muscles, she pondered once again how to tell Zach. Her shower lasted longer than usual as she stood hoping for divine intervention to help her cope with this monumental change in her life.

Beach Esplanade was quieter than usual as Anouska strolled along the promenade, most people opting to do last-minute Christmas shopping in the city centre. She'd be heading there shortly, too, to see Zach at Bean There.

But first she needed the bracing North Sea air to not only blow those cobwebs away but work their magic so she could work out how to tell Zach.

It was such alien territory to her that she wasn't sure how to broach the subject of her pregnancy. And she couldn't exactly hang about; they were rarely in the same time zone, for goodness' sake.

A father of twin girls with platinum-blonde curls, who were probably around the age of two or three, ran onto the beach, chasing them as they shrieked with delight. Anouska's lips curved into a smile. That could be her and Zach soon. Her right hand flew to her stomach, as if in acknowledgement.

As she followed them down onto the beach, she was glad she'd put on her walking boots. They made trudging along the sand that bit easier. At the water's edge, she felt once again captivated by the sheer power of the sea. Sometimes it was as if it held the answers to life's great secrets. She hoped that was true today as she was seeking those answers deep within herself and coming up short. Why didn't she feel ready to tell Zach about the baby? What was stopping her? Why was she hesitating? Zach loved her, she loved him. Simple. Except Zach had always been clear about one thing – he didn't want children.

Anouska approached Bean There with more than a little trepidation. This could be the end of something beautiful or the start of something even more wonderful. She hadn't the faintest idea how Zach would react, but she'd made up her mind – she was telling him today, now.

She meandered along Union Street, looking in all the shop windows, including a baby boutique. She smiled at the tiny Baby-gros and cute motifs, as well as the 'hand-knitted' cardigans.

Finally, she reached Bean There. She stood admiring the new window display, fully aware it was a delaying tactic, but she wasn't quite ready. So she drank in every detail about Moroccan architecture and cuisine, New Zealand's

Eastern Seaboard and Koh Yao Noi in Thailand. Three places she had never been, and most likely would never go now, or at least, not for the next seventeen years.

When she had no further excuse not to enter, she took a deep breath, urged herself to be strong and pushed open the door.

Zach was holding court with a group of regular diners so didn't notice her come in. One of the diners saw her standing waiting, and nodded in her direction, causing Zach to turn around.

'Anouska, I'm so glad you came. Sleep well?'

She nodded.

Zach turned back to his customers and said, 'Would you excuse me for a second?'

Anouska followed Zach into the office. He held her hands, gazed into her eyes, then pulled her towards him, kissing her then nuzzling into her neck.

When they broke apart, he said, 'How was Singapore?'

'Good. We got the contract.'

'I'd expect nothing less. Well done.' He kissed her again, this time with more passion, until she knew where the term 'weak at the knees' had originated. 'I've missed you. This trip more than ever. This hardly seeing each other is killing me. Will our schedules ever calm down? I just want some time for us. Just the two of us. Not the bistro, not the constant travelling, just us.'

Anouska's heart shattered into a million pieces.

How can I tell him now?

Monday 23 December

Over the past few days Anouska had looked for opportunities to tell Zach, but there had never seemed a good moment. She'd had plenty of time to reflect on her situation and work out what to say to him, but it hadn't helped. She had no idea how she was going to tell him, short of saying, 'Oh, by the way, darling, we're going to be parents,' or, 'Great news, I'm pregnant.' And since she knew pregnancy had been a dealbreaker with his ex, she wasn't finding it easy to confront the topic head-on.

After a jam-packed day of work, she'd decided to return to the harbour front to clear her head, literally this time, as her head was pounding. It had helped a little last time. However, although the weather had been cold but pleasant when she'd set out, it had changed in the past fifteen minutes and the wind gusting in from the North Sea buffeted her as signs of an impending storm increased. If she stayed out here any longer, she risked brain freeze.

She knew she should have paid more attention to the forecast, but she had other things on her mind. Anouska adjusted her scarf and tightened the belt of her woollen trench coat as she headed towards the city centre.

The warming glow of the lights of Bean There shone out like a beacon in the midst of all the drizzle and enveloping darkness as Anouska hurried towards it.

Five o'clock, almost. The bistro was busy despite the inclement weather, or perhaps because of it. A welcome blast of hot air greeted her as she opened the door to her refuge.

'Nush!' Zach's business partner, Todd, enveloped her in a cloud of Issey Miyake, then caught up on her news before taking her order.

'Hi, gorgeous.' Zach planted a kiss on Anouska's lips to smiles from some of the bistro's clientele. 'How was your day?'

'Busy. Yours?'

'The same. Todd said you've ordered some quiche. I haven't had my break yet, so if things start to quieten down, I could eat with you.'

'That would be great. We've hardly seen each other since I got back.'

'I know. It has been a busy week. Always is at this time of year. Tell you what, why don't I see if Todd can manage in here on his own for the last few hours tonight, and I'll come home and make it up to you?'

'Sounds good.'

Zach stood up, dropped a kiss on her head and strode over to the counter to talk to Todd.

'We need to do this more often.' Anouska snuggled into Zach's side as they watched a romantic comedy they'd seen countless times before, Gypsy purring contentedly at Zach's feet.

'I know. We both work so much. I'm always at the bistro and you're away travelling all the time.' After a brief pause, Zach said, 'Do you think you'd ever want to move abroad?'

Anouska considered this then said, 'Never really thought about it. I like Aberdeen, even if I'm rarely home these days. It's nice to have roots.'

'I know what you mean. I've lived here all my life and if I couldn't see the sea every day, it would feel as if the world had tilted on its axis.'

'Well, how about we buy somewhere bigger someday? This flat's nice but it's a bit bijou.'

'I like bijou,' replied Zach, feigning indignation.

'You know what I mean. We have to keep decluttering so we have enough room.'

'Everybody knows that if you buy a bigger house, you end up filling it up with even more crap.'

'But we can't live here forever. We need to have our own place, one we've both chosen.' It had always niggled at Anouska that she'd been forced to adopt the flat Zach's aunt had left him in her will. It would have been churlish to ask him to move at the time, but now she wanted somewhere to make her own, their own.

'Hmm,' Zach said. 'Let's not fight. C'mon, your turn to fetch the Pringles.'

As Anouska retrieved more snacks, she kicked herself. Her introduction of the house topic was meant to act as a lead-in to revealing her pregnancy to him, but that had fallen flat. The longer she waited, the harder it would be. She needed to do it, and soon.

Chapter Two

Ellie

Christmas Eve

Ellie was working from home when her phone rang.

'Ellie, it's Trish.'

'Hi. Are you looking for the proofs for next year's brochure? They're not quite done.'

'No, nothing to do with the proofs. Since I won't see you today, I'm calling to tell you I've handed in my notice.'

'You're joking!' Ellie loved working for Trish. She was a great boss, who made her staff work hard, but she wasn't a slave-driver. They respected her and she was decent, plus she gave praise where it was due.

'No, I've been headhunted by a luxury holiday company. Elite Holidays. Do you know it? They want me as managing director.'

Ellie recalled seeing their stand at a trade show.

'Yes, I've heard of it. Congratulations. That's a major step up for you.' She hesitated a second then said, 'But we'll miss you so much.' Her voice caught. She truly meant it. Who would be marketing director now?

'Thanks, and it is. Anyway, apart from wanting to keep you in the loop, I also thought you should know I've spoken to Mike.'

'Oh?'

'Yes. I made it clear I'd like you to take over from me.'

'Wh-a-a-t? But I don't have the—'

'Yes you do,' Trish cut in. 'In spades. It will still have to go out to interview, but hopefully that'll be a formality. You know the way this place works.'

She did indeed. 'So, when do you finish up?'

'Oh, I have to give the usual three months' notice, so end of March.'

Ellie was quiet for a second as she tried to take it all in.

'I don't know what to say. I mean, I know it's not in the bag yet, but thanks for championing me.'

'You're welcome. Also, although as you quite rightly put it, it's not a dead cert, I'm confident enough of your success that I'd like to offer you the possibility of shadowing me for the next few months, let me pass on my knowledge to you, introduce you to my contacts, that sort of thing.'

'That would be great, thanks.'

'There's one more thing. The powers that be have decided that the new marketing director is to work out of the Manchester office.'

'Oh!' Ellie's bubble burst almost immediately. That was that then.

'Is something wrong?' Trish asked.

'No, no, nothing,' Ellie lied. 'Quite the opposite.' Now she was protesting too much.

'In that case, once you're back in the office, we'll discuss it in more detail, but for now, I'll let you get back to work.'

'Thanks, Trish. I really appreciate it.'

'No problem. Merry Christmas.'

'Merry Christmas, Trish.' Ellie stared at the phone for a full ten seconds before she hung up, still in shock. The promotion she'd been after for, literally, years had landed almost at her feet but with a sting in the tail – she'd have to leave Scotland, and Scott.

Now she really did have a dilemma.

'Sorry I'm late.' Scott swept into her flat laden down with bags, kicking the door closed with his foot. As he reached her sitting on the sofa, laptop on her knees, he leant over and kissed her on the lips, before holding the bags up. 'Here you go. M&S Christmas dinner for two. We'll just have it today instead of tomorrow.' He frowned. 'You still working?'

'I know, I know. I'm nearly done. I promise. But since you didn't arrive when I expected, I just kept on working.'

'The traffic was crazy. I mean, I know it's Christmas, but it was nose-to-tail. We're going to a party in an hour and a half. Aren't you getting ready?'

'Well, yeah, but I'm not going to put on my dress until just before we go, am I? Don't want to get my dinner down myself.'

'Fair point,' Scott said. 'Right, let's get this party started. I'll hop in the shower and you can open the wine and let it breathe. Then laptop off. Do you hear?'

'All right, bossy.' Ellie softened when he kissed the nape of her neck as she turned round to face her screen again.

'I don't know if I can face going out now,' Ellie said as she stroked her stomach. 'I am absolutely stuffed.'

'There's a joke in there somewhere, but I won't go there.'

'Oh, please don't. I certainly couldn't think about that right now. I can barely move. Pass the remote, will you?'

Scott laughed. 'And I'm supposed to be the old fogey in this relationship.'

'You are, but your metabolism is higher than mine. Either that or I'm just greedier. I honestly think if I move, I might explode. Can we just sit quietly for a bit? We can go out later. It's Christmas Eve. We should be staying in to watch *Elf, Miracle on 34th Street* and *The Holiday,* anyway.'

'If you're going to make me watch romcoms, I need more wine. In fact, I may need some gin.'

'Ha, ha. It's not that bad. Let's settle in for the film, then later we can go to the party and arrive fashionably late.'

As Scott returned with his gin, Ellie snuggled into him, careful to keep the remote her side of the sofa. She didn't want to end up watching *Diehard* or some fantasy movie. She laughed at the realisation Scott probably thought her romcoms were fantasy – no reflection of real life. But it was the season of goodwill and she wanted to feel that warm glow that permeated the world at this time of year. She could honestly do without going out to the party. It was a colleague of Scott who had engineered it all, since their department hadn't had a Christmas party this year, and he'd suggested they bring partners. She was beginning to wish they'd just gone on their own. She'd quite happily watch back-to-back films on Christmas Eve and spend Christmas morning with Scott, but they'd committed to going now.

Christmas Day

'Merry Christmas.' Scott stood over the bottom of her sleigh bed, two mugs of tea in his hands.

'Merry Christmas,' she said sleepily as she took in the welcome sight of liquid sustenance and a potential hangover cure. Someone was bungee-jumping on her head. How much had they drunk last night? She knew she should have stayed home.

Scott set the mugs down on the pine bedside table, then climbed back into bed and hooked an arm around Ellie's waist. Dormant parts of her began to wake as he moulded his body the length of hers. The hairs on his chest tickled her back and she finally flipped over to find he was every bit as turned-on as she was. As he traced kisses down her throat, she feared the tea would have to wait.

Afterwards, as they lay entangled in the sheets, sweat encasing their bodies, Scott said, 'Oh, I almost forgot, present time.' He delved beneath the bed and came back up with his hand behind his back. Ellie had squirrelled his present away in the bedside cabinet and took the opportunity to remove it from its hiding place.

'Me first.' She handed over the carefully wrapped box, containing the Hugo Boss watch he'd been banging on about for ages.

Scott ripped off the shiny paper like a child on…well…Christmas morning. 'Aw, Ellie, this is just the one I wanted. Thanks!' His excitement made Ellie beam at him and gave her a warm glow inside. He placed the Ambassador on his wrist and admired it from every angle then said, 'Now you.'

Ellie took the envelope he held out, and undid the flap.

She opened the card and out fell fifty pounds' worth of vouchers for her favourite outdoor clothing shop. Useful, but not the most romantic gift ever. Exactly the same as he had bought her for her birthday in June, even down to the amount. She couldn't help but feel a little dejected, yet she did her best to hide her disappointment.

'I thought you could put it towards a new North Face jacket.'

'Yes,' said Ellie, distractedly. Did he have anything else to give her? She'd been dropping hints for months about wanting to go to see The Toussaints in concert. And if not, what of the other five presents she had bought him? Could she give them to him or would it look ridiculous? The watch itself cost two hundred and fifty pounds, and whilst she knew that had been an extravagance, she'd seen a light in his eyes when he looked at it in the jeweller's window, that would have rivalled the Christmas lights in London's Carnaby Street. Sure, the other presents were smaller: a Ralph Lauren shirt, a joke present of a cuddly reindeer, a subscription to *The Economist*, a Christmas jumper with everything on it – from Christmas puddings to candy canes, Christmas trees to snowflakes – and last but not least, tickets to the 3-D planetarium in Bristol. That would also involve trains or planes and a hotel stay. Maybe they could go Dutch on that.

Scott hopped out of bed. 'Right, I'm going for a shower.'

So that was the end of the gift-giving then. Perhaps she would give him the remainder of his presents throughout the day.

She pulled the duvet up around her and eyed the voucher. Why did she never learn? Every year she thought maybe he would put some actual thought into her gift, but he seemed to be making less effort, not more. Did familiarity really breed contempt? Or was he just one of those men who were rubbish at choosing presents for their partners? It was so frustrating. She tried to take her mind off her disappointment by thinking of seeing the excitement on Rosie's face later as she told Ellie Santa had been and showed her the presents he'd brought her.

Her niece was three now and for Ellie, Christmas was all about the kids. She'd love to have her own, in time. It was ridiculous that in six years of being together, Scott had always managed to sidestep the topic of having children. That said, the future itself seemed to be a taboo area. Every time Ellie made even the slightest noise about where they might be in a few years' time, Scott would say they were fine as they were. With a sigh, Ellie swung her legs over the edge of the bed and went to make proper coffee. She needed it.

'You look really good in that dress,' Scott said when she re-entered the room. Once he had finished in the shower, Ellie had luxuriated in the bath for half an hour then tamed her shoulder-length brown curly hair as much as was possible. The forest green vintage dress she wore set off her emerald eyes perfectly and made her feel Christmassy. All that was missing was a pair of reindeer deely boppers, which she had stashed in her bag, and she was ready to go.

Scott put his arms around her, pulling her towards him, an all-too-familiar glint in his eye. 'How long until we have to leave for your parents' house?' he said.

'An hour or so,' breathed Ellie, her disillusionment

with her gifts evaporating for now. She looked up at him. Scott was over a foot taller than her, and had a rugby player's shoulders, which made her feel so petite and feminine next to him.

An hour later, they resurfaced. And as Ellie dressed, she smiled to herself at their second lovemaking session – the man was insatiable – but her thoughts soon turned to the dissatisfaction she'd been feeling lately with her life overall. She loved her job as a marketing executive for a major travel firm, and she was, hopefully, on track to be the next marketing director, if her conversation with Trish was anything to go by. She had a loving, close family and she had plenty of time to indulge her adrenaline-junkie hobbies. But something was missing – she was ready for commitment. Wasn't Scott? Why did they never discuss it? Surely that couldn't be normal given how long they'd been dating. Ellie knew she could let this stew in her brain for days, weeks, months, but equally she knew she had to do something about it – she needed to call in the big guns – Chloe would know what to do. And she'd start on her plan of action this very afternoon if she could get her sister alone.

'Merry Christmas, sweetheart.' Ellie's mum enveloped her in a hug and only released her to accost Scott. 'Scott, dear. Come in. Lovely to see you. Give us a hug. Merry Christmas.' When her mum let him go, she said, 'The others are in the living room. Help yourself to a drink.'

Turning back to Ellie, her mum guided her into the kitchen, then said, 'What happened to the new shirt you bought him? That thing he's wearing is like a bag of rags compared with the Ralph Lauren one.'

'Shh, he'll hear you.' When her mother continued to wait for an explanation, Ellie blew out a breath and said, 'If you must know, I haven't given him all his presents yet.'

'Why not? It's two o'clock. We've always opened our presents on Christmas morning.'

'I know, but I just haven't. I gave him the watch and I'm keeping the others until later, OK?'

Her mum's eyes narrowed. Ellie knew her mother could smell a rat at ten paces, but she wasn't having this conversation now. She was looking forward to Christmas dinner, and she didn't want to spoil the atmosphere. Plus, she was hoping to talk to Chloe and spend time with Rosie. As if on cue the mini-whirlwind spun into the room.

'Auntie Ell, Auntie Ell,' she screamed, her blonde curls, as unruly as Ellie's own, bouncing everywhere in her excitement.

'Hey, gorgeous girl!' Ellie knelt down, picked up her niece and smothered her with kisses, making her shriek. 'Where's Mummy?' she asked when she'd lowered her to the ground.

'In there,' Rosie announced, dragging Ellie towards the living room.

'Hi, sis.' Ellie bent down and kissed her sister's cheek then nodded at her brother-in-law, Mitchell, who perched on the end of the couch, pretending to listen to her dad but secretly watching whichever Ice Age movie was on in the background, presumably for Rosie. Her dad could bore for Scotland on two topics – fly fishing and carpet bowls – and he liked to do both at every opportunity. Poor Mitchell was too nice to change the subject, so he let her dad witter on. Scott, who had endured her dad's anecdotes in the past, and had learned his lesson, had strategically positioned himself next to Chloe.

'Does anyone want a drink?' Scott asked. A chorus of yeses went up and shortly afterwards, Scott disappeared into the kitchen armed with his mental list. Ellie slid onto the sofa beside Chloe. 'Can we talk after dinner?'

Chloe arched an eyebrow. 'Everything OK?'

'Yeah, just looking for some advice.'

'No problem. Aargh! Rosie, don't jump on Mummy like that.'

'Your nipple has popped out,' Ellie whispered, leaning forward to shield Chloe from the others' view as Rosie jumped up and down on her mum.

Mortified, Chloe pulled her wrap dress back together, adjusted her bra and plonked her daughter on the floor. 'Go rescue Daddy.'

Rosie ran straight to Mitchell and pronounced, 'Daddy, I'm rescuing you, like the brave knight with the princess!'

'Rescuing me?' Mitchell's eyes crinkled in amusement.

'Yes, Mummy said I had to.'

'Out of the mouths of babes,' muttered Ellie as Chloe avoided her father's gaze, which could have rivalled Medusa's in the turning people to stone department.

'Drinks, ladies.'

Ellie could have kissed Scott. His timing was perfect.

After dinner, and once they were in the kitchen alone, Chloe turned to her. 'Spill!'

Taken unawares, Ellie said, 'Wha—?'

'Ellie, when you were born, I somehow knew I would always look out for you, even though I was only two, so what's going on?'

'Well…it's…it's…I don't know if Scott and I want the same things.'

'Has something happened? Have you had a fight? I'll kill him if he's hurt you!' she growled.

'No, nothing like that. It's just, where are we going? We've been together six years and we don't even live together. The only time we spend a full night together is if we go on holiday, or on special occasions.'

'Hmm. And that's not enough for you any more?'

Ellie sighed. 'No, I don't think it is. I mean, we have all the freedom we want, we go on our lovely two-week long-haul holiday, but we spend most of it on the beach or by the pool, so we could be anywhere. And we get drunk and go clubbing and have a good time, but is that it? Is that the sum of my life?'

Chloe eyed her. 'Have you discussed this with Scott?'

Ellie shook her head. 'No, I just had the epiphany this morning.' Pausing to think how to phrase it, she finally said, 'Whenever I try to talk about anything more than another holiday six months from now, he clams up.'

'Els, this isn't like you. You're a straight-talking girl. And Scott loves you.'

'Does he? Sorry, yes, of course he does, and I don't *do* insecure, but I can't be held in this no man's land until he wakes up and decides to make things more permanent.'

'Does he make you happy?'

Ellie hesitated then finally said, 'Yes.'

'Happier than anyone before?'

'I think so.'

'Well, either you continue things at his pace, which is making you unhappy, or you take the initiative, sit him down and talk it through. But before you do so, ask yourself one thing.'

Ellie stared at Chloe, but when her sister didn't elaborate, she said, 'What?'

'What if his answer isn't what you want to hear?'

Ellie bit her lip. She had been thinking the exact same thing herself.

Chapter Three

Jess

New Year's Day

'Five, four, three, two, one, Happy New Year!' the presenter shouted.

The fireworks in Princes Street Gardens lit up the night sky as Mark yelled, 'Happy New Year' in Jess' ear and kissed her.

His kiss still managed to make her melt. Pathetic, she knew, but she was in love with this man and had been for many years.

'Happy New Year.' She lay her head on his shoulder and wrapped one arm around him for warmth. Edinburgh was magnificent, but it was also bloomin' freezing. Minus eight.

They stood silently together, absorbing the impressive display, high over Edinburgh Castle: a smorgasbord of Catherine wheels, rockets and Roman candles.

'I love you, Jess Maitland.'

'I love you back, Mark Featherstone.' She did, and a part of her still hoped for the next ten seconds that he would propose, but when the clock chimed for the twelfth time, it appeared the opportunity had passed him by. Again.

As they cheered along with all the other revellers, Jess tried to suppress a soupçon of doubt over not starting the year quite as she'd hoped. There were more important things than getting married, although right now she was finding it difficult to focus on them. She should be grateful that she was here, on a mini-break, with the love of her life, her soulmate, her best friend, the boy who had fallen for her the first day she'd started at his school.

Mark hugged her to him. 'Come here, you. Let me heat you up.' He folded her into his open jacket, equally as puffy as hers, which effectively gave her another layer. It worked too. They stood enveloped in each other's arms, like the lovers in Rodin's sculpture *The Kiss*, but with more clothes on, yet still Jess felt as if something were missing. Guilt flooded through her at the thought, and she tugged Mark by the hand and led him to one of the food stalls nearby. 'I'm starving. I need some food to soak up the alcohol.'

'On that note, I need more alcohol to go with that food.' Mark's blue eyes twinkled as he leant in and kissed her full on the mouth.

Once the lion's share of the festivities had died down, they made their way back to their hotel in the west end of the city.

'So, where should be our first trip this year?' Mark asked as they strolled along, hand in hand, his thumb tracing small circles in her palm.

Jess had already thought about this in recent weeks, but for very different reasons. She wasn't yet ready to divulge her thoughts on that, though, so instead she said, 'Well, technically, this is our first trip of the year.'

Mark nudged her with his shoulder. 'I meant one that requires a passport.'

'Ah, now you didn't say that,' teased Jess.

'Well, we've done Lisbon, Copenhagen, Amsterdam and Pisa.' Mark ticked off the cities on his fingers.

'And we would have done Prague for New Year if Mum hadn't booked the tickets and the hotel here without us knowing. So we could do Prague. I know you went on James' stag a few years back, but I dare say there wasn't much sightseeing done.'

'I think you might be right there. I remember a clock, loads of pubs, a lot of other stag parties and not a great deal else,' confessed Mark.

'Lisbon was fantastic. And I loved that day trip we took to Sintra, and the monastery. But it was so hot.'

'Yeah, a little too hot, if I'm honest.'

'Any other ideas apart from Prague?' she asked, fishing.

'Hmm, let me think about it. Maybe I'll drop in to the travel agent's when we get back and pick up a few brochures. Sometimes it's easier to decide looking at a glossy brochure than picking something out of a million possibilities on the internet.'

'True. So, you don't fancy doing the independent holidaymaker thing again?'

'Thanks, but no. Not after last time. When we go on holiday, I want us to be able to relax, enjoy the high life, get jiggy.' He waggled his eyebrows.

She grinned. It had indeed been a fiasco, and Mark liked his high-end hotels and numbered seat.

At least the hotel Jess' mum and dad had booked for

them was lovely, and clean, a Georgian townhouse with an incredible view onto a park, where they had already sat earlier in the day admiring the view and people-watching.

They really needed these few days away. Even though as a teacher, Mark had just over two weeks off at Christmas, Jess had no such respite from the daily grind. She loved her jobs, and being self-employed suited her, but with no holiday pay and with clients in her dog-walking business expecting her to work almost every day of the year, it was difficult to take more than a few days off at a time, which was probably why they tended to opt for city breaks.

Edinburgh certainly knew how to bring in the bells, she couldn't argue with that, but it didn't feel like a real holiday the way their other breaks had, since they only lived forty-five miles away in Glasgow.

Perhaps that's why Mark hadn't proposed. She'd been so sure he would this time. Why hadn't he, for heaven's sake?

When Mark had mentioned the day after Boxing Day that they'd received an invitation to a university friend's wedding in March, she'd felt certain he was sowing the seed. But now nothing. Was he just clueless? They'd been together for, well, forever, almost, yet it didn't seem to occur to him they should be taking those next vital steps in their relationship. She knew he was super laidback, but c'mon, if he was any more laidback, he'd be reclining on a chaise longue.

They had one more day in Edinburgh, then it would be time for her to return to work for a day before heading off on Kelsea's hen weekend in Arran. Perhaps Mark would realise how much he missed her when she was in Brodick with Kelsea, Kelsea's sister Lauren and some of Kelsea's close friends.

She didn't begrudge Kelsea getting married, despite the lack of proposal from Mark. They'd been friends for such a long time, and although she didn't see her ex-neighbour so much nowadays, whenever they caught up, it always felt like they'd seen each other only the day before: a sign of true friendship.

She just wished her own path to married life was further along than its current stasis. But what to do about it?

Thursday 2 January

'Right, Coco, let's go, girl.' Jess led the greyhound down into Queen's Park where a grey squirrel paused to look at them, as if taunting Coco, who was on a lead, then scampered off into the nearby undergrowth. Jess waved to a fellow dog walker who was juggling four dogs on extendable leads. She shivered. Recipe for disaster, unless you knew what you were doing. Jess preferred stress-free walks, plus she wanted to enjoy the time with each dog. She pleaded over and over with Mark about getting a dog, even a small one, although she'd rather have a Pointer or a German Shepherd, but he stood firm each time, saying they tied you down – OK, they did, but they were so much fun, and gave so much affection.

She was so glad that in the absence of having her own dog, she'd had the brainwave a couple of years ago of supplementing her yoga and aerobics instructor work with her own dog-walking business. Pawsitive Pooches had been born and she'd never looked back since. In fact, she now had to turn business away. Fifteen dogs was quite enough.

There was only her, after all, and she already had a successful fitness business. It was as well she always had bags of energy.

As she passed the pond, ear buds in, listening to her favourite playlist, she breathed in the fresh air, and as she exhaled her breath formed a cloud in front of her. She was lucky living so close to the park. She wasn't made for being indoors all the time. An office job would have killed her. Fortunately, she loved her classes at Victoria Road Leisure Centre, and the mix of exercise classes and dog walking was a good one for her. Moreover, it meant she didn't need to worry about finding time to work out. How many people could say that? And it wasn't your traditional nine to five. Plus, she passed her days with her favourite people. Well, not people, her furry friends, but to be honest, she generally preferred animals, or at least dogs, to people. You knew where you were with dogs. And they were always pleased to see you. Always forgave you. Every little slight. Spending an hour with Coco, or one of her other charges, was the perfect antidote to not being able to cuddle up on the sofa of an evening with a dog of her own.

She dropped Coco back with Wilfred, her elderly owner, and chatted with him for a few minutes. He'd inherited her from his son when he died tragically in a car crash, but unfortunately Wilfred was in no position to walk her as he was too infirm, hence he'd engaged Jess' services. At least Coco provided him with some company, though, and he doted on her. Jess knew she was often the only person Wilfred saw in a day, so the fact he at least had Coco with him all the time made her feel a little better. Coco would bark the house down if anything were ever wrong with her owner.

With a cheery, 'See you tomorrow,' she headed off to pick up Rocky.

As Jess approached Rocky's house, she smiled. Mark called him Rocky the Riot, and sometimes Rocky the Rocket. He was your proverbial St Bernard in a china shop. Jess didn't allow herself favourites, but if she had, Rocky would have topped her list. Brown and white, enormous, even by St Bernard standards, he was a walking, running, knocking-you-over barrel of fun. And at two, he was still growing. Never mind her walking him, it was definitely the other way around, and at this rate, she'd be able to ride him soon. All that was missing was the saddle.

She was still about fifty yards away from the house when she heard him barking, then whining, then scrabbling at the door. His poor owner was at his wits' end and had to regularly repaint sections of the house as Rocky scratched and tore at everything. And then there was the chewing. She surveyed the mid-terraced house for a moment, wondering at why some owners chose certain breeds of dogs without truly considering the consequences or factoring into the equation the size of their home. At least Rocky didn't live in a one-bedroom flat like the Pointer she walked.

Since Rocky's owner was at work, she let herself in with the key, and the minute she opened the door, he almost bowled her over in his enthusiasm to see her and indeed go for a walk. She kept a lead in the van especially for him, because if she'd had to go in and fetch his from the kitchen, half the house would have been destroyed in the process, such was Rocky's eagerness to go for his walk.

Once he'd licked her to show his joy at her arrival, she gave him a puppy treat and he sat until she calmed him.

Then they set off. She was keen to reach the park as soon as possible, as handling a St Bernard in a park was one thing, being dragged through the busy roads of the south side of the city quite another. It wasn't the first time she'd almost been mangled under the wheels of a number three bus.

But once in the park, Rocky was happy to walk beside her, albeit he pulled on the lead a little, OK, a lot. They had an understanding, though. Rocky would stop at the same bench every day and await his puppy treat, which was problematic if there was someone else sitting there, although they soon vacated it, clearly not wanting to mess with a St Bernard, or perhaps be slobbered on. Then they would sit for five or ten minutes simply enjoying the view, until Rocky saw a rabbit, or more commonly a squirrel, or another dog. And then all hell would break loose.

By the time Jess returned from her walks, she was a little sweaty and dishevelled. She decided to shower before packing for the hen weekend. *Why is everything always so close together? First Christmas, then our New Year trip away, and now the hen weekend on Arran.* Even when you had a holiday, once you returned, it never really felt like you'd had one, as you always had to catch up after being away. She shouldn't complain though, as it was so rare for her to have time off, never mind so much time in only a few weeks.

She had to admit, though, she was really looking forward to seeing both Kelsea and Lauren, the sisters who'd lived next door to her when she was growing up. Apart from Mark, they'd been her two confidantes, and the four of them always got up to mischief. Nothing dramatic, just loads of fun. She couldn't imagine that Kelsea's hen weekend would be anything other than phenomenal.

Once she'd showered, she noticed the pile of mail on the table. It must have arrived before Mark left for school. Her hand rested on an elegant, posh-looking envelope. Cream. Embossed seal. The writing was as sophisticated as a calligrapher's. *What's this? Another wedding invitation. You have got to be joking. What is there, an epidemic? A fire sale on wedding dresses? Unprecedented discounts at luxury hotels? A run on the markets?* She'd almost missed it too, hidden as it was amongst all the late Christmas cards.

Carefully, she slit the envelope open with a paperknife – Mark's. He was very OCD about things like that. Hated his letters to be ripped open.

You are cordially invited to the marriage of Casey and Millicent.

Jess snorted. *Millicent.* Milly hadn't been Millicent since her christening, she expected. Certainly, when Mark had spoken of her, and on the few occasions their paths had crossed, no one had called her Millicent, not even her parents. *Millicent* was one of Mark's friends from his Cambridge days.

It was all becoming too much for her. No New Year proposal, Kelsea's hen weekend, yet another wedding invitation – they'd only just been to a wedding in October, for goodness' sake. Plus, they'd received one on Boxing Day for a wedding in March.

Jess' jaw clenched. No, she knew what she had to do: take control of her life. Fate was only good for so much. She had to put herself back in control of her own destiny. If he wouldn't propose, then she would. And by the end of the year, come what may, she would marry this man.

Chapter Four

Anouska

Saturday 4 January

Someone rapped at the door. 'Anouska, are you in there?' Lauren. 'Are you all right? You're not throwing up are you? Do you need me to hold your hair back for you? Wouldn't be the first time.' She laughed.

Anouska quickly wiped her mouth and cupped her hands under the tap to collect some water to drink. 'I'm fine. I'll be there in a minute.'

'OK.'

She knew it had been a bad idea to come to Kelsea's hen weekend. She'd never be able to conceal this from Lauren. Ever since they'd first met at Freshers Week at the University of Aberdeen, Lauren had had the uncanny ability of being able to read her – too well.

Hen nights and mass social gatherings weren't Anouska's thing anyway, but with a huge secret to hide and being unable to drink alcohol to pretend she didn't feel socially inept in these situations, the weekend was fast becoming her worst nightmare.

A few seconds later, the click clack of heels on the wooden flooring told her Lauren had taken her at her word.

Anouska freshened up, spritzing herself more liberally than usual with perfume, and gargled water to try to remove the acidic taste from her mouth, then sighed and headed back into the fray.

From the living area, the strains of Abba's 'Dancing Queen' filtered through, and the sound of raucous laughter and cheering. The celebration was in full swing.

As the girls murdered a few more songs, Anouska tried to block it all out. Already, only two weeks after discovering she was pregnant, she felt positively middle-aged. Did everything really have to be this noisy?

Everyone was laughing, joking and clinking glasses. Kelsea, the bride-to-be, had her arms around Lauren's neck, telling her she was the best sister in the world, whilst one of her friends belted out the next track, the others accompanying her with varying degrees of success. In fact, the only person who wasn't screaming at the top of their voice was Jess, the girl Anouska had mentally nicknamed Peaches because of her peaches and cream complexion, whom Kelsea had introduced earlier that day as her childhood next-door neighbour. She was sitting quietly, observing, sipping her Prosecco. Anouska plonked herself on the sofa beside her. If she couldn't have peace and quiet, she'd take the next best thing.

She wanted to be alone with her thoughts. If she kept a low profile, perhaps she could mask that anything was amiss. She didn't really know anyone else, only Lauren and Kelsea. Hopefully, Lauren would be so caught up in the evening's festivities that she wouldn't notice Anouska was preoccupied, or that she wasn't drinking Prosecco. The pretence was exhausting.

Jess caught Anouska's eye. 'I don't know where they get

their energy from. It's been a great night, but I've hit a wall now.'

Anouska sighed. 'Me too. I wish we'd had dinner. I tried to warn Lauren, but she and Kelsea were having none of it.'

'I know, I'm starving now. And I dread to think how much we've all had to drink. We'll suffer for it in the morning. I will, anyway. I'm not used to drinking so much.'

Anouska smiled at her.

Whilst the others screeched out yet another tune, Anouska saw Lauren watching her and averted her gaze. The last thing she needed was an interrogation. Lauren was too good at prising information out of her.

She chit-chatted with Jess until the weight of someone sitting down on the other end of the sofa caused it to dip and made Anouska list slightly. Lauren. *Drat! I knew I couldn't escape her scrutiny for long.*

'I'm parched. Give us a sip.' Lauren reached out her hand for Anouska's glass, which Anouska held away from her. She couldn't have Lauren knowing she was drinking water at a hen do. Then she'd definitely be suspicious.

'Sorry, I'm a bit funny about people drinking out of my glass. I'll get you one though,' Anouska said.

Lauren frowned. 'How did I not know that about you?' She shook her head as if to say 'No matter' then turned to Jess. 'You want anything?' she asked, before struggling to her feet and heading for the fridge. She came back with an open bottle of Prosecco and two glasses, as if she'd anticipated Jess' response.

As Lauren poured the drinks then sank into the sofa once more, the strains of 'I Will Survive' dimmed until

Anouska felt no one had survived.

She smiled. Clearly the hens were losing momentum, their batteries running low. One by one, they dropped away from the diehard karaoke singers and slumped to the sofa, or headed to the fridge for sustenance. Many returned with only the liquid variety.

Soon all ten of them, energy depleted, were chilling on the sofas murmuring and chatting.

'Kels, we've got some questions about your life with Cooper.' Lauren grinned as she pulled out a handful of postcards from her bag and held them up.

Kelsea groaned. Some of the hens cheered. One snored. Anouska tried not to laugh. Ten women, one luxury lodge, one hell of an excuse for a party, and look at the state of them. She'd normally be the same, but as she hugged the secret she was carrying to herself, she realised she wouldn't be imbibing like this for quite some time. Nine months of pregnancy, and then if she breastfed, it would be longer. Breastfed? Where had that come from? Last month she hadn't known she was pregnant, now she was channelling her inner earth mother.

Lauren stood up and tapped her champagne flute with a teaspoon to gain their attention, lending the moment a sense of drama and occasion. 'Ladies, shall we begin?'

Silence fell over the group and Lauren, glancing around, satisfied she had a captive audience, eyed her sister, then began to read.

'Question one: Where did you first meet Cooper?'

Kelsea stared up at her sister. 'Easy, the bar at the Hydro during the Muse concert.'

Lauren nodded. 'Very good. Question two: Where did you first have sex?'

'Lauren!' Kelsea turned crimson. 'I'm not telling everyone that. It's too personal.'

'Don't talk rubbish.' Lauren scanned the room. 'Is there anyone who doesn't know where Lauren and Cooper first had sex?'

Everyone shook their heads.

'I rest my case.' Lauren turned to Kelsea and quirked an eyebrow.

'OK, OK. It was in his car after the Muse concert.'

The questions continued in this vein, becoming progressively more risqué, until Kelsea called for a timeout.

'I think Kels might kill Lauren later,' said Jess.

Anouska chuckled. 'That's a distinct possibility.'

Once the quiz was over, Kelsea clapped her hands together. 'Right, what's next? Hey, I know. Lauren, where's that magazine you had on the ferry? The one with the wedding quiz.'

'In my bag.'

'Let's see it then.'

Anouska's eyes half-closed. How soon were you meant to feel the effects of being pregnant, the exhaustion, in particular?

'Are you tired too?' asked the girl sitting in the armchair beside her. Ellie, that was her name. Anouska smiled.

Ellie groaned as she shifted in the chair. 'Do you think they'd notice if we sneaked away? I can't keep up with them. I'm an early bird, not a night owl. And I feel like a right party pooper saying so, but I've simply run out of steam.'

'I think we're all fading fast,' said Anouska.

'Except Kelsea. Honestly, that girl could party all night,

and has done.' Ellie shook her head.

Anouska frowned, confused.

'When we shared a flat, we either had parties until all hours of the morning, or if she was out partying, she'd come in at four or five. Then she'd get up at ten, totally refreshed. So unfair.'

'OK, ladies, here we go. My turn to grill you.' Kelsea was clearly relishing her role. She licked her finger and turned the page. 'What's the minimum number of people you'd be happy to have at your wedding?' She glanced around for her first victim.

Anouska took the opportunity to zone out. She was having a hard time not yawning. Two o'clock in the morning and being in your first trimester weren't the best bedfellows, she was discovering.

A few questions later, Anouska was on the verge of falling asleep when Kelsea said, 'This is an interesting one. Would you propose on the twenty-ninth of February, like the old Irish tradition, where a woman can only propose to a man once every four years? That goes to Ellie.'

A shadow passed over Ellie's face, but she quickly recovered before saying, 'At this rate, I may have to.'

The others laughed.

'Yeah, but would you?' Kelsea pressed, before taking a sip of her Prosecco.

Ellie pursed her lips for a few seconds then said, 'I reckon I would, given the right circumstances.'

'Really?' Kelsea squeaked. 'I could never do that. It's a good thing Cooper asked me, or we'd just be living with each other forever.'

Marriage. Even with the weekend's surroundings, it wasn't something Anouska had ever thought about in any detail. She was too independent, too woman of the world. She had to be. It took a lot to run her own human resources company in twelve countries. And although she and Zach loved each other, they were perfectly happy with the status quo.

'What about you, Lauren?' Kelsea asked.

'I'd do it in a heartbeat. Why should the guys have all the fun, and make all the decisions?'

Kelsea's jaw dropped. 'Honestly?'

When Lauren nodded, Kelsea said, 'So why haven't you then?'

'It hadn't actually occurred to me until now. Maybe I'll ask Hunter when we get back.' A smile played on Lauren's lips.

Kelsea batted her on the arm, 'Don't you dare! Wait until my wedding's over first!'

'I would,' Jess whispered to Anouska. 'I'd never really thought about it either, but I would. Would you?'

Wrong-footed, Anouska gave Jess a tight smile and shrugged.

'What are you two whispering about?' Ellie leant towards them on the sofa again, glass of Prosecco swaying around, dangerously close to losing its contents.

'Leap-year proposals. I'd do it,' said Jess again.

'You would? Why?' asked Ellie.

Yeah, why? Anouska wondered.

'Well, since I already decided the day after New Year that by the end of the year we'd be married, it's not much of a hop, skip and a jump to do it on the twenty-ninth of February.'

Ellie gawped, whilst Anouska's eyebrows disappeared into her hairline.

Jess chuckled. 'Mark and I have been together since primary school, we live together and he's lovely and sweet, and he can be so thoughtful, but he is totally oblivious. It wouldn't even occur to him that it's high time he asked. Plus, I want kids in the next few years.'

Ellie nodded slightly at Jess' response. 'Good points. I'd consider doing it, but for totally different reasons.' When Anouska and Jess looked at her, urging her to elaborate, Ellie said, 'I'm beginning to think Scott has commitment issues. Every time I mention the future, he shies away from the topic. We've been together for six years, and we still live in separate houses.'

Anouska gave a sympathetic smile. 'That's tough.'

Ellie sighed. 'And as if that's not bad enough, I've now been offered a job in Manchester, a promotion, actually, *the* promotion I've been after for ages, and if I knew we were going somewhere – marriage, kids, the whole shebang – I'd turn it down. I don't know what to do. There's no chance Scott will move with me, so if I'm going to turn it down, I need to know I'm doing it for a good reason.' She looked at her Prosecco glass. 'This has a lot to answer for. Sorry for oversharing.'

Jess dismissed her concern with a shake of her head then said, 'How would you propose, if you did do it?'

Ellie thought for a moment then blew out a breath. 'I'm not sure, but I'm a bit of an adrenaline junkie, so maybe whilst we were doing a tandem skydive or something.'

Jess' cornflower-blue eyes bulged. 'Oh my God. I could never do anything like that.'

Ellie grinned. 'That would be the easy bit. The asking would be the terrifying part. And if he said no, that would be it. Game over. I think it really is make-or-break time for us.'

'I hear you.' Anouska's thoughts jostled with each other, vying for space in her brain. Jess and Ellie were talking about futures and kids, and here was she, alone with the knowledge she was already pregnant. But they appeared to think marriage and kids went hand in hand. Did it? Was it necessary nowadays?

Had her view on marriage changed now, knowing she was pregnant? She'd barely had time to process the idea of becoming a mum, never mind anything else.

'What about you, Anouska?' Ellie asked. 'Could you see yourself proposing ever, or rather, would you be against doing it?'

Anouska shook her head. 'No, I'm not against doing it. I'd just never really thought about marriage before.'

'You're kidding?' Jess looked gobsmacked and Ellie's eyes widened.

'What? Never ever?' Ellie asked.

Anouska shrugged. 'I'm happy in my own skin. I love Zach, but I've never felt the need to get married to show that. And I'm not very traditional or girlie.' She smiled.

'Each to their own,' said Jess. 'But my mind's made up. I'm going to ask Mark, and soon. This discussion has given me the perfect motivation. Now, I just have to figure out how.'

Ellie smiled at her. 'Well, good luck. I really admire you.' She laughed. 'Maybe I'll do the same.'

'You should,' Jess encouraged her. 'What's the worst that could happen?'

'He could say no.' Ellie grinned.

Anouska laughed. 'That won't happen. I'm sure of it.'

'I wish I was,' said Ellie.

'Hey, you three, is this a private party, or can anyone join in?' Kelsea asked, positioning herself, hands on hips, in front of them.

With a laugh, Anouska turned back to the main group, but not before noticing a complicit look pass between Ellie and Jess.

Chapter Five

Ellie

Sunday 5 January

Next morning, as she sat at breakfast in the hotel which owned the lodges, Ellie smiled to herself. Not a great turnout. Three of the ten had crawled out of bed on time. She wasn't surprised Kelsea and Lauren hadn't, they'd been plastered, but it tickled her that those diehards who had made it to the hotel for food were her, Jess and Anouska, the three who had been chatting late last night.

Anouska hadn't been knocking it back to the same extent as the others as far as she'd seen, and Jess must be hollow as she was chirpy and bouncy this morning. A tad annoying, actually. Not Jess herself, but the fact the alcohol had had little to no effect on her. How lucky. Ellie's head felt as if someone was trampolining on top of it. That's what she got for mixing her drinks. Either fizz or wine, not both. It never ended well. But she liked her food, and fortunately the sporty side of her combated piling on the pounds, so she was never one to pass up a cooked Scottish breakfast in a hotel: potato scones, hash browns, black pudding, sausage, egg and bacon.

She looked up to see Jess staring at her plate.

'What?' she asked.

'N-nothing,' Jess said, but didn't move her gaze. When Ellie stared at her, Jess sighed and explained. 'I wish I could eat all that and still be as slim as you.'

Ellie laughed. 'Look at you. There's nothing of you.'

'Ah,' said Jess, 'but that's because I treat my body like a temple. I'm a yoga and aerobics instructor and dog walker. If I were to eat a cooked breakfast, I'd balloon almost straight away.'

'I don't believe that for a second. Here, live a little.' She held out a hash brown to Jess, who waved her hand to dismiss the offer. 'No, seriously, take it. You could do with fattening up.'

'Hardly.' Jess looked down at her body.

'Jess, Ellie's right, you're rake thin, but, well, with muscles. Must be all that aerobics,' Anouska agreed.

'I wasn't always thin, though, and now I'm more careful of what I eat. Plus, I don't like to put crap into my body.' When Ellie looked at her then at her breakfast and went to push it away, Jess said, 'No, no, eat your breakfast. Sorry, I'm always going on.'

'No need to apologise, but did you really just say "my body is a temple"?'

Jess grinned. 'I sort of did. Sorry, I sounded like a right div, didn't I?'

Ellie nodded. 'Just a bit. So, how did you end up as an aerobics instructor?'

'And more to the point, how did the unusual combination of aerobics instructor and dog walker come about?' Anouska added, smiling.

'Well, I didn't do too badly at school, I suppose. I passed seven NAT 5s, including one in PE, and four

Highers, but I never fancied going to university or college. The concept of saddling myself with all that debt just never appealed.'

'I can't imagine why,' Anouska said dryly.

Jess nodded then continued. 'So after taking some Pilates and yoga classes, I enrolled in a yoga instructor course and managed fairly easily to get a job, even though it meant working two hours here and there, gaps in the middle of the day, then working late sometimes, but it suited me. And although it still does, I've recently supplemented my fitness business with a dog-walking one. And now Pawsitive Pooches is doing well too.'

'Wow, that's impressive.' Ellie stopped with her fork halfway to her mouth. 'I thought I was doing well being offered a promotion.'

'You are doing well,' Anouska and Jess said in unison.

Ellie resumed her breakfast and the conversation flowed, until they realised they were overstaying their welcome, the hovering waitress and the empty restaurant testament to that.

Jess looked at her watch. 'Is that the time? Oh my goodness, we'd better get back. They'll be sending out a search party.'

'They're probably still asleep,' Anouska pointed out.

'Let's settle the bill and then we can text them to let them know where we are. Actually, it's not snowing, or raining, or windy. How about we go for a walk? We've ages before the ferry yet, and I wanted to get a couple of wee things at that gift shop we saw last night. I wonder if it's open today.'

'It's Sunday. Might be shut,' Anouska said.

'Worth a try.' Ellie was determined to be optimistic. 'I

really liked that shop with the handmade soaps and stuff. Plus, I have some Christmas money to spend.'

'That's true.' Jess pulled out her phone. 'I'll text Kelsea.' Her phone rang. 'Ooh, Mark, hi. I wasn't expecting you to be up this early. You've been tidying? At this hour?'

As Jess chatted to Mark, Ellie pulled out her phone and said to Anouska, 'I'll text Kelsea.' She nodded to Jess. 'She may be quite some time.' But she noticed a text from Scott. *What time will you be home? I was thinking of cooking you dinner at yours. Nice bottle of wine? What do you say?*

'I say yes.' She then typed back those exact words, before texting Kelsea the girls' whereabouts, then allowing herself to bask in the prospect of a night of Scott pampering her.

The girls spent a pleasurable afternoon browsing in the very few shops Brodick had to offer, particularly on a Sunday, and hiding from the elements in the cafés. Whilst Ellie, Jess and Anouska nursed mugs of hot chocolate, the others tucked into brunch. All too soon it was time for the ferry and as they trudged on board, dejected at their break having come to an end, Jess said, 'We should keep in touch.'

Anouska eyed her. 'Definitely.'

'Yes, we need to hear all about your plans for your leap-year proposal and how it all goes.' Ellie winked.

'Indeed. But who knows, maybe I won't be the only one proposing.'

'Maybe,' Ellie said, a smile playing on her lips.

'This looks fabulous,' Ellie said as she shrugged off her coat and dumped her bags in the hall. The aroma of spices greeted her as she walked towards Scott, who was wearing a full-size chef's apron, which was already splattered red. What was that spice? Paprika? She wasn't sure, but she was ready to eat. It had been a long time since lunch.

Scott snaked a hand around her waist before leaning down to kiss her on the lips. 'Did you have a good time?'

Ellie dipped her head. 'I did. In fact, I might keep in touch with a couple of the girls I met. Kelsea and Lauren were wild as usual. Karaoke went on way too long. I enjoyed being on Arran itself, the scenery, all that, much more than I did the singing.'

Scott grinned. 'Didn't you have a go yourself?'

'I didn't have much choice. There was no reprieve for anyone. Even if Kelsea had let me off with it, Lauren never would.'

'Sounds like quite a hen party.'

'Oh, it was. But, I *was* one of the few who made it down to breakfast this morning. I'm quite proud of that fact, especially since we were still up at three.'

'Wow, you really were going all out.'

Ellie yawned. 'It's starting to catch up with me now. I think Kelsea was trying to see if we could pull an all-nighter.'

'Glad you enjoyed it. Right, why don't you relax and I'll pop the prawns in?'

Ellie sniffed the air appreciatively. 'What are we having? It smells delicious, whatever it is.'

'Prawn fajitas, but with a twist.'

Ellie raised an eyebrow. 'Ooh, exciting. Right, I'll wash up and then veg on the sofa, if that's OK, until it's ready.

I'm shattered.'

As Ellie went off to freshen up, she couldn't help thinking that when Scott behaved like this, it was so easy for all her doubts and insecurities about the future to vanish. For now she decided to live in the moment without caring what tomorrow would bring.

'Mmm, this is incredible. Is this the first time you've made this?' Ellie asked as she held her tortilla up to her mouth and took another bite.

Scott shook his head. 'I've made it for myself at home a few times. You need to have good quality tiger prawns for it to taste just right. I saw these on offer and figured now was a good time to make it again.'

As Ellie chewed, she gave Scott a thumbs-up.

Later, reclining on the sofa, replete, Ellie decided to test the waters. 'Did I tell you Trish was leaving?'

Scott sat up straighter and plumped a cushion behind him as he turned to face her, his head tilting to the side as he said, 'No, I don't think so. Where's she off to?'

'She was headhunted by Elite Holidays.'

'Very swish. When does she leave?'

'Not for a couple of months yet. They need to find a replacement whilst she works her notice.'

'Surely you must be in with a chance,' Scott said.

'Maybe, but they've moved the role to Manchester.'

'Manchester? What the hell for? What's wrong with Edinburgh? Well, that's that then. Better luck next time.'

A stab of irritation shot through Ellie at his summary dismissal of her applying for the role. How presumptuous of him.

Well, if he wanted her to remain in Edinburgh, he'd need to give her a damn good reason to stay. Maybe Jess had the right idea after all.

Tuesday 7 January

Ellie sat at her desk, her head spinning. She had two new proposals to submit by tomorrow but neither her heart nor her head were in it. This wasn't her, she loved her job, but right now she was having difficulty focusing. She'd been so psyched about the very real possibility of getting the promotion, but now, with a different set of problems to face, it was beginning to overwhelm her.

She couldn't break her thoughts away from her and Scott. Six years. It was a long time to invest in someone, a bit like investing your time in working for a company. She laughed under her breath at the irony. Now she potentially had to choose between her relationship and her dream job. Would another opportunity like this present itself anytime soon? Could she afford to risk it? Was Scott worth fighting for? The very fact she didn't feel she could openly discuss the promotion or its terms definitely added to her stress levels. Was that telling in itself? Surely she should be able to share everything with someone she hoped to spend the rest of her life with. And there it was, the crux of the matter: Did Scott want to spend his life with her?

Ellie doodled on her notepad as the thoughts tumbled over and over in her mind. Maybe Jess did have the right idea. Maybe forcing his hand would be the way to go. Not that she thought that's what Jess was doing. If she'd read the vibe right from Jess, Mark was definitely still into her; he just had blinkers on about getting married or progressing things. Was that the case with Scott? But then she and Scott didn't live together, Jess and Mark did.

Aargh. Her head was pounding with it all. Round and round it all went, no solution ever presenting herself. She was sick of it. She was sick of herself right now. And most of all she was sick of her situation.

Ellie didn't like feeling out of control in her personal life, well, her love life. She far preferred her risk-taking to limit itself to the extreme sports segment of her life. Talking of which, maybe taking some time off would help sort her head out. If she did get the promotion, she knew it would be difficult to get any annual leave for a while, and she had so many days to take.

If she worked late tonight, she could finish these proposals and still hit the slopes at Glenshee tomorrow. Although she loved her job, she was never happier than when outside, not exactly at one with nature, but just out, in the open, breathing fresh air, not being cooped up or hemmed in.

She was sure Trish would go for it and she had no other great plans as she'd been intending to work on both these proposals until close of business tomorrow.

Firing off a text to Trish, who was out of the office today, she sat back in her chair and breathed heavily. This could be just what she needed to clear her mind. She loved the conditions at the Glenshee Ski Centre and the diversity of the slopes. If Trish did give her the day off, she'd book an Airbnb and dig out her skis and snowboard.

Ellie drew her keyboard towards her and soon her fingers were flying over the keys, the proposals virtually writing themselves. What a difference motivation made. By lunch, she'd finished the draft of one proposal and was gearing up to start the next, but she was beginning to fret a little as she hadn't yet heard from Trish. She knew she was probably in meetings, but it didn't make her any less antsy.

She was just slurping down a homemade tomato soup she'd bought at the café two doors down when her phone pinged. Great. Trish must finally have seen her message. But it wasn't Trish, it was Jess.

Hi, Ellie. Hope you're well. You know how you said you'd be happy to meet up? Well, I was wondering if you'd be free on Thursday night. I'd come to you, of course. Not sure if Anouska will be able to make it as she's all the way up in Aberdeen, but I'll ask her, if you can make it. Would be great to see you again and I've had some ideas for my proposal. Squee! Jess x

Well, that was a surprise. She had actually thought they would meet up again, but not so soon. And she supposed Edinburgh did make sense as a meeting place, what with Anouska being in Aberdeen and Jess in Glasgow. Edinburgh kind of formed the right angle of that triangle. Mentally shrugging, Ellie decided why not? She wasn't doing anything on Thursday as she had agreed to go out for dinner with Chloe on Friday and meet Scott on Saturday, so she'd originally intended to have a night in. But hey, there would be time in her thirties and forties to stay in.

She texted back: *Count me in. Does half seven work for you? There's a great café I know called Cirque. It does really delicious hearty soups and has a fab range of grilled panini. It's in Rose Street, the street behind and parallel to Princes Street. Let me know if Anouska can make it. Will be great to see you again x*

Things were looking up. Now, no matter whether Trish sanctioned her holidays or not, she felt galvanised into action. With Jess stepping up and having the courage to propose to Mark, it really hammered home to Ellie how not taking any action was the worst possible thing she could do. Perhaps she could learn something from Jess. Maybe Jess could hand her some of her bravery pills in dealing with her relationship. Despite being fearless on the slopes, when falling out of a plane, dangling from the end of a bungee rope or when base jumping, Ellie did not consider herself brave when it came to talking her mind to her other half, especially when that other half was closed-book Scott.

This was good news. Meeting the girls would do all three of them good. She was sure of it. She really hoped Anouska could make it too as she'd liked her, even if she'd come across as a little reserved.

Ellie started on the second proposal and in two hours it was done. Now all she had to do was check both proposals over, and even though she hadn't heard from Trish, and even though she couldn't go to Glenshee tomorrow without her approval, she didn't care. Fate had taken her life in a new direction. At least tomorrow she'd have a more relaxed work day.

Her phone pinged again then again. *Jess has set up a group chat. Leap-Year Proposals (LYP).* Ha! How perfect. Then, just as she started typing a reply, two messages arrived almost simultaneously.

Look forward to seeing you both on Thursday, Love, Anouska

Hi, girls. Thought it best to set up a group chat. See you both at half seven at Cirque in Rose Street. Can't wait to tell you my ideas. Jess x

Ellie couldn't wait. She emailed her proposals to Trish and gave Ramon, her colleague, a thumbs-up when he asked if she wanted a coffee.

As he passed her the coffee five minutes later, her phone rang.

'Hi, Ellie, it's Trish. How are you?'

'I'm good, thanks. You?'

'You ready to start shadowing me yet?'

'Of course.'

'Great, because I'll be in the office on Friday, thought we could start then.'

'Fantastic.'

'That's sorted then, and you can have tomorrow off.'

Ellie fist-pumped the air, lowering her eyes at Ramon's startled expression as he scuttled past her open office door. 'Thanks, Trish.'

'You doing anything nice?'

'Just a bit of snowboarding.' Well, she was hardly going to say soul-searching, was she?

'Enjoy yourself. If you land the promotion, time off will be but a distant memory.' Trish laughed.

'I will, and I know. Thanks, Trish.'

Ellie replaced the receiver. Time to get her ducks in a row.

Chapter Six

Jess

Thursday 9 January

Jess pressed play on her iPod and the instrumental music for the final class of the day filtered out into the room.

'Ready, ladies?'

A chorus of nods welcomed her and she smiled and said, 'Then let's begin.'

A few minutes later, the women, who were a mixed bag of ages, anything from mid-twenties to mid-sixties, were busy doing the plough pose when the door opened again and a rather dishevelled guy strode in, murmuring a 'Sorry I'm late' and shooting Jess an apologetic glance. She was just about to ask him if he had the right class when she clocked the yoga mat attached to a clip on his back.

Jess gave him an encouraging smile and he unrolled his mat near the back of the class, but not before several of the women's heads had turned in his direction. Gawked would be more accurate. She supposed he was pretty good-looking, with deep mocha eyes, and he was reasonably tall, around five eleven, and there was the fact he was the only male in the class. Jess grinned to herself. Those coming to class to meet a mate had slim pickings, so they'd probably view him as fresh meat. Poor bloke.

She guided them through the bridge, the locust and the tree before switching to autopilot, finally finishing with the mountain pose.

Throughout the class, she'd had to cover her smirk more than once as the women none too discreetly made every excuse to turn in the cute guy's direction. She'd never seen so many dropped water bottles in her life. Her class had become clumsy all of a sudden.

As she tidied up afterwards, saying goodbye to each person as they passed her, a woman stopped to ask her about the times of her Pilates classes. She was deep in conversation with her when she became aware of someone hovering on the edge of her peripheral vision. Turning slightly, she saw it was the cute guy. She gave him a brief smile, which he returned.

'Sorry, I didn't want to interrupt, but I just wanted to say how much I enjoyed the class. I've never done yoga before.'

The woman beside Jess stared at him, and Jess didn't think it was because he'd never done yoga before.

'Excellent. Will we see you back next week then?' Jess asked.

'You can count on it. Oh, I'm Nathan, by the way.' He slapped his head as if annoyed at himself for failing to introduce himself earlier.

Jess smiled. 'Jess.' She was about to thank him for coming when the woman she'd been speaking to interrupted. 'Hi, Nathan. I'm Maureen. A few of us are going for a drink. Do you fancy it?'

Jess tried but failed to hide a smile. She didn't hear what Nathan said as Maureen shepherded him out of the class. A shame. A lamb to the slaughter. He'd never survive.

An hour and a half later, and after a relatively uneventful train journey, Jess approached Cirque, amazed at how few people were around. Did she have the right place? There were no tables outside, but then it was January. They'd freeze to death if they sat outside, even those hardier types and smokers.

The bell dinged gently as she entered and a lilting voice called, 'Be with you in a minute.' She glanced around but saw no one. Maybe they'd missed the rush. It *was* twenty past seven, she supposed. Most people would be safely ensconced in their living rooms under a blanket to ward off the chill, or eating dinner.

She guessed she could sit anywhere since it wasn't exactly busy. She hoped that wasn't testament to the quality of the café's wares. As she glanced round, she took in the mismatched cups and saucers set out on the tables, some with floral patterns, others with postbox-red love hearts, and yet others with various colours of polka dots adorning them. Porcelain teapots in assorted bright colours stood on each table, with cast-iron tea kettles the only items at the other end of the colour spectrum.

A head popped up from behind the counter, making Jess jump.

'Sorry, didn't mean to startle you. I've been reorganising,' the middle-aged woman with the bright fuchsia plaits said. 'Have you booked?'

Jess didn't like to point out it hardly seemed necessary, so she settled for, 'I'm not sure. It was my friend who chose to meet here.'

The woman's brow furrowed. Surely she didn't think Jess was questioning her not being the one to choose her locale. Oh, maybe she thought she had something against it. Hurriedly, she explained, 'I'm from Glasgow. I don't know Edinburgh very well.'

Suitably mollified, the woman introduced herself. 'I'm Marion. Sit wherever you like. Would you like something now or would you prefer to wait for your friend?'

Still trying to accustom herself to Marion's rather eclectic look – tattoo sleeve, pink dungarees and a periwinkle blue beanie – Jess mumbled that perhaps she could have a peppermint tea whilst she waited.

She chose one of the tables with the tea kettle as its unusual shape intrigued her. She'd just parked her bottom on the edge of one of the mismatched accent chairs when the doorbell dinged again.

Anouska.

'Hi, Jess. Great to see you,' she breathed as she hugged Jess briefly before setting her briefcase down on the seat opposite Jess and taking off her coat.

'Wow! You look like you've stepped out of a tailor's in Savile Row.'

Anouska grinned. 'Workwear. A necessary evil.' She popped her handbag on the table. Gucci, Jess noted.

'I think I'm doing well if I buy something from Next,' said Jess.

'Ha ha. There's nothing wrong with Next. I get my pyjamas from there sometimes.'

Somehow Jess couldn't imagine this high-flying businesswoman, the epitome of sophistication, wearing the navy print daisy pyjamas Mark had bought her for Christmas.

The doorbell dinged again and Ellie swept in, bringing a blast of ice-cold air with her. 'So sorry I'm late. Can't believe I'm the one who lives in Edinburgh, yet I'm last here.' She hugged them both as they stood up to greet her. She then waved to Marion. 'Hi, hon, how are you?' To Marion's response that she was fine, Ellie added, 'Can I have a luxury hot chocolate when you have a sec?'

'Sure. I might be a bit, mind you. I'm rushed off my feet in here.'

The three women smiled at Marion's sense of humour, and Anouska added her order before Marion took off again.

Ellie shrugged off her coat then put her long, curly hair up in a scrunchie and collapsed into a seat. 'That's better. What a day.'

'Busy at work?' Jess asked.

'Yeah. That's what I get for taking the day off yesterday.'

'Oh? Did you do something nice?' Anouska asked.

Ellie beamed. 'Actually, yes, I went skiing.'

'Well, you definitely got the weather for it,' Anouska said.

'I did. It was fabulous.' Ellie broke off as Marion placed their drinks in front of them.

'I've never been skiing. I've always fancied trying it,' Jess said thoughtfully.

'You should come with me sometime.' Ellie wiped whipped cream from her top lip and sat the mug down. 'Especially midweek. It's fabulous as there's hardly anyone else around.'

'But you'd be whizzing down all those black runs and red runs. I'd need to go on the baby slopes,' Jess said glumly.

'I could slum it the once, you know.' Ellie grinned. 'Anyway, it was brilliant. Gave me time to clear my head.'

'Oh?' Anouska raised an eyebrow.

'I had a lot of thinking to do.' Ellie sidestepped the question and cupped her hands around her mug. 'So, Jess, tell me, when did you decide for certain you wanted to get married?'

Jess tapped a finger against her lips then said, 'Years ago, I don't remember exactly when, but it was only on New Year's Day that it seemed more urgent, and that I realised it had to happen this year.'

Ellie's eyes bulged. 'Wow, you don't do things by halves, do you?'

'Ha, ha! No, not really. Once I've made up my mind, I tend to just get on with it.'

'But how did you know it was the right time?' Ellie pressed. Jess wondered for a second if she was asking about her or for herself.

'Well, I'm twenty-four, we've been living together for two years, and we've known each other since we were seven.' She took a sip of her water. 'I want kids, loads of kids, always have. I'm from a big family myself. Five of us.'

At their expressions, she smiled. 'I know, a handful, so Mum says. Anyway, I digress. Let's face it, I'm never going to be in any better physical shape than I am now, and I'm not particularly good with pain, so I figure the sooner I can have kids, the better. Since I look after myself and my body, it should be easy, right?'

Anouska frowned. 'I'm not sure it's quite as simple as that, but certainly being in good health physically, and fit, would go in your favour.'

'And I don't want to be an older mum. Not that there's

anything wrong with that,' she hastened to add, 'but I don't want to be the mum who can't play sport with their kids or has no energy because they're in their forties and not physically in their prime.'

Ellie bit her lip. 'But surely you don't only want to get married because you want kids whilst you're still young.'

Jess shook her head. 'No, of course not. I love Mark to bits, always have, always will. I just believe that if it's right, it's right. Why wait? And it is right with me and Mark. I can't imagine myself ever with anyone but Mark, or him with anyone but me. In fact, the thought of him with someone else makes me feel ill.'

Both women were nodding at her, so she continued. 'Mark gets me. He's never been possessive, nor I with him. We don't need to be. Neither of us is jealous, nor gives the other any reason to be. He doesn't mind if I have friends who're male, and likewise I don't mind if he has female friends.'

Ellie's eyebrows lifted at that.

'I don't. Honestly. What we have is special. I've always known we'd end up together. Call me crazy, but I think I knew when I was seven.'

'That's forward planning.' Ellie laughed. 'I can barely plan my next meal.'

They all laughed.

'Well, when you're sure, you're sure,' Jess finished.

'What's the problem then?' Anouska stared earnestly at Jess.

'He hasn't asked. It's as if we're already married. You know, living together, it's too easy to slump into a routine of not making an effort.' A thought occurred to her. 'Do you live with your boyfriend, Anouska?'

Anouska nodded. 'Yes, in a flat his auntie left him.'

At Jess' scrunched-up face, she laughed. 'Bone of contention. So why was New Year your catalyst? Was it simply the romance of it being New Year, a New Year's resolution, or something else?'

Jess thought for a second then said, 'No, if I'm honest it's because I really hoped he'd propose at the bells – and then he didn't.'

'Ouch.' Ellie shot her a sympathetic look.

'Exactly.' Jess let the word hang there for a second then waved her hand dismissively. 'Anyway, enough about me. Tell me about you and your other halves.'

'I'll go first.' Anouska leant forward slightly. 'Zach and I have been together for three years. We met at a wine-tasting event here in Edinburgh, funnily enough, even though we're both from Aberdeen. So you can probably guess we both love wine, and we're both foodies, although I like eating food and he likes cooking it as well as eating it.'

Ellie and Jess laughed before Anouska continued. 'I run my own human resources business. I'm thirty-four, he's thirty-two. I love him to bits, but marriage hasn't really been on the table for us.'

Jess raised an invisible eyebrow at this. That wasn't the same as saying she didn't want to get married; on the contrary, it sounded like Zach didn't.

At their silence, Anouska clearly felt she needed to fill it. 'I'm constantly travelling for work, all over the world, and Zach and his business partner, Todd, are always so busy with their bistro, we're just grateful to have some time with each other when we can.'

'How long have you lived together?' Ellie asked.

Anouska thought for a second. 'Just under two years, I

think. Your turn, Ellie.'

Jess couldn't help but think Anouska wanted the spotlight turned away from her.

Ellie exhaled. 'Like I told you on the hen weekend, Scott and I have separate houses, and we've been together six years. He's a molecular biologist, doing his PhD at Edinburgh Uni. We're very different, although he also likes extreme sports, so we bond over that.' She drew breath as Jess and Anouska stared at her.

'Wow, extreme sports. That's so brave,' Jess said eventually.

'Rather you than me,' Anouska said. 'I prefer après-ski.'

They all laughed.

Anouska turned to Jess. 'So, have you thought any more about your proposal?'

Jess sighed. It was all she was thinking about. 'Yes, but now I've discounted all those I've considered.'

'Isn't there anywhere on your wish list that you haven't visited yet?' Ellie put in.

'We were supposed to go to Prague for New Year, but then Mum and Dad bought us a mini-break in Edinburgh, so we ditched that idea.'

Anouska frowned. 'So why not go there then?'

Jess twiddled the ends of the scarf she still wore around her neck, hoping to ward off the café's chill. 'I don't know if it's special enough. Prague's always associated with stag parties. I wanted a more romantic location.'

'I can understand that,' said Anouska.

'And the hotel I really wanted to go to, and that I know Mark has always wanted to stay in in Prague, was full. It's booked out for months.' When the other two looked at her, she confirmed, 'I did check.'

Ellie raised her hot chocolate to her mouth and said, 'It sounds like you have your work cut out for you. Time's marching on.' She replaced her mug on the table, eyes gleaming as an idea struck her. 'Tell you what, why don't you make a list of places and if you haven't decided by next week, we can meet here again next Thursday.' She glanced at Anouska. 'You can make it next Thursday, can't you?'

Anouska appeared to think for a moment then said, 'Yes, I'm not going to São Paulo until the day after.'

'And you, Jess?'

'I'm sure I can.'

'That's settled then. You make your list and we'll dissect it next week.' Ellie sat back, looking pleased with herself.

As Ellie's words sank in, Jess couldn't help feeling energised. She was really doing this.

Chapter Seven

Anouska

Monday 13 January

Anouska was so engrossed in her group chat messages with Ellie and Jess that she didn't even hear Zach come in. She started when he said, 'Still up, sweetheart?'

She quickly locked her phone and put it in her bag. That didn't look guilty at all, she thought belatedly. 'Yes, I was finishing up some work.'

Zach kissed her passionately on the mouth. 'I feel as if I haven't seen you for ages. How was your day?'

'Oh, you know, just catching up with things in the office and with Leigh-Ann.'

'How's she doing?' When Anouska hesitated, he said, 'Everything OK?'

'Yeah, she could do with some help, that's all. I've been away a lot recently. I was thinking I might start cutting back on my trips for a while once I return from São Paulo.'

'Hurrah! I get my girl back!'

Not quite, thought Anouska, and she wasn't lying by using Leigh-Ann as the reason she was curtailing her travel; she simply wasn't divulging the whole truth.

'Actually, I've been thinking,' he said.

'Should I be worried?' Anouska teased him.

'No, not at all. You should be elated.'

She frowned and he continued. 'How's about you and me, just the two of us, start looking for a long-haul holiday somewhere?'

Anouska paled, and Zach must have seen something in her expression as he said, 'No, hear me out. You said yourself you're going to cut back on your trips, how about in a few months we go on one of these all-inclusive breaks? We could shop around for a good deal. I certainly have plenty sources of inspiration on where to go at my fingertips.' He smiled.

With the travel bookshop part of his business, he wasn't wrong there.

'We could go on safari to the Masai Mara, or trekking in Nepal…'

Anouska's eyes fluttered closed. No, not now. Another panic attack was bubbling up from inside her. She knew the signs.

Normally, she'd have bitten his hand off to go on a break, and not cared where they went, but Kenya involved injections for yellow fever and she'd need to take malaria tablets. Plus, in a few months she'd be five months pregnant.

'Or,' Zach said, possibly noticing her change in breathing, 'if that's too strenuous we could maybe bag a good price on an all-inclusive at a Sandals resort in the Caribbean.'

Anouska's vision swam and she struggled to stay upright. Zach was moving in and out of focus.

'Anouska, are you OK?' He sounded awfully far away.

'I'm not feeling very well.'

'Let me get you some water.' Zach's voice was laced with concern.

She sipped the water gratefully, and gradually she was able to refocus and breathe normally again.

'You've been overdoing it. It's just as well you're going to travel less for work.' Zach pulled her to him and kissed her on the head.

'Probably. I think I'm going to turn in, get an early night.'

He smiled fondly at her. 'Sounds like a plan.'

Anouska relaxed into Zach as they snuggled together in bed not long afterwards, both too tired for different reasons to engage in any energetic pursuits. They had a good life together. She just wasn't sure how he would react to any change in it. Guilt crept over her at the thought of the next day's appointment, an appointment he'd miss. She hoped he'd forgive her.

As Zach was drifting off to sleep, she said, 'By the way, Mum phoned today. She's coming for a shopping break.'

'Oh?'

'At the end of the month.'

'End of the month? Sounds lovely. And you're sure you'll be here?'

'Yes, we checked our schedules.'

'Great, it'll be nice to see Maura again, when I'm not working. Anouska, I'm shattered. Can we talk more about this tomorrow?'

Did she detect a note of irritation in his tone? She realised also that once her panic attack had passed, he hadn't mentioned the holiday again. Was he pissed off about that? She'd never know. Aargh. Hormones were so annoying, all this self-doubt.

'Sure.' Anouska kissed him on the cheek and within thirty seconds he was asleep. She lay there studying him as his dark hair flopped over onto his face. He really was handsome. He wasn't the tallest man in the world, at five feet eight, but he was hers and she cherished him. Their baby would be beautiful. She wondered if it would be a boy or a girl. What would they call him, or her? Did she care if it was a boy or a girl? Now that she was having a baby, would she want more than one? If so, how many? So many questions. She decided she didn't care if it was a boy or a girl, as long as it was healthy.

She tossed and turned, willing herself to go to sleep. She was exhausted, and now that she was pregnant, until she managed to make arrangements to take some of the weight off her shoulders and poor Leigh-Ann's, she had to ensure she took care of herself. She stroked her stomach, whispered, 'Night, Bean,' and started counting elephants; it had always worked as a child. The last thing she remembered was five hundred and seventy elephants.

Tuesday 14 January

'Morning, sweetheart. Here's a caffeine injection for you. Did I hear you say last night your mum was coming?'

Struggling to wake up, Anouska cleared the grit from her eyes and gingerly sat up.

'Sorry?' She yawned.

'Is Maura coming in a few weeks?'

Anouska reached for her coffee cup, yawned again then said, 'Yes, she's arriving on the thirty-first.'

'That's great news. I know you haven't seen much of her recently. And, with you not travelling so much for a bit, that'll work out well.'

Anouska nodded her agreement. She was too tired to form any more sentences right then.

'Right, I've got to go to work. You dropping in tonight for some food? You haven't been in for a while. Todd's beginning to get a complex.' Zach planted a kiss on her lips and headed for the door.

A wave of nausea struck Anouska and she managed to blurt out, 'Sure, see you later,' and wave Zach off, before she sprinted for the toilet. She got there in the nick of time, depositing the contents of her stomach into the toilet bowl. *Bloody morning sickness.*

As she freshened up, a thought occurred to her: How on earth was she going to keep her pregnancy a secret from her mother when they were living in the same house?

Twenty-five days. Twenty-five days since she'd found out she was pregnant and she still hadn't mentioned the pregnancy to Zach. Today she was seeing the midwife for the first time. She hadn't been able to get an appointment that suited until now, what with all her meetings. She knew, particularly today, she should be focusing completely on her and the baby, but she couldn't help reproaching herself for not having told Zach yet. He might be hurt by the fact she had gone without him, and she would have loved for him to be there. Uncertainty crept into her mind then. What if, when she told him, he still didn't want kids and suggested she get rid of Bean? She knew she couldn't. Now that the baby was real, she wanted it. She wanted it with a fierceness she couldn't explain. Maternal instinct? Hormones? Who knew, but she couldn't escape the protectiveness she felt towards her unborn child, even if she wanted to.

Anouska walked through the park to the doctor's surgery, as the sun melted the frost on the pavements, taking extra care where she put her feet. The last thing she wanted to do was slip on the ice.

In the surgery, she pored over her iPad, head down, trying not to draw attention to herself. It was unlikely anyone she knew would be there, as she and Zach tended to keep themselves to themselves, and didn't overly mix with the neighbours; however, it would be just her luck for someone to see her going in to the midwife and congratulate Zach before he even knew himself.

She knew she was procrastinating, but if she was truly being honest with herself, she was afraid.

'Anouska Bennett?'

Anouska rose to her feet and followed the midwife through the double doors to her room.

'I'm Cara. Please take a seat.' The midwife smiled at her. She was young, not the matronly, plump nurse Anouska had conjured up in her mind.

'So, you're pregnant.' It was a statement rather than a question.

Anouska nodded. 'Two to four weeks the test I took said, but that was twenty-five days ago.'

Cara smiled. 'Not that you're counting. Right, that's a start. Just so you know, those tests count your pregnancy from the date of conception. We count it from the first day of your last period.' Cara checked Anouska's particulars were correct then said, 'So, when was that?'

Anouska shook her head. 'I'm not sure. I know I had one in November, but can't quite recall when, perhaps the middle.'

'Nothing at all that jogs your memory, a concert you were at, someone or somewhere you visited?'

Now she thought about it, she had been in the Philippines in November. And she'd had to go and buy tampons. When was she there exactly?

'Can you give me a minute? I might be able to work it out.'

'Sure, go ahead.' Cara waited patiently whilst Anouska scrolled through her phone calendar.

She'd arrived in Manila on the seventeenth of November and left on the twenty-second, and she seemed to recall having her period for most of the time there. She told the midwife as much.

'And how long is your cycle usually?'

'Standard twenty-eight days.'

Cara made some notes. 'Excellent. So I have a due date for you of the twenty-fifth of August, give or take. A summer baby.'

Anouska couldn't stop the smile from spreading over her face. She was having a baby. Later this year she'd be celebrating her baby's first Christmas.

She could barely take in what Cara told her about future appointments, when the scans would be, ways to look after herself, dos and don'ts. She tried her best but the elation she felt at believing, finally taking in, that she was having a baby, made everything else fade into the background. As she drove to the office, she decided she'd tell Zach tonight. She had to.

'Your four o'clock's in the boardroom.' Leigh-Ann placed

some papers for signature on Anouska's desk.

'Thanks. Could you bring some coffees in, and do we have any of those cinnamon twists left we had at lunch? See if we can sweeten them up?' They shared a conspiratorial smile.

Anouska frowned at her inbox. Two hundred and twenty-seven unread messages.

She opened her file on Bell Communications. It was a mid-sized firm, which until recently had their own in-house human resources. However, times were tough and the company had been downsizing in certain areas and outsourcing in others. Tax and payroll had been subbed out to Mumbai, and human resources was ripe for the picking. Javier LaPuente was Bell's UK managing director, but he would be interviewing Anouska's company for all fourteen countries they operated in, having already liaised with his counterparts in each country at a summit the previous month in Berlin. It would be a lucrative contract to win and Anouska loved a challenge. It was why she had set up the Impress Me outsourcing agency for IT and communications firms ten years ago.

She ruffled her hair with the aim of making it look tousled as opposed to greasy after a hard day in the office. Bring it on! Following her appointment with the midwife today and her connection with her baby feeling even stronger as a result, she felt invincible. She'd have no problem closing today.

'So, you're saying we could have all of our countries run through one hub? Your team could service all our needs worldwide?'

Anouska, ever the professional, replied, 'That's right. Although we're a small corporation, we have a huge global reach, everywhere from Dakar to Istanbul, Tokyo to Tehran,' she said, touching on some of her client's key locations. She had done her research well.

Javier smiled, nodding at her response, and started to ask her specifics. Yes! He was hers. She had reeled him in. She recognised the signs.

At the end of the meeting, they arranged to have a conference call the following Monday prior to signing contracts. Once Javier left the office, Anouska gave a huge sigh of relief. 'Thank God that went well.'

'You had it in the bag the whole time,' Leigh-Ann said loyally, and Anouska felt a rush of affection for her.

'Do you fancy joining Lucas and me for a pizza?' Leigh-Ann asked.

'Thanks, but I'm going to drop in to Bean There on the way home, see if Zach or Todd can fix me something. I also might actually get to see Zach then.'

Leigh-Ann smirked. Anouska knew that meant she wasn't surprised as Anouska was a regular fixture in the bistro. When she did leave the office at a reasonable time, which was rare, more often than not she went via Bean There and ended up having dinner at her usual table, drinking countless coffees, or the odd glass of wine, and reviewing client data on her laptop.

With Zach often at the bistro until gone midnight, there was usually nothing to rush home for. That was all about to change.

Chapter Eight

Ellie

Tuesday 14 January

'What's this?' Scott frowned as he picked up some papers from the table in the hall. 'Property brochures?'

'Yes. I fancy something bigger and with a garden. It would be nice to sit out in the summer. I think it's time to find somewhere new.'

'But people would bite your hand off to have a flat like this, and in Stockbridge of all places.'

'Like I said, I've outgrown it. I wouldn't mind moving out of the city if I could have something bigger.'

'Hmm.' Scott's eyebrows knitted. 'If you say so. I'll see you around twelve. I just need to pop into work for a bit.'

'But you're on annual leave. *We're* on annual leave.'

'I know, and I'm sorry, but I won't be long. I promise.' He gave her a quick peck on the forehead and the door swung closed behind him as he left the flat.

And there it was. Scott's lack of interest, or even awareness. He couldn't even commit to a full day off together. A pre-arranged full day off.

She was twenty-eight, her boyfriend of six years was thirty-six and they still lived in separate homes: Ellie in this one-bedroom flat in Edinburgh, and Scott in a three-bedroom house in Livingston. They'd gone on numerous long-haul holidays and got on well when in close quarters: no nagging, no fighting – it had been like a dream. Yet Scott had never once broached the subject of them moving in together, let alone anything else.

So she'd decided to force the issue. Whatever happened, her efforts wouldn't be wasted, but she wanted to see how Scott reacted to her looking at moving.

She'd also scheduled an estate agent to visit so he'd know she was serious. She intended to make him really think, if he was capable of doing so, about their relationship and what her selling up and buying something bigger might mean for them. Surely he had to have an opinion one way or the other.

Since she'd met the girls on Thursday, and with Jess' confirmation that she was one hundred per cent proposing to Mark, her mind had been racing with possibilities and outcomes. Should she go for the job in Manchester? It was her dream job. Could she afford, in every sense, to pass it up? And just when she'd convinced herself that she couldn't possibly leave Scott and her family – Chloe would be seriously narked when she found out, and who could blame her? – her mind flipped to the fact she was turning down the job she'd worked so hard for, and she decided she couldn't do it.

She'd written down all the pros and cons in the notes app in her phone, and she had driven herself to distraction sneaking a peek at the list every so often – far too many times to count – to see if anything had become clearer for her. It hadn't.

Trish had called her into the office yesterday to tell her

she was ready for Ellie to increase her shadowing of her to three days a week. The thrill she'd had working alongside Trish, being shown her boss' job and seeing how her future work life could be, was second only to base jumping. OK, she might be stretching the truth a little there, but she'd loved it. It was as if she'd been born to do it. The thought of turning that down, and for a relationship that might not be progressing, left her sick to her stomach.

Chloe had asked her to come over last night but she hadn't been able to face her sister when all of this was roiling around inside her. Because of her potential new job's location, she still hadn't told her that the interview for the promotion was coming up soon, nor that Trish had offered to mentor her, nor, well, any of it.

Ellie couldn't bear the thought of leaving her family behind in Edinburgh – she adored them – but if she wanted her career to advance, couldn't she move for a little while? Manchester wasn't so far, after all. Perhaps they could come visit every month or so, or she return home. In fact, now she was in that mindset, couldn't she just have a long-distance relationship with Scott? They barely saw each other anyway, only a couple of times a week. It's not like they were living with each other or anything.

Ellie clasped her head in her hands. She was getting nowhere fast. This was driving her insane.

Hopefully, the estate agent she'd booked on a whim for one o'clock would make Scott sit up and take notice. It was only half a ploy after all. She wanted his attention, but if things went south with them, then she may really be renting out or, worse, selling her beloved flat.

She leant heavily against the couch and surveyed her living room. She'd had it painted only six months before. A friend of her dad's was a painter and decorator, and he'd given her mates rates, so the flat was pretty fresh-looking. A blessing. It saved her forking out money now for her grand plan of seeing which way Scott jumped regarding her potentially selling up.

Fortunately, she'd chosen neutral colours throughout, no glaring terracotta or duck-egg blue like Scott's house, whose décor looked like a painter had tripped and their palette had flown out of their hand. Maybe she should be grateful they didn't live together, she thought with a wry smile.

She tried to appraise her flat as a potential viewer might, and also played with the wording the estate agent might use to sell her flat. By her reckoning: 'Recently redecorated throughout, this incredible one-bedroom property in the heart of Stockbridge offers all the benefits of modern living whilst retaining some wonderful period features, including original fireplace, decorative cornicing and case and sash windows.'

One thing Scott probably had right – the estate agent would snap up her flat in double-quick time. Property in Stockbridge was much sought-after.

She wandered from room to room, wondering how she'd manage to give up her little flat, the only home she'd had since leaving her parental one. Her first scrap of independence. Originally, she'd been a tenant, then she'd bought it from the owner two years ago.

She took in the huge bedroom; the dining area tucked at the back of the living room; the dual aspect windows which satisfied her people-watching hobby; the galley kitchen with its sloping ceiling – the bane of Scott's life. It didn't bother Ellie. She never hit her head off it, but it had made Scott scowl on occasion when he moved back too quickly and hit his head on the lower part of the ceiling. She loved her flat. It was quirky, just like her. She hoped if she did have to sell, that whoever bought it, treated it with the respect and love it deserved. Oh, she was being silly, she knew, thinking about a flat as if it were an actual person, but it had become very dear to her over the years, and she definitely considered it a part of her, which was why the thought of leaving it was such a wrench, but times moved on. Life had to move on, and she with it.

But now she felt life was moving too fast. She hadn't discussed the potential promotion with Scott, she hadn't discussed it with her sister or the rest of her family, and she hated herself for her duplicity. Sure, the promotion wasn't in the bag yet, but the fact she was actively avoiding her sister spoke volumes. She knew she'd be gutted. It wasn't as if Ellie wouldn't be, too, but she had to spread her wings. Chloe had her little family unit, which she'd always been wonderful at including Ellie in, but Ellie wanted the job of her dreams, eventually her own happy ever after, with a family of her own, a baby of her own, just not yet. She did, however, want to take steps to facilitate her getting there eventually.

She massaged her temples to help rid herself of the beginnings of a tension headache. She knew she'd have to tell everyone sometime, soon, actually, but her heart ached at the thought of doing so, and she still didn't know if she needed to. Oh, why was life so complicated? Why couldn't she just get her dream job in her own city, buy a house with the man she loved and live happily ever after? *Because life isn't like that. Stop sugar-coating things.*

The only people who knew about the promotion were

two virtual strangers who were fast becoming friends.

Ellie whipped her phone out of her back pocket and texted:

Morning, girls. I have an estate agent coming out to value my flat later. I left property brochures lying around and Scott was dismissive of me selling up. I've been shadowing my boss in case I get the promotion once it goes to interview. I haven't told my family I may end up moving to Manchester. I'm avoiding my sister as I can't look her in the eye. Help!

As she waited for someone to reply, she fluffed some cushions and tidied the remainder of the already tidy flat. The one good thing about having a one-bedroom flat was it didn't take long to clean or tidy.

Ping!

Jess: *Go see your sister x*

Anouska: *Go and visit Chloe and explain everything to her. She's your sister and she loves you. She'll understand x*

That seemed pretty definitive.

Ellie: *I'll call her now. Thanks, girls. Will keep you posted on everything else x*

'I'd think, having seen it now, that you'd be looking at a price in the region of three hundred and thirty thousand pounds,' the estate agent told Ellie.

Scott, who'd come in just as the estate agent arrived, and for some bizarre reason seemed to be following him around like a puppy, repeated the number back to him, his voice a decibel higher than usual.

'Yes. Or rather, I'd suggest you put the property on at offers over that price. You may well get around ten per cent more than that. At the moment, buyers are being recommended to offer between eight and ten per cent above the home report price.'

'Really' Scott gawped, incredulity written all over his face.

Ellie felt it was time to intervene. It was, after all, she who was selling the flat, not him. She, however, preferred to play it cool with the estate agent, not let him see that she too was stunned by the number. Until now she hadn't followed the property market, at all. Since she'd bought her flat from the landlord two years ago, she'd never needed to deal with estate agents. Yet the fact she'd paid three hundred and ten thousand pounds for it two years ago also made her head spin. She could have potentially a fifty grand profit in two years. That was mind-boggling.

She knew she was lucky to be able to buy a flat in Stockbridge in the first place, but her mum had bought Premium Bonds for both her children from birth until their eighteenth birthdays. Ellie's had come up, and although her mum had split the money between her and Chloe, it had left her a sizeable sum as a deposit for this flat.

'Thank you,' said Ellie with a smile, without revealing too much of her inner thoughts. She may well want to get another valuation if she did go ahead and sell, and it didn't do to look too keen, although Scott's reaction may have scuppered any chance she had of playing it cool with the estate agent.

Once she'd dispatched the estate agent, Scott dragged her into a kiss. 'Let's go out for brunch. My treat.'

Crikey, wonders never cease.

'Let me just go change.' Ellie began to pull away from him.

'Don't be daft. You look perfect just as you are.' He

pulled her in for another kiss.

It was over a lovely romantic lunch at Howie's in Victoria Street, one of Ellie's favourite restaurants, that Scott leant across the table and took Ellie's hand. 'I've been thinking.'

'Don't do that, it's dangerous,' Ellie said.

'Ha, ha. No, seriously, what with you saying you'd like to move somewhere bigger, and that you've outgrown the flat, it seems silly for you to do it on your own.'

Ellie raised her eyebrows. 'Oh?'

'Yeah. Surely it's only a matter of time before we move in together, so it makes no sense for you to buy somewhere else, only to sell it again in a year or so.'

'What do you suggest then?' She tried to keep the excitement out of her voice, but she wanted, no, needed, to hear him say the words.

Scott's chestnut eyes glinted with merriment. 'Ellie, would you like to move in together? Will you buy a house with me?'

'Oh, Scott, yes, yes, of course I will.' Then she leant forward until her lips met his as her entire being zinged with happiness.

Chapter Nine

Jess

Wednesday 15 January

'This is just like old times, Mark Featherstone,' Jess said as she rested her hand on her minigolf club.

'Well, if we're going to be true to form, I'm going to win.' He smirked as Jess pretended to swat him with her club.

'You're lucky I'm slightly too far away. Anyway, I don't fancy your chances tonight, do you?'

'Oh, I absolutely fancy my chances.' He waggled his eyebrows.

Jess rolled her eyes. 'At minigolf. And if you continue like that, you can extend that outcome to other areas too.'

Mark laughed as he lined up his ball for the eighth hole. 'I don't see you winning tonight. I beat you on the shark, the octopus and if I had to bet on it, I'd put money on me winning the manta ray hole too.'

Jess stayed silent. He had a point.

'You're not holding your club properly, and your stance isn't wide enough,' Mark went on.

'Well, we don't all have a lucky red ball,' Jess said.

Mark grinned. Never a game went by when he didn't

make a reference to how he always chose the red ball at minigolf as it was a tradition he'd had since he was little, because he had red hair. She didn't like to tell him it might have been cute when he was four, but not so much at twenty-four.

'Mark, stop trying to coach me. I'm not one of your pupils. If I want to play minigolf badly, I will.'

'Your choice. And you're so good at it … playing badly, that is.'

He ducked as Jess threw her balled-up hoodie at him. Mark was so annoying when he insisted things had to be done a certain way, particularly when it came to any kind of sport, competitive or otherwise. Not that minigolf was exactly a sport, but he applied the same rules.

'Drat!'

Ha, he'd missed. 'Aw, what? No hole in one, or two, or even three? Would you like me to give you some pointers?' She grinned as he shot her a dark look. He was so competitive it made her laugh.

She took her shot, straight under the manta ray's fin, and it kept going, going, going. *Yes! It was in. Take that, Mark!*

Mark groaned. She was only three points behind him now, and he'd hate that. Jess scanned her band and input her score. She wasn't doing too badly, actually. Maybe Mark was trying to put her off so he could win. Well, two could play at that game.

As Mark lined up to take his shot at the starfish – she was loving the under the sea theme of this particular minigolf – she whispered in his ear, 'How about we cut this short and go home and…?'

Mark's shot went wide, he cursed and, looking around

to ensure no one else saw, dived for Jess, tickling her, then kissing her until she felt literally dizzy.

'Think you can put me off, do you? I'm still going to win, but you had better deliver on that promise when we get home.'

'I have no idea what you mean,' Jess said as Mark swept her into a passionate kiss, halted eventually only by the arrival of some wolf-whistling teenagers.

'Are any of them in your class?' Jess asked, reddening.

'Let's bloody hope not,' Mark muttered, 'or I'll never hear the end of it. Right, much as I'm really enjoying this course, let's hurry up, so we can get home and get started on your suggestion.'

Spurred on by his comment, and warmed by the thought, Jess resolved to do her best to take the win. She'd find a way to console him once they got home. With a smile, she struck out for the great white shark hole – the irony of its killer instinct not lost on her.

Thursday 16 January

'Jess, have you seen my rugby shorts? I'm playing against the science department tonight.'

Jess was standing in their miniscule utility room wading through the clean laundry basket, finding all her yoga pants and workout tops when she heard Mark calling her. Between two pairs of yoga pants nestled a pair of black rugby shorts.

'Laundry basket,' she called back. She replaced the items she didn't need and set up the ironing board.

'What time will you be in tonight?' she asked Mark as he gave her a peck on the cheek then shoved the shorts into his sports bag.

'Don't know. Might go for a couple of beers with the guys. You don't mind, do you?'

'No, I have classes and dog walks until five, then if I have time, I was going to nip to Parkers for some supplies, and then I'm heading through to Edinburgh to meet Jess and Anouska.'

Mark frowned. 'Didn't you meet up with them last week?'

'Yep. We got on really well. Thought we'd make it a weekly thing. Actually, who am I kidding? I won't have time to get to Parkers if I'm to make that train.'

Mark raised his eyebrows. 'A bit of a trek on a Thursday night, but it's clearly worth it to you. Text me a list and I'll pick up what you need.'

'Really? That would be great. You know how little choice the supermarkets' health-food sections have compared with Parkers.' He really was so thoughtful.

Mark nuzzled into Jess' neck, gave her a lingering kiss on the lips, which made parts of her fizz with delight, then grabbed his man bag containing all his classes' assignments. 'Yeah. Right, I need to go. I've S2 this morning – back to back, and they're a tough lot this year. Have fun tonight. Bye.' He was out the door in two seconds. Thirty seconds later, he returned, flashing her a megawatt smile. 'Sports bag,' he explained, retrieving it from behind the door, before about-turning and heading back out.

'Think of your core,' called Jess to her final class of the morning. 'You are in control of it, yep, even the beginners. Lie on your back, pull your left knee towards your chest and hold for ten, twenty, thirty. That's it – feel the burn. Now, the right knee, and ten, twenty, thirty.'

By the time she had worked her class up to the double leg stretch, half were zen-like and half were in agony. One thing was for sure, they'd all feel it in the morning, possibly herself included.

'And we're done,' Jess called as she picked up her towel and wiped her forehead.

She checked her watch. Fifteen minutes before her Pilates class started. She'd grab some water and a protein shake and get back to it.

'And now into downward dog, and relax.'

Jess' eyes strayed to the clock. Five past five. Phew, what a day. Sometimes having the classes spaced out helped. Other times she was in the zone and could happily keep going for hours without a break. Her phone vibrated. Whoever it was would have to wait. They still had triangle and upward-facing dog to do.

'That's us, guys. Well done, everyone.' Jess smiled at them and picked up her gym towel to wipe the sweat from her face.

The twenty or so people in the class, mainly women, thanked her and filed out of the room or stood in little groups chatting or making plans to go for coffee the following week. As Jess went to leave, Nathan stopped her.

'Jess, you coming to the pub with us? A few of us are heading over to The Crooked Chimney.'

'Thanks, Nathan, but I have plans tonight.'

He shot her a cheeky smile. 'Our loss. Maybe next time. See you next week.'

'Maybe. Yeah, see you. Enjoy yourselves.'

'We will.'

Jess shook Nathan's sexy grin from her mind and strode towards the changing rooms. She showered quickly then grabbed her kit bag and headed for the station. Perhaps tonight wasn't the best time to be taking public transport over to Edinburgh for their second meet-up. It must be close to freezing at the moment, which meant by the time she returned it would probably be minus temperatures.

As she waited for the train, she checked her messages. *Got everything you asked for from Parkers, my little health nut, M x*

She smiled. Mark wasn't exactly averse to exercise himself and had the body to show for it, but she was glad he'd managed to go to the health-food store for her, one more thing off her to-do list. Although she was overjoyed to have set up her dog-walking business, some days, the mix of walks combined with the exercise classes she led meant life was pretty full-on.

Once the girls had all arrived, greeted each other and settled in Cirque again, Ellie got straight to the point. 'So, have you had any more ideas about where you're going to propose?'

'Of course. I haven't been able to concentrate on anything else, and I've done a ton of research,' Jess admitted. 'But before we get into all that, congratulations on you and Scott moving in together.'

Ellie flushed. 'I can't quite believe it's really happening. I was so annoyed at his disinterest in me putting the flat up for sale and then wham, he's suggesting we buy a place together.'

Anouska shook her head. 'I'll never understand men, but I'm really happy for you.'

'Thanks, Anouska.'

As their attention turned to Jess' situation, Jess took a bite of chicken whilst gathering her thoughts then whipped out her phone. 'I had a look online earlier. How about this? Oporto, five nights B&B, dept. Gatwick, £549, 27 Feb.'

'Hmm, maybe.' Ellie screwed up her face. 'Why Oporto?'

'It has one of the teams Mark likes best in European football.'

At their amused expressions, Jess said, 'I know, I know, not the most romantic of reasons, but it's a pretty city too. I checked it out. And they have port!'

Muted murmurs of agreement came from Ellie and Anouska. They weren't convinced, she could tell.

Jess scrolled through her phone then glanced up at them. 'Or St Petersburg. I know it will be freezing, but it's so picturesque and has so much gorgeous architecture. Four nights, full board, £649, 26 Feb.'

'That sounds good,' said Anouska. 'But wait, you need a visa for Russia. How will you swing that without Mark being present? He'd need to sign the form.'

Well, that ruled that out.

Riga? They'd always talked about going to the Baltics. And that was probably only a couple of hours' flight. And the Baltics wouldn't be so expensive, would they? Not as cheap as a few years ago, mind, but not as dear as Central or Southern Europe.

'How about Riga? Mark loves Henning Mankell, and one of his books is set there.' At their vacant expressions, she went on. 'He likes the Wallander series. Do you remember, there was a TV version with Kenneth Branagh?'

Anouska nodded, whilst Ellie's blank look remained.

Whichever city she chose, if it was a city, she felt sure she should decide upon either a landmark they'd visited or wanted to visit. It was so difficult. There was so much choice, but it was such an important thing to get right.

Jess worried at a ragged piece of her pinkie nail that had been bothering her for days. He would say yes, wouldn't he? Doubt crept in. She ninety-nine per cent knew he'd say yes, but that other one per cent was starting to haunt her dreams. In reality, she knew it was because it was on her mind all the time; if she wasn't thinking how to propose or where, she was trying to work out the exact words to use. The downside of being a dog walker was it gave her a lot of headspace, too much time to reflect.

Yes, of course she would say 'Will you marry me?' but she did feel there should be some sort of precursor to the proposal. Something along the lines of 'Mark, you've been my soulmate since we were seven, how about you remain it until we're in our dotage?' or 'Mark, I've known since I first met you that you were the one I wanted to marry. Will you do me the great honour of being my husband?' or 'Mark, we've been inseparable since we were little – let's make it more permanent.' The possibilities played out on a never-ending loop in her head, but nothing stuck. She simply couldn't seem to make a final decision. Her head was aching from overthinking.

'I don't suppose you two have come up with any great ideas for me then?'

'How about at the rugby ground? You said last week he was into rugby. You could have it come up on the board during the game,' Anouska offered.

'I'm not sure Mark would like that. It's a bit public.'

'Or how about through the medium of karaoke? You could sing Train's "Marry Me",' suggested Ellie.

Jess did like that song, but she hated karaoke, albeit Mark loved it. She huffed out a breath, despondent.

Anouska said, 'And that's pretty public too. Well, one thing's for certain, he'd know from that single act how much you love him and want to marry him.'

'No, more like he'll be mortified and leave me, never mind marry me.' Jess wasn't known for her singing voice, or rather she was, but for all the wrong reasons.

They went through the possibilities, one by one, but it seemed that all those Jess put forward had snags. Even those Anouska and Ellie came up with were either improbable or likely to have Mark booking a solo one-way ticket to Australia.

Jess sighed. The search was far from over.

Friday 17 January

The next morning, Jess had already been up for an hour working in the living room on some new music for her Zumba class, when she noted she still hadn't heard Mark in the shower. She glanced at the clock. Twenty past eight.

She marched into their bedroom and shook him awake. 'Mark, wake up. You're going to be late for work.'

'Ugh...what?' Mark grunted.

'Mark, stop messing about. You've overslept. It's twenty past eight.'

'Oh shit!' Mark bolted upright. 'I'll never make the bus in time now.'

'No, you won't. You look like crap, by the way. And you stink. You can't go to work like that. Jump in the shower and I'll see if I can find you some mints. I'll drive you to work. There's no way you can take the car. You'll still be way over the limit.'

Jess was more than a tad annoyed that Mark's impromptu midweek drinking session was going to disrupt her day, but saw no way out of it, short of Mark arriving late to work. She made him a coffee in his to-go cup and prepared her own things, ready for the day. She wasn't working until eleven, as one of her dogs was going to the vet and the other was away on holiday, so she had planned to pop into her parents' first. Now she'd have to cut short her visit, given her impromptu chauffeuring session.

Mark appeared, fresh from the shower, yet still managing to look as if he'd been dragged through a hedge, with bloodshot eyes, hair sticking up and a vacant expression on his face. He smiled as soon as he saw the coffee mug.

'Not until you're dressed. We need to go.' Jess was firm. Honestly, sometimes it was like having a child. She loved Mark to pieces, but on occasion he didn't seem to have matured much from the seven-year-old she had met almost two decades earlier.

Mark quickly shaved and dressed and by twenty-five to nine, he was ready to go.

They got into Jess' little-used Honda Civic and headed for the school.

'Thanks, Jess.' Mark's eyes were full of sincerity as she deposited him at the gates at five to nine. He'd still be playing catch-up for part of the morning, but at least he would turn up in time for his class, and the coffee seemed to have energised him.

'Don't make a habit of it,' she said in her best schoolmarm tone.

'I won't. I'm sorry. One of the lads had just found out he's about to become a dad, and well, he thought it was a good idea to wet the baby's head already, rather than waiting until it's actually born.'

She rolled her eyes at their antics and at his sheepish expression.

'All right, you're forgiven. Don't forget these.' Jess leant out of the window and pushed some mints into his hand.

'What would I do without you?' He leant through the open window and kissed her full on the lips, to the excited catcalls of some nearby teenagers, pupils of his, no doubt. Well, that was good enough for him. It would serve him right if they took the mick out of him, this morning.

It wasn't the first time he had said that to her, but she did wonder sometimes what he would do, as he was so scatterbrained. The only thing he seemed able to focus on properly was teaching.

Funny how some people pigeon-holed her or stereotyped her as being airy-fairy, expecting her to believe in astrology, worship crystals and follow the teachings of Buddha, just because she was a yoga instructor. But that wasn't her, and she was more grounded than most people she knew. She simply liked to keep fit and had always loved exercising and music. Sometimes, before she was an instructor, she felt she needed something less energetic than her body attack class, and one day a friend had invited her to Pilates and she'd loved it, and from that first class had grown the germ of an idea for an exercise business.

As she drove to her parents' house, she mused that life wasn't too bad, apart from inconsiderate boyfriends coming home drunk and being too hungover to get up in time for work. Fortunately, he didn't do it very often. He'd have some serious making-up to do tonight when he got home, though.

She was reversing into the driveway when her mobile buzzed with a message. Ellie, in the group chat.

Just wanted to say thanks!

Jess frowned. Thanks for what?

As if reading her mind, Ellie texted: *It was Jess who clinched it for me, plus I had all that thinking time out on the slopes last week.*

What? came Jess' reply, followed by *Don't keep us guessing* from Anouska.

I'm going to do it. I'm going to propose on the twenty-ninth of February too.

At Jess and Anouska's explosion of shocked and delighted emojis, Ellie sent back about ten laughing emojis with tears in their eyes.

Jess grinned then bashed out, *Here's to our leap-year proposals!*

Chapter Ten

Anouska

Sunday 19 January

Anouska kicked off her shoes and sat down on her hotel suite sofa with her iPad. She'd grabbed a Diet Coke from the fridge when she came in and she took a thirsty swig of it. A gin and tonic would have been preferable but that was out for at least a year.

Today's meeting with her Brazilian manager had been gruelling. Plus, she hadn't felt as refreshed as she usually did when flying out over a weekend. Although she'd left on Friday, she'd only arrived yesterday, and the flights had taken a lot more out of her than she was used to. There was no way she'd be able to do this on a regular basis, or even semi-regular, until the baby came. It was good she was putting her contingency plans in place now, which was difficult as she had no real explanation for her staff as to why – she hadn't told Zach or Leigh-Ann yet, so she couldn't exactly tell anyone else.

She'd honestly intended to tell him last week, but when she'd called upon leaving the office to tell Zach and Todd she was on the way over for a bite to eat, Todd had answered and suggested she grab a takeaway that night as they'd had a bit of an incident at the bistro. He hadn't been in a position to elaborate greatly at that point, because as it turned out Zach was talking to the police, but Zach had filled her in later.

A jealous ex-husband had burst into the bistro and punched his replacement almost unconscious before Zach and Todd and other diners were able to come to his rescue. Todd had not long waved off the ambulance whilst Zach had, together with other diners, restrained the perpetrator until the police arrived. Then, once the police had taken the guilty party to the police station, Zach had needed to give the police a statement whilst Todd dealt with the other diners and offered them all to-go boxes, refunds or vouchers for a replacement meal. Many had waved off his generosity, but a few had taken him up on the offer, despite it not being Zach or Todd's fault. But Zach and Todd both had excellent business sense and knew reputation was everything, so were more than happy to dole out a few vouchers to stop negative reviews.

By the time Zach came home that night, the last thing she had any intention of doing was telling him he was about to become a father. Talk about choosing your moment. If there was ever a bad time, that was it. And from then until she left for São Paulo, Zach had been withdrawn, morose even.

So the chance had passed her by once again. Yet a tiny piece of her couldn't help being relieved. Here, alone with her thoughts, she could process why she was so afraid. Afraid that Zach wouldn't want the baby. Afraid that Zach would no longer want her. People changed once they had babies, didn't they? It happened all the time. One minute you were a high-flying executive earning a six-figure sum and the next the extent of your conversational topics was limited only to those directly regarding your infant: breastfeeding, dual pumping, the best nappies to buy, or worse, when they did focus on you as a person again, it was by how much your perineum had torn during labour, why having a C-section was the worst thing ever, why bottle-feeding was akin to introducing your child to Satan himself. In many respects you ceased to exist as an actual person once that small human came into the world.

She really needed to stop reading these blogs and articles. Despite all of the frightening comments, she couldn't wait to become a parent, and what scared her most was that Zach may not feel the same way.

Anouska took another sip of her drink. One thing about travelling alone, it gave you plenty of time to think. Great, just what she needed, even more time inside her head.

She smiled, though, as she thought of one of Ellie's recent texts. She was proposing on the twenty-ninth too. Scott was finally committing to her. She was pleased for Ellie, really she was, but was she cursed, or was the universe hellbent on telling her something?

Jess and Ellie were going to propose.

Time to be honest with herself. She wanted to get married. Listening to the girls tell her their ideas for their proposals had infiltrated her subconscious somehow and made her revisit her feelings. She'd always thought she'd eventually get married, although she hadn't been one of those girls who have vision boards of their wedding from the age of eight, nor their bridesmaids picked out by the time they're teenagers. But she'd genuinely assumed she'd meet the right guy and at some point they'd marry. She'd met the right guy, but he hated marriage. He hadn't always hated marriage, but a certain someone, a certain *Marcie*, had forever tainted his view of it. His ex-fiancée had let Zach down so badly he could barely remain civil when the subject of marriage cropped up in conversation. He always quickly changed the subject, or made himself scarce when in company and it was possible to do so.

Now, here she was, having a baby with the man she'd always wanted to marry, but whom she'd never told so, given his very vocal negative viewpoint on the matter, and now she was spending a significant amount of her free time with two friends who were about to propose. Either someone up there was having a good old laugh at her expense or it was a sign.

But how could she propose when she couldn't even tell Zach she was expecting his baby? Crikey, how screwed-up could you get? If there were awards for it, she'd be top of the podium.

She figured there was no harm in doing a little research, and she definitely wasn't in the mood to do any work, so she typed 'leap-year proposals' into Google, which returned the following results: Leap Day Customs and Traditions; Leap-Year Proposals: Why women traditionally propose; Leap-Year Proposal – what's the story behind it? The last one – 'How To Get It Right' – sounded right for her. She didn't want to make a complete hash of it, after all, did she?

She clicked on the 'How To Get It Right' one and read through why they should get married and prerequisites for it: common goals, next logical step, previously discussed marriage. She couldn't tick that last one, but the others were solid. Then it suggested where and how they should get married, obvious stuff about not tailoring it to your likes and dislikes but your partner's. That was something else she'd have to consider. Where? Definitely in private. Zach was a very private person. Although he played the role of extrovert restaurateur, when it came to his personal life he was the exact opposite. That's why she had to make sure no one knew before he did about the baby, as he'd be devastated and would view it as a breach of trust. First, though, she had to gather her thoughts. Should she wait until after the proposal? Should she tell him then propose? Should part of her proposal be having a little gift made which read, 'You're going to be a father'? Her mind was awhirl and she didn't know where to start.

A text coming in on the group chat interrupted her thoughts. Ellie. *How's Brazil? Are you living it up at a samba club? Hope you're having a* caipirinha *or two for me. And some of that delicious* picanha. *A string of emojis followed: hearts, a ballerina – Anouska guessed there was no specific samba dancer emoji – a steak and two different cocktail glasses.*

Anouska appreciated the irony. Usually, when she came to Brazil, she did partake of both the cocktail and the steak, but not the dancing. She knew her limits, and embarrassing herself in front of a huge roomful of stunningly beautiful, amazingly talented samba dancers wasn't her idea of a good time. Maybe if she'd been there with Jess and Ellie or the girls from the hen party it would have been a different dynamic and outcome, but there was no way she'd put herself through that relatively sober and with her male territory manager.

However, this trip to Brazil would encompass neither caipirinha nor picanha as cocktails and potentially undercooked meat were most definitely off the menu for her right now.

All these thoughts of food were making her hungry. She grabbed the room service menu, and after flipping through, selected the slow-cooked prawn stew with coconut milk. It was the best thing in this area. She'd have gone to her favourite restaurant, Camarões, tonight – funnily enough, it meant prawns – but she simply didn't have the energy. She'd have to pass on her favourite dessert of *quindim* because of the egg yolk in the custard, but she'd settle for her second favourite of *bolo de rolo*. The fruit roll was one of the prettiest desserts she'd ever had, and it didn't taste half bad either.

Oh no. Now she was salivating. Time to get that order in then she'd reply to Ellie. Her mobile pinged again. She glanced at it then logged on to the room service app and placed her order. Now to kill some time before it arrived.

Thanks for that, Ellie! I've now had to order room service as I was starving. Long day today and I don't seem to have recovered so well from the flights. Still shattered. However, tonight's dinner should perk me up. She then attached images from the hotel website of the meal she'd just ordered. Ha, revenge was sweet!

Then she noticed Jess' message. *Hi, ladies. Hope you're well. I've had a couple of other ideas for locations. How about Luxembourg City, or Piazzale Michelangelo in Florence – a bit commercial, but gorgeous – or how about Santorini? How's the weather in Brazil, Anouska? Got to be better than here. It's -5 °C. Brr!* X

Anouska smiled. One of the things she was struggling with most was the heat. Her iPad showed it was still 23 °C and it was eight o'clock in the evening. Earlier, it had been above thirty degrees.

She reread Jess' message. Personally, she thought all

three of those options sounded lovely, although a great deal depended on Jess and Mark's personal taste. Despite the three of them sharing a little insight into their other halves' likes and dislikes, Mark in particular, as when they'd last met, they'd only known Jess was going to propose, they'd really only scraped the surface of getting to know them. How well could you really know anyone when you'd never met them and everything you'd learned about them was second-hand information?

Her phone buzzed again and images of the three locations came through from Jess. She'd been right with her gut feeling. They did all look great places to propose. Aware her food would be arriving soon, she tapped out, *All of those look gorgeous, Jess. Go for it x*

As she waited for room service to arrive, Anouska's thoughts inevitably returned to her baby, their baby, her and Zach's baby. She already knew she wanted to spend the rest of her life with this man. With an unexpected surge of resolve, Anouska decided enough was enough. It was time to face up to her fear of rejection.

She checked the time again in the UK. Not too late, hopefully. The bistro didn't close until eleven. She had to do it. She had to. She couldn't wait any longer. She dialled Zach's number. No dial tone. Drat. She walked over to the window in case reception was poor where she was sitting. Ah, better. Just as she was about to dial Zach again, a knock came at the door. 'Room service.'

Anouska sighed and then tried to control a hysterical laugh that bubbled up from deep inside her. Something or someone was conspiring for her not to tell Zach about the baby. A wave of exhaustion swept over her as she strode towards the door.

Half an hour later, with two almost empty plates, a half-empty cup of guava juice beside her and her hand resting on her swollen belly – not from pregnancy but from the amount of food she'd consumed – Anouska sat back sated, but unable to move an inch. It was as well she was busy texting the girls. Ellie had had her in stitches over her ever more bizarre proposal ideas for her and Scott – Anouska was really glad she wasn't Scott. Proposing whilst swimming with sharks, whilst white-water rafting or a marginally more sedate possibility, whilst hot air ballooning over the Serengeti desert in Tanzania were Ellie's top three of the moment.

As she lay thinking of the girls' intention to propose and her own situation, she came to a decision. She wanted to get married. She needed to get married. She had to take back control. Perhaps if she proposed to Zach, instead of the other way around, that would be enough to make him realise it needn't be like it was with Marcie. She wasn't going to cheat on him. She wasn't Marcie. He had to have faith, and believe in her. He had to believe in them.

Chapter Eleven

Ellie

Thursday 23 January

'You're what?' Chloe gawped at her and almost fell over a stack of Rosie's toys as she reeled from Ellie's revelation.

'I'm going to propose to Scott on the twenty-ninth of February. A leap-year proposal.'

'Ellie, are you sure about this?' Chloe's eyes didn't leave Ellie's face as she handed Rosie a colouring book with one hand and a packet of colouring pencils with the other. She was exemplary at multitasking.

'Yes, you know me, sis, once I've made up my mind, that's that.'

'I know, but you've only just decided to move in together. Proposing less than a month after deciding that, and without even having moved in together yet, seems a bit…'

'Organised? Adventurous? As if I'm taking control of my own destiny?' Ellie threw at her.

Chloe's eyebrows knitted. 'No, I was thinking more "extreme".'

Ellie shot her an exasperated look. 'C'mon, Chloe, we've hardly just started dating.'

'I'd probably be happier if you had,' Chloe muttered.

'But you're the one who told me to take the initiative if I wasn't happy with the status quo.' Ellie raised her hands then let them drop to her side in incomprehension.

Chloe sighed. 'You're right, I did, but it just all seems to be happening so fast. You've gone from almost being ready to ditch him a few weeks ago if he didn't step up and commit, to buying a house with him and proposing marriage.'

Ellie slumped down on the kitchen bench. 'I was hoping for a bit more support, Chloe.'

Chloe came round the table and put her arms around Ellie's shoulders. 'Ellie, I'll always be here to support you, but I wouldn't be doing my sisterly duty if I didn't point out the whimsical nature of what you're about to do, would I now?'

Ellie studied Chloe's kind-hearted face and knew her sister, as always, was only looking out for her. She leant in to her, nudging her head slightly against Chloe's arm. 'I suppose not, but I really do think I'm doing the right thing.'

'I know you do, and I'm not saying you aren't, I'm just saying, stop and think. Don't get too swept up in the moment. Romantic as it might seem, buying a house and planning a wedding and marriage are two of the three biggies in life. That's why it's best not to do them simultaneously.'

Ellie chewed on her lip. 'I hear what you're saying, but I've waited so long to be at this stage, I just want to get excited about it all.'

'And that's fine, but, please, exercise a little caution.'

Ellie's heart plummeted. She'd been all fired-up at the

prospect of sharing her news with Chloe, but her sister wasn't telling her what she wanted to hear. Part of her knew she was right to be the voice of reason, but she was fed up with reason, where relationships were concerned anyway. She'd had her fill of waiting around for something to happen, so she'd made it happen, by having the estate agency value her property, and now not one but two positive things were happening, or three if you counted Scott's commitment. She just wanted to bask in this moment, at least for a bit longer, then she'd put her serious pants back on again and consider the ramifications of her recent decisions and perhaps rein it in a bit.

'And, Ellie, how does this affect your potential promotion?'

Ellie's face fell. She hadn't allowed herself headspace for that yet. The bottom line was she couldn't have the best of both worlds. She either had Scott, living with him and hopefully marrying him, or she had the promotion. But there'd be other promotions, surely. If not with her current employer, she'd manage, eventually, to get one at another firm. Or would she? Plus, she liked it at Faraway Shores Travel.

'I haven't processed that part yet,' she confessed.

'Ellie–' Chloe rubbed Ellie's hand gently '–last week, you came to see me, gutted that you had to tell me you may, if you were lucky, be moving to Manchester for the job of your dreams.'

Ellie's eyes remained fixed on Chloe's.

'We were both distraught at the thought of you upping sticks and leaving, but ultimately we both accepted it may be the best course for you and your career right now. Correct?'

Glumly, Ellie nodded.

'Then, in the space of a few hours, you show your house to an estate agency and Scott asks you to buy a house together, and now your dream job is not only up in the air, but you're going to propose.'

Ellie's misery intensified as a tear slid down her face. 'I don't know what to do, Chloe. I want to have it all, but it seems I can't.'

Chloe let Ellie cry it out on her shoulder. 'Look, all I'm saying is think things through. I'm not trying to rain on your parade, I promise I'm not, you know me better than that anyway, but I'm worried you're making some major life decisions without considering all the consequences.'

'You've always got my back, Chloe. I know that. I just want to be excited about the fact my life is progressing. The problem is, it all seems to be doing so at once.'

Chloe nodded. 'Ellie, I'm here for you whatever you decide. Just, keep your options open on the job front, that's all I'm asking. You've worked too hard, to simply throw it all away.'

Ellie sniffed then took out a tissue and blew her nose. 'I will.'

As Ellie drove back to Stockbridge, she mulled over what Chloe had said. When she got home, she slung her bag on the hall floor, and for once was delighted to be alone. She had an hour before she had to meet the girls, so she popped the kettle on, put on an album by one of her favourite indie bands and logged on to the Rightmove website to check out the properties she'd bookmarked for her and Scott to look at.

Maybe if she took some action in this direction, actually showed Scott some of the houses she thought might be a good fit for their first home together, she could gauge his opinion and they could start making plans. Perhaps if they visited properties together, she'd know which way to jump when decision time came.

Could they get married and initially commute up and down between Edinburgh and Manchester for a year? Was it a foregone conclusion that she had to turn the promotion down, if she was lucky enough to get it in the first place, if she and Scott moved in together or got married? Actually, the buying a bigger property made less sense than getting married if she took the job in Manchester. They could be married but potentially live apart for a little while, even if it wasn't ideal, but buying a bigger house with a bigger mortgage, in a neighbourhood she'd want to live in, whilst simultaneously paying rent in Manchester or its suburbs made no sense. Aargh. Her head was about to explode again.

Right, enough of this nonsense. She stood up and strode around the room. She'd always thought pacing helped her think. After less than a minute, she knew what she had to do.

She picked up her mobile and dialled. 'Hi, I was interested in viewing a couple of properties you have on at the minute.'

Ellie was last to arrive at Cirque. This was becoming a habit, although today it had more to do with her conversation with Chloe and no longer really wanting to share what she'd intended to with the girls, but they weren't letting her off that easily. She'd promised them the goods and now they wanted her to deliver.

'C'mon then, don't keep us in suspense, what have you got for us?' said Jess.

'No, you give us your update first.' Ellie smiled but she knew it wouldn't reach her eyes.

Anouska frowned. 'What's wrong?'

Ellie sighed. 'Nothing.' She sighed again, more heavily this time. 'Everything.'

'Well, that's specific,' joked Jess.

Ellie gave a half-smile.

'I had a chat with Chloe. She thinks things are moving too fast and she's worried about me.'

'But that's what sisters do, especially big sisters,' Jess reassured her.

Ellie shook her head. 'No, it's more than that. She was definitely giving off a seriously concerned vibe, and even though I know she's in my corner, it's really making me reassess everything – again.'

'That's not necessarily a bad thing, Ellie,' Anouska said. 'Sometimes, we can get caught up in the heat of the moment and act or react without fully allowing ourselves to absorb what's going on.'

Ellie grimaced. 'That's sort of what Chloe said.'

'She's a wise woman.' Anouska grinned. 'But that doesn't mean you can't be excited about the things you've planned, nor that you have to rule anything in or out just yet. How's about this, tell us what progress you've made, and we'll listen, without interrupting, so you can lay it all out. Then, if you want, we'll tell you what we think. Agreed, Jess?'

'Absolutely. Ellie, we don't always have to have

everything figured out all at once, you know. It's fine to arrive at decisions in stages. So, in your own time…'

Ellie laughed. 'No pressure then.' She took a deep breath. 'Well, me being me, I went hammer and tongs at everything, and I've made a shortlist of properties I want us to view.'

'Well done.' Anouska smiled. 'You're in the zone.'

'A-ha, but not only that, I've nailed the proposal location!'

Jess' eyes widened.

'All in good time.' Ellie grinned. 'I took on board your thoughts on anything related to extreme sports, and I've decided that perhaps you were right.'

'We were?' said Jess.

Ellie nodded. 'Yes. So I'm going to propose at…drum roll, please…Eilean Donan Castle!'

'Oh, that's gorgeous,' breathed Jess. 'So romantic.'

'That's definitely far safer than skydiving,' Anouska put in.

'Yep, and I'd like to arrive by speedboat.'

'In February? It'll be freezing,' said Jess.

'I know, but I think it lends a touch of drama and occasion to the, well, occasion! A bit James Bond. Scott will love that.'

'He might not love his privates shrinking to the size of walnuts, though, very small walnuts,' Anouska said pointedly.

'Ha ha, you're so funny.'

'No, but seriously, what if it snows?' Jess said.

'If it snows, it will be even more picturesque.'

'But what if the loch is frozen? Isn't that a bit dangerous? Maybe you should have a contingency plan,'

Jess persisted.

'Hmm.' Ellie wasn't convinced.

'I've got it. Scott likes fast cars, doesn't he?' Jess clearly didn't want to be beaten.

'Ye-e-es.'

'Why don't you hire a Lamborghini for the day and arrive in that? That would make it a memorable experience.'

'So would vomit all down his shoes. No, I know where you're coming from, Jess, but if Scott's in a fast car, I don't want to be in it with him. I hate his driving at the best of times. Plus, I'd prefer to be the one driving at speed!'

'Good point. I'm still not convinced the speedboat's a good idea, though.'

'Well, that's a shame because I booked and paid for it this morning.'

'Arriving by speedboat does rather add to the romance of it all,' Anouska said, taking the sting out of Jess' inadvertent faux pas. 'Sorry, Ellie, we weren't trying to stomp all over your idea. Just make sure you take warm clothing.'

'We will.' She smiled. 'I can't wait to see his face.'

She proceeded to tell them about the viewings she'd arranged, one in the city, one in Dalkeith and one in North Berwick, because of its seaside location.

Ellie ordered another round of tea for them and as she sat back down, Anouska steepled her fingers on the table and said, 'Confession time.'

'Oh?' Ellie raised an eyebrow and glanced quickly at Jess to see if she knew what was coming.

A half-smile played on Anouska's lips. 'I promise I'm not simply jumping on the bandwagon, but I did a lot of thinking in Brazil, and–' she paused '–I've decided to propose too. And if you guys can do it on the twenty-ninth of February, I don't see why I can't.'

I wasn't expecting that. Ellie patted Anouska on the arm in a gesture of solidarity.

'This is amazing!' Jess jumped up and hugged her.

Ellie smiled. 'Wow, look at us, the leap-year proposalers.'

Jess said, 'I don't think proposaler is a word, Ellie.'

Ellie made a face. 'Who cares?'

Anouska laughed then added, 'I'm now absolutely terrified, have no idea how to propose, and am already doubting my decision, but at least I've come to it.'

Ellie wagged a finger. 'You've obviously thought long and hard about it, so don't talk yourself out of it now. Welcome to the club!'

Chapter Twelve

Jess

Wednesday 29 January

'Hi, honey, I'm home,' Jess called.

Silence.

None of the lights were on anywhere in the flat, so she switched on the lamps on either side of the room, then the radio for company and cranked up the central heating. She was tired tonight. It was already half past nine and she hadn't had dinner yet. The club had put on an extra two classes and then the new instructor had bailed at the last minute, accepting an offer elsewhere, so she'd been asked if she could step in as a favour, just for this week. Now she was wrecked.

Where was Mark? He didn't have rugby tonight and he hadn't said anything about going anywhere. Had she missed him telling her about a departmental meeting or something? She checked the kitchen calendar where they kept a note of all their appointments so they didn't double-book themselves. Zilch. Oh well, she'd make herself a chicken stir fry and have an early night with a book.

She pushed the chicken, peppers and onions around the frying pan, then realised she hadn't checked her phone to see if she had any messages. She rummaged in her bag for her phone then returned to the kitchen to stir her food so it didn't burn. Two missed calls. One voicemail. As she listened to her voicemail, she removed the pan from the heat and poured its contents onto a plate.

'Message received at 5.35 p.m. *"Hi, Jess, just to say I'm going out for a pizza with the English department tonight. Tony's fault. He's roped us all into it at the last minute. Hope that's OK and you didn't have anything planned. I figured you'd be working anyway. See you when I get in. Love you."*'

Ah, so that's where he was. Fair enough. She took her plate through to the dining room and sat down at the oak dining table, staring into space, her eyes resting on the Matisse print of a black cat at an open window. Mark had bought it for her the year before and it now took centre stage in their dining room. Although she was more of a dog person, she loved that picture. Absent-mindedly, she reminded herself she needed to have the frame changed out so it matched the oak of the others dotted around the dining room and living room. Her gaze swept around the living room, and she smiled at the dent in the sofa cushions Mark had made that morning. They really needed a new sofa, this one was second-hand and in dusky pink, but after shelling out for the flat, they hadn't been able to afford everything new. But first a wedding ... and that likely wouldn't come cheap.

She popped another forkful of chicken into her mouth as her thoughts turned to the girls and their proposals. She considered Anouska's decision to propose. That had come out of left field, and she couldn't help thinking something else was going on in the background with Anouska, but she couldn't quite put her finger on what it was. Oh well, if she wanted her to know, or if she had anything troubling her, she'd tell them in her own time.

She smiled at how different they all were, and she hugged to herself the thought that she had been instrumental in these two wonderful women coming to the decision, partly because she herself had been brave enough to make the decision first. It tickled her to think that if it hadn't been for the hen do, or the marriage quiz, none of them might have considered proposing, and certainly wouldn't be making a leap-year proposal. And she chuckled at Ellie making snap decisions and storming ahead with her plans. Good on her.

Mark still wasn't home when she went to bed, and worn out, she fell asleep almost immediately. She woke up with the weight of a body sitting on the edge of the bed.

'What time is it?' Jess yawned.

'One o'clock?'

Now she was wide awake. 'You just home?'

'I've been in about half an hour. I met Jared when I was out with the department. He convinced me to go to the pub with him.'

'Was Livorna with him?'

'No, she was out with her friends, so he was in no hurry to get home.'

'Must have been quite a night.'

'I know. It just sort of progressed and I felt I needed a night away from marking.'

Jess didn't say he could have spent it with her, free of his red pen for once, as she knew she'd been in no fit state to be decent company.

'Are you getting in then? You're creating a draught,' she said, half joking.

'I need to pee first.'

Lovely.

As Mark went to the toilet, Jess realised he hadn't even kissed her. They were like an old married couple already.

It hadn't always been this way. When they were first going out, they'd been all over each other, couldn't get enough of each other, and Mark was very demonstrative, including in public. She supposed that couldn't last forever though, in the same way as they'd outgrown partying every weekend. That had progressed into long walks on a Sunday and lunch or dinner out at their destination. Friends' birthday celebrations had also featured heavily in their social life, and now it seemed to be weddings. But bit by bit the time for just the two of them had evaporated. Somewhere along the line, the romance in their life had started to fade. Somehow she had to reverse that trend.

Thursday 30 January

Jess slid her finger around the rim of her empty cup, deep in thought, until a rap at the café window startled her. Anouska was waving at her and grinning. A second later and she'd

plonked herself on the velour chair, which was very Paris chic, undoing her scarf from around her neck as she did so.

'So, any news?' Anouska asked after kissing her cheek.

Jess clapped her hands together repeatedly. 'Yes! I've decided on Sicily. I've found a hotel in Taormina and checked flights. Hopefully, I can book them tonight, but I wanted to show you two first.'

'Well, let's see the hotel then. You bring up the details

and I'll get the drinks in. More tea?'

Jess nodded. 'Peppermint, please.' As she waited for the page to load, her mobile rang. Ellie.

'Hi, Ellie. How far away are you? I'm about to show Anouska the hotel I've chosen.'

'Please don't start without me,' Ellie begged.

'We'll wait for you, but hurry up.' She hung up and turned to Anouska, who held out a colourful mug with nine yoga poses on it.

'Thought it was perfect for you.' She smiled.

Jess gratefully accepted the tea and took a sip. 'Mmm, just what I needed. We've to wait for Ellie.'

'I got that. Is she far away?'

'Ten minutes.'

'Excellent, we can grill each other until she gets here. How was your day?'

'Fine.' Jess nibbled on a macaron, which Anouska had had the foresight to order at the same time as the drinks. She made a note to buy some to take home with her later. 'But I'm actually much more interested in you and your decision to propose. I must admit it was a shock and I felt as if we didn't have enough time to cover it last week.'

Anouska's hazel eyes twinkled. 'That's the way I planned it. No, just kidding.' She sighed then leant her elbows on the table.

'Is everything OK?' Jess asked, her concern heightening at Anouska's change in expression.

'What? Sure. It's just that when I was in Brazil, I gave myself a bit of a talking-to, and admitted that I'd always wanted to marry Zach, but because of his issues around marriage – his ex-fiancée cheated on him – I'd shut that option off to myself.'

'Wow! I wasn't expecting that. That is a lot to deal with. And you've not told anyone about this?'

Anouska shook her head and Jess leant forward. 'Well, I'm glad you told me. That couldn't have been easy, but hey, you've made a decision to do something about it.'

'I have. Just like you and Ellie. Your strength and resolve gave me the incentive to act.' Her eyes watered and she blinked rapidly. 'Anyway, enough about me. Just because Ellie hasn't arrived yet, doesn't mean you can't discuss the proposal plans. Does Mark have any inkling, do you think? You have been careful, haven't you? Not left anything lying around.'

'No.' Jess embraced Anouska's swift change of subject. She clearly needed to collect herself. 'He hasn't a clue. I've even been deleting my history on my laptop in case he uses mine when it's open and starts typing something into the search engine and it suggests something I've been looking for.'

'You'd make a great private detective.' Anouska grinned.

The bell over the door pinged again and Ellie blew in, hair streaming over her shoulders like one of Titian's muses. Several shopping bags weighed her down as she tried to negotiate the door. 'God, I'm freezing.' She glanced at the hot drinks. 'Did you order me one?'

'I'll get you one. Why don't you sit down and heat up?' Anouska suggested.

'Hot chocolate, please.'

Once they were all comfortably ensconced with hot drinks and they had chosen from the menu, they huddled together over the distressed wooden table, hands around their mugs for extra warmth.

'Right.' Jess beamed at their expectant faces. 'I've decided on Sicily.' She sat the phone on the table facing the girls so they could both see.

Ellie scanned the screen. 'That looks lovely. So authentic and charming.'

Jess nodded. That's what she'd thought too.

'One thing though. With Mark being a teacher, how much time will you have in Sicily? It's after half-term, isn't it?' Ellie said.

'Don't worry. I've sorted all that out.' Jess clasped her hands together. 'So, here's my plan. It's expensive, but there's an evening flight on the twenty-seventh, which gets us into Catania at ten. The hotel have offered to send their courtesy bus for us. We would then have two full days there, then the flight back is on the first of March, getting us into London for eleven thirty, so we won't be back in Glasgow until the early hours, and we'll be exhausted, but who cares?'

Anouska and Ellie nodded.

'So why Sicily?' Anouska asked.

Jess grinned and leant forward. 'Well, I did say I wanted something that meant something special to Mark, had some sort of significance for him, so since his favourite movie is *Cinema Paradiso*, I figured Sicily fitted the bill.'

'Nice,' said Ellie. 'But didn't you fancy somewhere a bit warmer at this time of year?'

'Of course,' said Jess, 'but I can't exactly hop over to Mexico for the weekend. I'd have to fly back almost the minute I landed.'

'Fair point,' conceded Ellie, who then spoke into her phone. 'Temperature in Taormina, Sicily in February.' She waited a minute then shrieked, 'Nine degrees! Christ, that's cold. Never mind, all the more reason to warm each other up.' She winked at Jess.

Jess rolled her eyes. 'We'll have coats.'

'You had better buy him one of those puffy jackets and thermals – or maybe not, that could be a real passion killer,' joked Ellie.

'But kidding aside, make sure you take hats, scarves and gloves. It's difficult to feel romantic when you're freezing,' said Anouska.

'Sounds brilliant. What are you waiting for? Let's get these flights booked!' Ellie was clearly never one to hang around when a good plan could be concluded there and then.

'I take it you've checked the hotel has availability,' Anouska piped up.

'Yes, they even have the room I wanted.'

'That's good. Well, I think you should go for it,' Anouska said.

Ellie agreed, then the waiter appeared with their food and silence reigned.

After they'd eaten, the three of them sat back to discuss in more detail how Jess would propose: in the hotel, in a nearby restaurant, if she would buy him a ring and what she would wear for the occasion.

When Jess returned home, she settled down at the dining table in front of her laptop, her plans taking shape. She couldn't wait to get away, not simply so she could propose, but because even the cosy glow from her Anglepoise lamp – an indulgence – did little to brighten up the cold winter's evening.

By the time Mark arrived back ten minutes later, she'd booked the flight and hotel on the personal credit card she kept for buying birthday and Christmas presents, not their joint one. That way, he wouldn't see it on the itemised bill and ruin the surprise. As she hugged him, she equally hugged her secret to herself. She knew he would love Sicily. It was a pity they couldn't go for longer, but perhaps they could return on honeymoon, maybe to a different part of the island. Or there was Sardinia. Alghero was supposed to be stunning and the Costa Smeralda, playground of the rich and famous, was famed for its beaches and turquoise waters.

'Hi, gorgeous, how has your day been?' Mark stifled a yawn as he pulled her in for a kiss. 'Sorry, long day, and the rugby went on longer than expected. We were picking teams for Saturday's game. But I did stop by Sugar and Spice and pick these up for you.' From behind his back, he withdrew a pink-and-white striped box bearing the red ribbon that was her favourite bakery's signature.

'Mmm. Yum. Thank you. I had a fabulous day, thanks. I met the girls in Edinburgh again tonight.'

As he handed her the box, he said, 'You three seem to be getting on really well. Ooh, where did you get the macarons?' He picked one up and popped it in his mouth before she could say 'Edinburgh.'

She'd forgotten about the weekend game. Once a month, Mark volunteered to take the boys in his school rugby team to their game, whether it was at home or away. This week, if she recollected correctly, it was away, although she didn't know where. That meant she was free on Saturday. Picking up her phone, she texted Lauren and Kelsea to see if they fancied doing a bit of shopping with her, to help her choose a new wardrobe for her trip to Sicily.

Excitement bubbled in the pit of her stomach. She was really doing this. She was going to propose. It suddenly hit her how massive a deal this was. Mark would say yes, she had few doubts on that front, but she wanted to make the proposal perfect. Absent-mindedly, she wondered if all men went to these lengths. It was nerve-wracking stuff.

She half-listened to Mark telling her about an accident at the rugby training, which had ended in him taking a boy to A&E with a suspected broken arm, but she couldn't give him her full attention as she was fizzing with happiness. She was getting married.

Friday 31 January

Jess' aerobics class started at eleven and she was running late again. This was becoming a habit. She arrived just in time, out of breath and cracking jokes about how she was already exhausted pre-workout and it was all down to her bus being cancelled. Sometimes taking public transport to be more environmentally friendly didn't seem that worthwhile.

She was so distracted as she set up her music and eased the class into some stretching exercises that she didn't initially see Nathan at the back of the class. She must have been blind as at almost six foot and with those mocha eyes, how could she miss him? When she finally did, her first thought was to wonder what on earth he was doing there. He'd been to her yoga and Pilates classes, but never to aerobics and he stood out like a fox in a henhouse as he was the only male in the class.

Throughout the one-hour session there were plenty of

covert glances in his direction by almost every woman there. Well, who wouldn't? He was gorgeous, and that smile, and those eyes. Some of the women didn't even hide their interest in him, flashing him full-on smiles. It was like watching a mating ritual, albeit a bizarre one-sided one, as Nathan seemed oblivious to his charms.

When the class was over and they were all suitably hot and sweaty from their exertions, Jess started packing up.

'Hey.'

She turned to see Nathan standing over her.

'Oh, hi, Nathan. Enjoy the class?'

'Yeah, I fancied a change. Something more high-impact.'

'Hopefully, it did the trick. It usually gets the muscles burning.'

'Yeah, I'm shattered. Using different muscles than usual, I suppose. Anyway, do you fancy a drink? Just at the bar here. Seeing as how you weren't able to make the pub the other night.' There was a definite twinkle in his eye.

What was the harm in it? They would be in full view of the gym staff and other gym-goers and it was only a smoothie. In fact, she told herself, she'd be silly not to say yes as she'd risk offending him. She could also feel the hard stares of almost every woman in the room as they listened to the exchange.

'Sure. Give me five minutes.'

Chapter Thirteen

Anouska

Friday 31 January

'Mum!' Anouska wrapped her arms around Maura, revelling in the personal contact. She didn't see her mum as much as she would like, but they were very close. Her father left when Anouska was three, got remarried to an American woman and lived in California. They weren't in touch. Fortunately, Maura showered her children with enough love for both parents.

'You look wonderful,' her mother told her. It was true. That pregnancy glow she had read so much about was real, except when she was throwing up into toilets. Keeping this baby thing under wraps was proving tricky. But she had noticed that her skin was smoother than usual and overall she felt good. She hadn't yet put on any weight or changed shape, for which she was thankful, as it would make it much easier to avoid detection this weekend whilst her mother was staying.

As they crunched over the compacted snow back towards the car, they filled each other in on all the gossip, well, almost all. Some things had to remain unsaid for another few weeks.

They drove straight to Bean There as Maura loved Zach's food and they got on well, almost like mother and son. Zach had been unable to come to the airport to collect her but had asked Anouska to bring Maura in for brunch.

Maura was known for being effusive, but she enveloped Zach then Todd in such tight hugs that they were soon gasping for air. Normally, Anouska would have been embarrassed, but she was used to her mum and so were Zach and Todd. Anouska sat in peace eating her chocolate chip muffin and drinking a decaf latte. She'd read caffeine was bad for the baby so had switched. When Zach asked her what prompted the change, she told him drinking too much caffeine had made her shaky of late, so she was trying to detox. He'd bought it and she hoped that meant he would put other anomalies in her behaviour down to the same thing.

She took another bite of her chocolate chip muffin and breathed. So far, her mother hadn't twigged about the pregnancy and she wasn't one to hold back. Had she noticed something at the airport, she would have said. Anouska could relax, for the time being at least. Glancing around at the bistro patrons, she wondered at their secrets. She'd bet good money none of them was hiding from their boyfriends the fact they were pregnant or that they intended to propose in a few weeks' time. No, she bet they all lived remarkably normal lives that hadn't been disrupted in the past few weeks and changed beyond all recognition.

Yet Anouska was glad she was pregnant. She knew her life would change irrevocably, and for a career woman it was difficult to reconcile that fact, but perhaps there was something in this concept of maternal instinct, because now she knew the most important thing was the baby, then her relationship with Zach, with her company coming a distant third. How had that happened?

After brunch, Anouska agreed to nip into the office so her mum could see Leigh-Ann – they'd always got on well. She'd man the phones whilst Leigh-Ann and Maura caught up over coffee and cake. There was always coffee and cake involved when Maura was present. It was the Irish upbringing. It never left you. She was almost surprised her mother hadn't arrived with soda bread or the Swedish equivalent in her suitcase.

They spent an hour or so in the office, then headed off to do some shopping.

'Will we go into Trinity?' Maura asked. 'I haven't been in for years. I used to love it there.'

Anouska nodded and Maura's shopping expedition began in earnest. Clothes in Sweden were so expensive, as were most other things, that Maura shopped till her credit card started to cough up its lungs.

'Early dinner at JoJo's?' her mum suggested.

'Why not?' It was their go-to place when Maura was in town. How could she refuse?

Maura sprinkled some lemon juice on her smoked salmon then rolled some onto her fork as Anouska bit into her bruschetta. Maura raised her glass of Merlot and said, 'Cheers. Ah, you're on a health kick, I see.'

'Sorry?'

'No wine.'

'Oh, right. Yes, detox. Been knocking it back a bit

recently. Thought I'd take it down a notch.'

'I see,' said Maura, but quite what she saw Anouska wasn't sure.

After a few mouthfuls of her meal, Maura said, 'So, were you going to tell me at some point you were pregnant?'

Anouska almost spat out her bruschetta and began to choke so fiercely, her mother had to come round and pat her on the back. She then handed her a glass of water.

'Wha-a-a-t?' she finally managed.

'Anouska, I'm your mother. I will always know when something is different with you, even if I don't see you for a long time. I carried you in my womb for eight and a half months. That bond cannot be broken. I sensed you were pregnant because you're glowing. And you radiate happiness.'

Anouska had tears in her eyes. 'I'm sorry, Mum. I wanted to tell you, but I haven't even told Zach yet.'

Maura's mouth fell open. 'Whyever not?'

'Because we always said we didn't want kids, and I've also decided…' she took a deep breath then motored on '…to ask him to marry me on the twenty-ninth of February.'

'Oh my word. That's so romantic. Can I get a ringside seat for the proposal?'

Anouska stared at her incredulously. 'No, Mum, you can't. This is real life, remember, not a soap opera.'

'Sorry, it's just you're always so together. I think I like this more vulnerable, hormonal side of you.'

'Thanks…I think,' Anouska said.

'So–' Maura leant forward '–when are you going to tell him?'

'I don't know. I'm having difficulty getting him on his own and when I do manage, the words won't come.' She exhaled heavily. 'And what if he freaks out?' Anouska folded her napkin in half and then again.

'He won't freak out. He may be a bit taken aback, surprised even, but he'll adapt. No man is ever ready to become a father,' Maura pronounced sagely.

'That's a bit of a sweeping generalisation, Mum,' Anouska said.

'Well, sometimes they just need it thrust upon them.'

'Hmm. But you don't understand. Marcie, Zach's ex, wanted a baby, and Zach didn't, and things didn't end well for them as a result. They didn't end well for them at all,' she muttered. She bit her lip. 'Maybe I should wait until after I propose to tell him.'

Maura vigorously wagged a finger at Anouska. 'No, no, no! That's a terrible idea! And too much for him to take in at once.'

'Perhaps. But I need to know that he'll marry me because he loves me and not because I'm carrying his child or because he feels duty bound.'

Maura nodded in understanding. 'I get it. But I still think you're doing Zach a disservice. That boy adores you. Don't you think he'll be mad at you keeping this from him? And, Zach aside, apart from not drinking wine, do you know how to prepare for a baby? Have you been to see a midwife? When's the baby due? When are the scans? Do you want a boy or a girl…?'

'Mum, breathe,' instructed Anouska. 'I know it's a lot to take in, it was for me too, but we can do this, as a family.'

'Sorry, I'm just excited.'

'Yes, I can see that.' Anouska accepted her mother's

hug.

'I'm going to be a grandmother! Oh, my goodness, I'll be able to spoil the baby rotten. Buy it lots of tiny Babygros and cardigans. When are you due?'

'August.'

'Ah, a summer baby, although that will make your last trimester a little trickier. Having to go through the summer pregnant is so hard because of the heat.'

'Mum, I was born in May, Kian in April. How would you know?'

'I've been told.' Maura huffed. 'Will the baby call me Granny or Nana?'

'I don't know.' Anouska threw her hands out. 'What would you like to be called?'

'I can't work out which one seems older. Does Nana seem more fun? I definitely want my grandchildren to have fun with me.'

'What do you mean grandchildren? There's only one baby. And can I point out that this isn't all about you. In fact, it's not about you at all, but about me and Bean.'

'Bean?'

'Yes.' Anouska smiled. 'That's what I nicknamed it. I had heard babies were the size of kidney beans at eight weeks. It made me think of Bean There, and I thought how appropriate that was.'

'It certainly is. Anyway, back to Zach. When are you going to tell him?' Maura popped a forkful of smoked salmon in her mouth.

'I'm not sure yet, but I'm going to make him a meal at home, propose, wait for his answer, then show him the positive pregnancy test.'

Maura waved her hand in front of her mouth, indicating she was still trying to swallow, then said, 'Uh-oh.

That's a terrible idea. What if you freak him out and he scarpers?'

'Mum, what an awful thing to say! Zach's as reliable as they come.'

'Yes, he is, and I don't dispute that fact, but believe me, with years of experience, I can happily say no man likes to have a major surprise like that sprung on them. I think you should tell him about the pregnancy first. I could make myself scarce one night if it helps.'

'There's no need to do that. We barely see you. But please don't say anything to Zach until I figure out how to tell him.'

'OK, OK,' Maura said. 'But tell him and tell him soon.'

Anouska rolled her eyes. 'I will.'

'Why don't we head home shortly and you can have a bath and relax whilst I make something for tomorrow's dinner?'

'You sure?' Anouska picked up another slice of bruschetta.

'I'm sure.'

Anouska took a long, hot bath, even managing to read thirty pages of a book as she luxuriated in the bubbles. She had read she should avoid certain oils so had stuck to bubble bath. Zach had come home for an hour earlier but had already left for the launch of a friend's restaurant.

'Anouska, that documentary you wanted to watch is starting,' her mother called.

Maura was making her traditional chicken cassoulet, French, of course, and to die for, for the following evening's dinner. The smell was incredible.

'I'll be there in a minute.'

They watched the documentary about climate change, Gypsy snuggled in to Maura – traitor – then Anouska made plans to take her mother to do a little more shopping in the morning. Again the smell of the cassoulet reached her. It was heavenly; her mum got certain things right, albeit dispensing relationship advice wasn't one of them. She wondered if her senses were heightened because of her pregnancy. Her appetite certainly seemed to be. As if in confirmation, her stomach rumbled.

As they relaxed with cups of tea, Maura said, 'So, have you thought much about the proposal?'

'Not really, Mum. I've had a lot on and I'm so tired all the time.'

'That's pregnancy for you. Let me get my thinking cap on. I'm here to help.'

Now Anouska was worried. She could almost see the speech bubbles coming out of her mum's head, and they said 'mariachi band', 'string quartet', 'harpist', 'Red Arrows fly-past', 'plane streaming through the air with a banner flapping behind it in the wind, saying "Marry Me, Zach, love, Anouska"'.

She wanted something simple, especially given the double whammy she was hitting him with. Perhaps she would get flash cards made up then display them to him one by one, kind of like Andrew Lincoln did with Kiera Knightley in *Love Actually*.

It wasn't that she didn't want her mother's help. She did, in certain areas, but this was *her* proposal. Her mother was from a different generation and their ideas didn't match on this. She only ever intended to make one proposal and it had to come from the heart. Oh, she could study the websites, take notes, choose parts that might work for her, but she'd mould it into something personal to them both.

She just had to get through this weekend with her mum and Zach in the same room without Zach cottoning on, as no doubt there would be an undercurrent. Hopefully, Zach would put it down to Maura's occasional eccentricities and be none the wiser. It was a godsend that he would be working most of the time.

When the documentary finished, she could recall virtually nothing about it. Her head hurt. There was too much to process. Maura chose a romcom and they settled down companionably to watch it, but soon Anouska's eyes became heavier and heavier, then finally drifted closed.

The blaring of the theme tune that accompanied the closing credits jolted Anouska awake.

'I think it's time for bed. Pity Zach isn't back yet,' Maura said.

The clock read eleven thirty. Disappointment coursed through Anouska. Zach had told her he would make time to see Maura during her trip, although she supposed they had crossed paths briefly this morning and again before his friend's launch. But the other part of her was glad. My goodness, having all these hormones raging around inside her body was weird, and they seemed to be making her dimmer too. On the one hand she wanted Zach to *want* to spend time with her mother, but on the other hand she had to keep them as far apart as possible. This was getting far too complicated.

She trudged off to bed. *Roll on the twenty-ninth of February.*

Chapter Fourteen

Ellie

Tuesday 4 February

Ellie was frantically trying to finish off the brochure she had been pulling together with the heads of the other departments, ready to go to the proofreader tonight. If she didn't manage it, there wouldn't be enough time to have it all checked properly before it went to the printer's.

She was meeting Scott at Caprese, their favourite Italian restaurant. They hadn't been out much recently, but she had insisted. She wanted to ask him to take a few days off work, including the twenty-ninth of February, and she didn't intend to do it by phone or text. She wasn't taking no for an answer.

When she arrived at the restaurant there were only four other diners and no sign of Scott. She was already five minutes late, as she'd left later than intended, and had had to put a spurt on and speedwalk there, particularly since the rain was coming down in torrents. So her temperament wasn't improved by the fact she was soaking wet. The February weather was shaping up to be just as horrible as January's.

The waiter, Luca, whom she knew because they had

once been frequent diners here, showed her to a table by the window, and more importantly the radiator, lit a candle in the centre of the table and left her two menus.

Whilst she waited for Scott, she perused the menu and ordered herself a Bellini. Why not? Quarter past six. He was supposed to be meeting her here at six. She checked her phone. Nothing. She texted him, asking how long before he would be there. Rather than opt for something she knew she loved, she chose *involtini* for starters but stuck with her old faithful *Bolognese alla ragù* for her main course. She'd wait for Scott to arrive before ordering though. She checked her phone again.

By half past six, she was seriously unimpressed. She called him but it rang out, so she left a voicemail, then ordered her starter. The two breadsticks she'd nibbled on hadn't quite filled her up. What was keeping him? Eventually, she called him again. Straight to voicemail. Now she was beginning to worry. Should she stay in the restaurant or go home and make some calls? She would look a right clingy mare if she called his friends after his only being 'missing' for half an hour. He couldn't have forgotten. She had reminded him only this morning. She called his house – no answer.

Ellie ate her starter but had no appetite for it. She couldn't even drive to Scott's house to see if he was all right, as she'd drunk that Bellini. Finally admitting to herself that Scott wasn't coming, she asked Luca for the bill. His concerned expression had her almost in tears.

From the taxi, she called Chloe and burst into noisy sobs when she answered the phone, then tried to pull herself together in case her sister was worried something had happened to her.

'It's Scott.'

'Has he been in an accident? Is he OK?'

'No. I don't know. I don't think so. But I can't get hold of him and we were to meet at Caprese, and I waited for more than half an hour but he hasn't turned up, and I've texted him and he hasn't replied, and I've phoned him and left a voicemail and phoned him again and it didn't even ring…' Ellie paused for breath. Her chest was tight, as if she were having a heart attack.

'Slow down, slow down,' Chloe said. 'Where are you now?'

'I'm on the way home.' She hiccoughed.

'Do you want to come here? Or I can be at yours in five minutes.'

'Would you mind coming here? I don't want Rosie seeing me in this state.' She hiccoughed again.

'She's in bed, but that's fine. Mitchell can look after her. I'll meet you at the flat.'

'Or shall I get the taxi to swing past yours? I'm not far away.'

'No, I'll bring the car. It'll make it easier for getting back.'

'Thanks, Chloe. I appreciate it.'

Ellie put her phone back in her bag and sat back in her seat. Where the hell was Scott?

By the time the taxi reached Ellie's flat, Chloe's car was pulling into a parking space. Ellie paid the driver and hurried over to Chloe, who stepped out of the car and hugged her.

'You OK?'

'Not sure.' Ellie continued to hug Chloe then drew back and said, 'I've just had an idea. Can you drive me to Scott's flat? I'd have driven myself, but I've had a Bellini.'

'Sure. Get in.'

As they drove the sixteen miles to Livingston, Chloe tried to reassure her. 'Maybe he's been held up at work.'

When Ellie remained silent, Chloe continued. 'Why don't you call Caprese to check if he has turned up?'

Ellie scowled. 'I think he's made me look enough of a prat for one night, thanks. I don't need anyone else to know my boyfriend is still AWOL.'

Chloe sighed. 'Fair point.'

Even though she obviously didn't want anything bad to have happened to Scott, Ellie was furious as she had never been stood up before. Why would he not turn up? If he had a meeting that ran late or if he had to go and be wined and dined by some pharmaceutical company, why not text or ring her? Anyway, he worked at the university. They mainly kept office hours, so the latter scenarios were unlikely, although he could occasionally get so caught up in his research that he forgot the time.

No, she was sure he would be home, but why not answer her calls and how could he have forgotten when she'd texted him to remind him only that morning? Come to think of it, had he actually replied to confirm? She'd been so busy working on the brochure, it hadn't occurred to her to double-check.

She explained her thought process to Chloe and checked her phone. He hadn't replied. However, he had said yes a few days before when she'd initially asked him. Now she felt a bit of an idiot. Maybe he was delayed at work, or had something else on and had forgotten, but it still didn't explain why he hadn't answered her text that morning or her calls or texts that night. Unless he'd left his phone at home. He was forever doing that.

She divulged her thoughts to Chloe, who asked if she wanted them to turn around. Ellie felt silly having dragged her sister out of her home and away from her husband on a cold winter's night and even more foolish for making her drive out to Livingston, but well, they were here now, and Scott's house was only two streets away, so they'd be as well to go and check.

Ellie showed Chloe which way to go, then as they approached Scott's house, she noted his car in the drive. There was also another car, one she didn't recognise. Ellie's brow creased in puzzlement and she shot Chloe a look. Who was he with? She wasn't the jealous type, but she'd just made an idiot of herself, sitting in a restaurant waiting for him to turn up. She had a right to know why he hadn't appeared. And if he was home, which seemed likely as the lights were on, the blinds partially drawn, then he'd have his mobile with him.

'So he *is* home.' Confusion swirled in Ellie's stomach as dread and uncertainty vied for supremacy within her. 'Why didn't he answer his bloody phone then?' she muttered almost to herself. 'Asshole. He made me look a right prat.' She jerked the car door open. 'Wait till I give him a piece of–'

As if sensing her whirling emotions, Chloe undid her seat belt and hauled her back in just as she was about to step out. 'I'll go. You stay here and think things through. Don't do anything rash in the heat of the moment, Els.'

'You're not going to ring the bell, are you?' Ellie was horrified.

'No, not yet. I'm just going to scope the place out.'

'What are you, a cat burglar?' Her defence mechanism was kicking in – making light of things when there was a serious problem. 'Watch you don't fall,' Ellie whispered as Chloe slithered her way across the icy road. 'I'm not fit to take you to A&E.'

'Shh,' warned Chloe. Like a character in a slapstick comedy, she scuttled up to the side of Scott's house. Ellie hoped they didn't have Neighbourhood Watch in this area or CCTV cameras in operation or her sister might end up on *Crimewatch*. Chloe edged around to the front of the house and was about to peek into the living room window when she stopped and about-turned, racing back the way she'd come, then ducked down.

The next moment, the front door opened and a tall blonde woman whom Ellie had never seen before emerged. Then Scott appeared, smiled at the woman and pecked her on the cheek. Who was she? A cousin? A friend? A friend's wife? At least it wasn't a lover. It hadn't been a passionate kiss. Ellie visibly relaxed. Her eyes peeping over the rim of the car window, she made eye contact with Chloe. Fortunately, she wasn't under a streetlight.

Chloe's eyes widened and Ellie turned back to see Scott fold his arm around the woman's waist and pull her to him, capturing her in one heck of a passionate kiss. Ellie couldn't believe it. She simply couldn't believe it. Her nostrils flared and her heartbeat accelerated faster than a sprinter out of the starting blocks. Her Scott. Well, he wasn't her Scott now. Six years. For what? Why? Why had he done this to her? She punched the inside of the car door. *Sorry, Chloe.* She wanted to march up to him right now and have it out with him, but Chloe was gesticulating wildly to her to stay in the car. Scott and the mystery woman broke apart and he walked her to her car whilst Ellie slunk lower in the seat to avoid being seen. After another passionate kiss, the woman reversed and waved. Ellie thought she was going to be sick. Scott waited until the woman's car was out of sight then went back inside.

A few minutes later, Chloe returned to the car to find Ellie banging her head off the dashboard.

'Why am I so fucking stupid?'

'Els, I'm so sorry.'

'What a shit! Why?' she sobbed.

'I don't know, hon. Come here.' Chloe held her as Ellie cried it all out on her shoulder, tears dripping onto her sister's T-shirt. 'Let's get out of here. Do you want to stay the night at mine?'

'I'll tell you what I want to do. I want to grab that piece of shit by the throat and ask him what the hell he's up to. I mean, why not just break up with me if he wanted to be with someone else? I wonder how long it's been going on.' The blood drained from her face like water down a plughole. 'Oh God, do you think there have been others? We only saw each other a few times a week. It's possible. He could have been stringing me along for months. Years.' She drew breath. 'I think I'm going to throw up.'

'Els, I'd feel the same if I were you. But I don't think having it out with him now when you're so wound up is a good thing. You know what he's done. Why don't we go home and talk it through rationally?'

Mutely, Ellie nodded. 'I hired a fucking speedboat for him. I was going to propose at Eilean Donan bloody Castle.'

'Look, you're upset. C'mon, let's go home, and if you

don't feel up to going to work tomorrow, I'll call in for you, say you're ill.'

Ellie obeyed as if she were on autopilot. She had thought she'd be arranging the details for a proposal tonight; instead, she'd discovered her boyfriend had been cheating on her. What an anti-climax.

When they arrived at Chloe's, Ellie slumped in a chair in the kitchen whilst Chloe went into the living room to talk to Mitchell. Ellie heard their whispering voices, then the sound of feet on the stairs. It seemed Mitchell was making himself scarce.

Chloe returned soon afterwards and put the kettle on, then prepared their cups and a plate of chocolate Hobnobs, essential comfort food, before putting everything on a tray and carrying it through to the living room.

Ellie followed her and sank into the sofa. Wordlessly, Chloe handed her a cup of tea, which Ellie took gratefully. She was still trying to gather her thoughts. This couldn't be happening to her. Was this denial? No, she'd been through that when she'd deluded herself he'd either left his mobile phone at home or was working late. Had her subconscious somehow known something was amiss? Was in fact her intent to propose spurred on by a warning signal in her head telling her something was seriously wrong in their relationship? Was the fact she would rather have been without him than not take their relationship to the next level an indicator they weren't meant to be together anyway? A moot point now, of course.

The questions tumbled one after the other into her mind, jostling for position. Nope, she still couldn't get her head around it. Sure, recently they hadn't had many nights out together, but they'd still seen each other twice a week, still joking and laughing together, still making love.

God, had he been sleeping with that other woman whilst he was with her? Then she chastised herself for her stupidity. Of course he had. Did that mean she'd have to get tested for STDs? Their only contraception in the past six years had been the pill, because she'd assumed, wrongly it turned out, that as a couple they no longer needed to use condoms, since they'd only be sleeping with each other. The tears welled up again and soon her whole body was heaving and she was emitting low, pitiful mewling noises like a scared newborn kitten. What should she do now?

Chloe held Ellie to her. 'Shh. You'll be OK. He doesn't deserve you. You're strong, stronger than you think. You will get through this.'

As her sister stroked her hair, she calmed down, steeled with a new resolve. She would not let him get the better of her. She would sleep on it then figure out how to end their relationship officially, because of course he had no inkling she'd been to his house tonight, or that she'd seen him kissing the blonde.

Had she always known their love wasn't the real thing? It certainly had never been the way Chloe was with Mitchell. Scott was more aloof, cold some would say, but she had put that down to him being scientific, more clinical, not emotional. Boffins weren't like normal people, were they? And they'd had a lot in common, their love for extreme sports just one example, although, in retrospect, had he taken up the extreme sports after meeting her? She couldn't quite recall.

'Sorry, Chloe.'

'Don't be sorry. I'm only glad I was here for you.'

Ellie sighed. 'What did Mitchell say?'

'I didn't tell him. I just said something had happened and I'd fill him in later, but we needed the room.'

Ellie shook her head as if trying to eradicate the scene she'd witnessed earlier. 'Can you tell Mitchell for me? I don't think I'm up to putting it all into words at the minute.'

'I'll tell him in the morning. Let's put on something with superheroes in it and chill for a bit. Here, I'll get you a blanket. If you want to drift off on the sofa, you can crash there. The spare room is made up too. Mitchell said he'd see to that before he went to bed.'

'Thanks, Chloe, you're the best. I love you.'

'I love you too. Now, Spiderman or Batman?'

'Definitely Batman, with Christian Bale. *The Dark Knight.*'

Ellie snuggled into the couch with Chloe at one end and her at the other, sipping her tea and chewing on a Hobnob, although it tasted like sawdust in her mouth given the evening's events. As she dedicated part of her attention to the film, she found herself appreciating just how wonderful her family were. They had always been close, but right now she wondered where she would be without them.

Chapter Fifteen

Jess

Tuesday 4 February

Jess wrapped her scarf around her and pulled her gloves out of her jacket pockets as she left the house to go pick up the first dog of the day. The sun blinded her as she turned the corner of her street and she almost jogged back to get her sunglasses. No doubt she'd regret not doing so later, but for once she'd actually overslept, so she needed to get a wriggle on. She never overslept, but her mind had been whirring like the propellers of a light aircraft, not giving her any respite.

She was beginning to feel anxious about the big day. It was, after all, only three and a half weeks away. The very thought almost brought her out in a cold sweat.

Self-doubt had plagued her as she catastrophised over all the things that could go wrong, or the negative responses Mark could give. She knew he wouldn't, but that wasn't the point. Her insecurities wouldn't leave her head, so she'd ended up rolling around in bed and fidgeting half the night. As a result, today she was exhausted, and one glance in the mirror had told her she looked every bit as awful as she felt. Not what she needed to see when she had a busy day ahead.

Time to pick up Betsy Boo. She loved the three-year-old Bichon Frise. She was so cute. Even as a dog lover, she could appreciate Betsy Boo had a perfect teddy bear appeal. Jess didn't want to just walk her, she wanted to take her home and snuggle with her on her lap whilst watching TV. The one downside to living with Mark was their home was a strictly dog-free zone. He could just about cope with her walking dogs, but with his allergies he couldn't have them in the house.

Betsy Boo's owner was already out at work, so she greeted her little friend, clipped her lead on and then headed over to get Teddy. Betsy Boo and Teddy adored each other, and for that reason, and because Betsy Boo's owner had told her so when Teddy's owner was looking for a dog walker but Jess' schedule was full, she had relaxed her rule of only walking one dog at a time. And the owners were right – the dogs were in love. They doted on each other, followed each other around religiously when Jess took them somewhere they could go off lead. And since Teddy was a Cockapoo, he was small enough that she could handle both dogs easily.

Her phone rang just as she was about to pick up Teddy. It was Bella's owner. Bella was the russet-coloured cocker spaniel she walked. She was due to pick her up in an hour and a half, but her owner was phoning her now. She hoped nothing was wrong with Bella.

'Hi, Jerry.'

'Hi, Jess. Listen, I'm really sorry to ask, but could you pick Bella up early? I've got to go to the airport in half an hour, and I've had to give the tiler who's doing my bathroom this week the spare key, and he's gone to the warehouse to get more tiles and I don't know when he'll be back.'

That was quite a bit of info to digest. Jess paused. Teddy's owner was eyeing her oddly through the window, so she smiled at her and waved in acknowledgement.

She didn't like letting anyone down and Jerry was lovely, and didn't usually take advantage. Clearly, she was in a jam.

Jess decided to throw caution to the wind for once and said, 'Sure, give me fifteen minutes.' Jerry's house was only half a mile away. She'd collect Teddy and then pick Bella up before taking them all over to the private field she sometimes used rather than walking them all in the park. Two she could manage, three not so much.

She rang the bell and two minutes later, Teddy was on the lead, walking obediently alongside his beloved. Even though these two were easy to manage, there was always the unexpected to account for, like a dog appearing from nowhere or a loud noise, like a motorcycle racing past, which could spook them. They were so little, after all, especially Betsy Boo.

When she arrived at Jerry's, she was already standing in the doorway with Bella on the lead, ready to go. *She really is in a hurry.*

'Off somewhere nice?' Jess asked.

'Sorry?' Jerry asked, distractedly.

'The airport,' she said, as she took Bella's lead, carefully, so as not to entangle it with the other two she was holding.

'Oh, no, I'm picking my dad up. Listen, I've got to run, but Rich will be here when you bring Bella back, OK? I'll pay you extra for the inconvenience.' She eyed Betsy

Boo and Teddy. 'I hadn't realised you'd already have two dogs with you. Are you sure you can manage the three of them together?'

'Yeah, it'll be fine. This pair are lovebirds, so don't care about anything or anyone else except each other. I'm going to take them to the private field, let them have a run around, rather than the park.'

'Oh, Bella will love that, won't you, darling?' She patted Bella on the head, then checked her watch. 'Sorry, I really need to go.'

'No problem. I've got it all in hand.'

'Thanks, Jess. You're a star.'

Jess smiled and said, 'Right, guys, let's go.'

She crunched along the frost-covered pavement, Betsy Boo and Teddy on her left, walking adorably in step with each other, and on her right, the jumpier and more excitable Bella, who was clearly enjoying being let loose after being indoors all night.

They passed a few people Jess knew by sight: an elderly man whom she met each day as he returned from buying a newspaper, a couple of high school kids going for the bus and two friends power-walking round the neighbourhood.

It was so handy having the field nearby. Well, they all called it the field, it was a large square patch of grass the size of a football field, but with no goals, and it was overgrown, but as it was hemmed in on all sides, and had a gate, it was the perfect place to let the dogs off lead so they could burn off some of their pent-up energy, without worrying about them running off.

'Hi there,' she greeted the postman as he passed without incident. The dogs were really on their best behaviour today. No jumping up from Bella, nor barking.

What was going on? She must have been at obedience classes again.

She approached the field, her thoughts drifting to the rest of the day ahead as she ran through her mental checklist for the afternoon's classes.

A cat shot out of the open gate of a nearby house, pursued by a Lurcher. The lead on her right pulled taut as Bella, excitedly, clearly thinking this was a game, tried to break free.

'Bella, no!' Jess reprimanded her, but Bella wasn't letting up, and as she tried to calm Bella down and stop her from pulling, Teddy started playing up, yipping and tugging on his lead, which agitated Betsy Boo, who whined and tried to run round in a circle, confined though she was by her lead.

As Jess tried to stop Bella from pulling, and sort out the other two errant dogs, she vaguely registered something in her peripheral vision.

'Look out, I can't stop!'

Jess looked up in horror to see a boy of about ten hurtling towards them on a skateboard. A second later, he crashed into her, knocking her flying, and the wind out of her, as she scrambled to hold on to the three leads, and ensure the dogs were all right.

Oof! That hurt. Ow, ow, bloody ow! She'd landed on the frosty path on her coccyx and boy it was letting her know. She'd also scraped her hands as she fell.

'Are you OK?' she asked the boy, reflexively.

'I think so,' he said. 'Sorry.'

She shook her head. 'It's all right.' She was still holding three leads, so apart from being shaken and a bit bruised, there was no harm done.

'I'm sorry about your dog,' the boy said.

Oh my God, is one of the dogs hurt?

Then she realised that although she was holding three leads, only two had dogs attached to them. Bella's lead had snapped or come undone somehow and she had made her bid for freedom.

'Oh no, I've got to go. Sure you're not hurt?'

The boy nodded.

She began to jog with the other two dogs beside her. They might be a little traumatised, but she'd sort that later. She had to find Bella.

As she ran, she called her name, occasionally stopping to ask people if they'd seen a red cocker spaniel.

She was almost in tears when she rounded a corner, glancing back to check she hadn't missed Bella go down a side street, and ran straight into a solid mass. Oh God, what now? She'd been so upset she hadn't even seen anyone coming.

'Jess?'

She looked up. 'Nathan!'

He smiled. 'I thought it was you.' He frowned. 'You all right? You look upset.'

'I've lost one of my dogs. A red cocker spaniel. I don't suppose you've passed her, have you?'

Nathan shook his head. 'No, but c'mon. I'll help you look.'

Jess gave a sigh of relief. She could have hugged him. 'You will? Oh, thank you, Nathan. Hopefully, between us we can find the little monster. She might be with a Lurcher, as one shot after a cat and that's what got Bella agitated in the first place.'

'Ah, the old dog-chasing-a-cat scenario.' He grinned.

'Don't worry, we'll find her. Best if we split up, though. Where have you checked already?'

Jess quickly filled him in and Nathan thought for a second then said, 'OK, so we still have Larch, Poplar and Maple to cover, as well as Indigo Drive. Why don't you take Larch and Poplar and I'll take Maple and Indigo. They're slightly further away, and unlike you, I don't have two little dogs slowing me down.'

'Perfect, thanks, Nathan. Will we meet back here in fifteen minutes?'

'Sounds good. See you.' He jogged off in the other direction as Jess resumed her search.

Ten minutes later she was beginning to panic. There was still no sign of Bella and Betsy Boo seemed very distressed. Teddy, fortunately, was plodding along placidly.

How was she going to tell Jerry she'd lost her dog? She'd give it until she met Nathan and then if he hadn't found her, she'd post on the community Facebook group asking if anyone had seen her.

Five minutes later, crestfallen, she returned to the spot where she'd left Nathan. He hadn't returned yet. She took the time to reassure Teddy and Betsy Boo and to check they didn't have any injuries from the skateboard incident, and once she'd ascertained they were fine, she tapped out a message on Facebook ready to hit send when Nathan inevitably told her he hadn't been able to find her.

An excited bark from behind her almost made her drop her phone. Bella!

'Bella!' She leant down and cuddled the mischievous dog, receiving multiple licks for her efforts. Jess straightened up and looked into Nathan's smiling face. 'You're a lifesaver. Where did you find her?'

Nathan grinned. 'You were right. She'd gone after the Lurcher, who was in the park, under a tree, barking like a maniac at the cat, who had understandably sought refuge up there. Last I checked, Lurchers can't climb trees.'

'Thank God.' Her heart sank at the thought of how many streets Bella had crossed to get there.

'I was thinking, as I'm at a loose end this morning, why don't I walk these guys back with you and then we can go for a coffee or something?'

'Aw, thanks, Nathan, that's kind of you, but I actually have a few other dogs to walk later, too.'

'So you're like the dog whisperer or something?' he joked.

She smiled. 'Not exactly, but it's a job I get a great deal of enjoyment out of.'

'Job? You mean you're a dog walker?'

She bristled slightly, unsure if his tone was condescending or not. 'Yes, I have my own dog-walking business, Pawsitive Pooches.'

He smiled. 'Alliteration, I like it.' He paused. 'So, woman of many talents, do you have any more space on your dog-walking schedule?'

Jess scrunched her eyebrows, wondering why he was asking. 'A little, one or two slots maybe.'

Nathan remained silent for a moment then seemed to come to a decision. 'Tell you what, let's take these guys back, and you can tell me all about your dog-walking business. You may be the answer to my problem.'

Chapter Sixteen

Anouska

Wednesday 5 February

Now that her mum had returned to Stockholm, Anouska felt she could breathe more easily in every respect. She was gearing up once again to tell Zach about the baby, and wishing she was in a position to confide in the girls. It felt almost deceitful not to tell them, but until Zach knew, she couldn't tell anyone else. It was bad enough her mum knew.

She was feeling more positive generally, and since she had an early meeting in Edinburgh, she decided to see if she could meet Ellie for lunch.

There was no immediate reply from Ellie, so she figured she'd play it by ear, and if she heard from her before lunch, they'd find a way to meet, otherwise it wasn't a problem. She'd eaten lunch often enough on her own not to baulk at the idea.

By eleven o'clock, Anouska had secured another two-year contract and she came out of the meeting feeling elated that she still had it. Who said women couldn't have it all? Career, motherhood…oh yeah, she still had to address that, and soon the proposal, with Zach. Yes, maybe she should wait before getting all smug.

Her phone pinged. Ellie. *Hi, Anouska, yes, I can meet, but I'm not in a good way, so I'll understand if you'd rather not. I could do with some advice though and a friendly face. Sorry for garbled text, Ellie x*

What the heck? She immediately typed back, *Hope you're OK. Yes, I'll definitely meet you and hopefully I can help, Love, A x*

Her phone pinged again almost at once. *Thanks, Anouska. Can you meet me at Cirque at 12? Ellie x*

See you then, and hang in there, A x

Anouska arrived at Cirque early. There seemed little point trying to go anywhere first, so she parked close by, had a chat with Marion, sat in the only booth, at the back of the café, as she guessed Ellie might want some privacy, and made some calls.

Ellie arrived on the dot at twelve, wearing sunglasses and a puffy jacket with a collar so high it almost completely obscured her face.

'Ellie.' Anouska rose to greet her.

Ellie began to smile, but tears slid out from beneath her sunglasses and ran down her face.

'Oh, Ellie, what's happened?' Anouska asked, guiding her to a chair.

Ellie gulped several times, took her sunglasses off, used one of the café's napkins to wipe her eyes then blew her nose and blurted out, 'Scott's been cheating on me.'

Whoosh. It was like a sucker-punch to the stomach. Anouska had not anticipated that revelation.

'Oh my God, Ellie, I'm so sorry. Are you sure?'

Ellie gave a bitter laugh. 'Unfortunately, yes. Chloe and I caught him red-handed last night.'

The colour fled from Anouska's face. Surely Ellie hadn't caught him having sex with someone else? How horrific.

'What happened?' she asked.

Ellie filled her in, stopping only to burst into tears, wipe her eyes with her sleeve or blow her nose in a tissue every so often. Marion, sensing something was sorely amiss, wisely kept her distance.

Anouska couldn't begin to comprehend the pain Ellie must be in. She'd never been in that position. All she could do was be here for her, be a sounding board, allow her to vent.

Ellie rubbed her eyes. 'I can't take it in. I barely slept last night.'

'Not surprising. Any idea what you're going to do?'

'Not really.'

Anouska thought for a moment then laid out her suggestions. 'You could wait for him to contact you and explain why he didn't meet you, or call it all off, or go and see him.'

Ellie pursed her lips. 'Hmm, I don't know. I thought after I slept on it, I would know. The only thing I know for sure is that I won't ever take him back, no matter what the lying, cheating scumbag says. And to think I wanted to marry him…'

'The one consolation in all of this is that you weren't married.'

Ellie gave the briefest inclination of her head, although Anouska felt underlining this would provide her friend little comfort at the moment.

'It's the betrayal and the why that gets me.'

'Have you heard anything from him yet?' Anouska asked.

Ellie shook her head. 'I haven't checked since this morning.'

'I thought you'd have been checking every five minutes,' confessed Anouska.

'So did I, but I can't bring myself to.'

They talked some more about the events of the evening before.

'Never mind me, what about you? Seriously, I am so sick of hearing the sound of my own voice. Have you made any progress with your proposal?'

'Are you sure you want to talk about this? You don't have to. We could talk about something else.' Anouska felt uncomfortable touching on the subject when Ellie's pain was so raw, and it wasn't as if she had anything to report.

'Don't worry. I'm not so bitter I can't be glad for you two. Oh no, I haven't told Jess yet.' She looked at Anouska. 'I don't suppose you could fill her in for me. I don't think I could cope with going over it all again.'

'No problem. Leave it with me and I'll message her later.'

Ellie sat bolt upright. 'Do you know what? I'm going to wait until the cheating bastard contacts me, if he does, with whatever pathetic excuse he comes up with for standing me up last night. Then I'll arrange to meet him somewhere public, and calmly tell him exactly what I think of him. I won't rant or rave; instead I will be dignified in my exit from his life.'

Anouska raised an eyebrow, but Ellie held up a finger as if to stop her from saying anything.

'To have proper closure this break-up has to be done in person. Otherwise, it'll always feel as if there are loose ends to address. And I want to embarrass him the way he embarrassed me.'

Anouska frowned. 'Are you sure that's wise?'

'Nothing too dramatic. No shouting or swearing, but I'm still working on location. I could do it at Caprese, then he'd never be able to show his face there again, as I know Luca would take my side. Or I could go to his work, which is my preference at the moment, and diss him in front of his colleagues. He would look a right tit then. But I'm still playing around with ideas. So all suggestions are welcome.'

'I'd suggest doing it at Caprese. You said it was his favourite restaurant, as well as being yours. That would be a good punishment and also, you'd be on neutral-ish territory, and if this were tennis, it would be advantage Ellie, but if you go to his work, you might come across as some crazy ex-girlfriend. And…'

'What?' Ellie asked.

Anouska hesitated a moment, then blew out a breath. 'Has it occurred to you the woman might work with him?'

Ellie hesitated. 'No. I hadn't got that far in my thought process.'

'Or that their colleagues might already know, so it wouldn't be a surprise or the showdown you'd hoped? That's if they let you into the building.'

'Hmm, that's a good point. They do have quite advanced security at the uni. Maybe Caprese is the best plan then.'

Anouska set her empty cup down on the saucer. 'What will you say to him?'

'Don't know yet, but I won't make a scene, just let

myself be overheard so people know how much of an asshole he is. Then I'll get up and walk out, leaving *him* sitting there like a prat on his own.'

'That sounds revenge enough – classy too.'

'That's cos I'm a classy chick!' Ellie grinned. 'In fact, now I've decided upon a course of action, I feel so much better. I've turned this victim scenario around. I'll tell him straight, albeit at a decibel level that won't shatter windows.' She smiled.

'Good for you. I'm glad you're not taking this lying down,' said Anouska.

'No way is that happening. The more I think about it, the more I realise we haven't been in a real relationship for some time. The fact that he couldn't commit, that we never lived together, that six years on, my thirty-six-year-old boyfriend never suggested we move in together, until last week, or get married, proves that.'

Anouska nodded, silently allowing Ellie to continue.

'How could I have been so blind? The good news is, I'm not mourning the death of our

relationship. I could so easily have found out further down the line. Crikey, what if I'd proposed, he'd said yes and then I discovered after we got married what he'd been up to? That would have been catastrophic – divorce settlement, solicitors' fees, the works. I have *some* things to be grateful for.'

They were on their second cup of coffee and Ellie was even managing a bacon roll, at Anouska's insistence, when Ellie's mobile rang. 'It's Scott.'

'Answer it then,' urged Anouska.

'I haven't worked out what I'm going to say yet.'

'Be unamused but suggest he takes you out for dinner ASAP, as in tonight or tomorrow to make up for it.'

Ellie nodded her agreement, then accepted the call and put it on speakerphone. 'Yes?' Her tone was clipped.

'Hi, Els, sorry I didn't get back to you yesterday, I was tied up at work. So, what time are we meeting at Caprese tonight then? I accidentally deleted the text.'

Ellie let silence hang in the air for a few seconds then said, 'It was last night, Scott.'

'What was last night?'

'Our dinner.' Ellie rolled her eyes.

He was smooth, Anouska would give him that.

'No way. You didn't go to Caprese, did you?'

'Yes, I did, and sat like a right lemon for half an hour waiting on you. Didn't you get my messages?'

'I've only now charged my phone. In fact, there have been a few pinging noises since we started this call. I wonder if that's your messages.'

'Whatever.' Ellie gestured at Anouska as if to say 'Can you believe this guy?'

'S-s-orry?' Scott appeared confused.

'Look, Scott, I'm busy. I wasted enough time last night sitting in the restaurant waiting for you, so if you don't mind…'

'Ellie, I'm sorry, it was a genuine mistake. I need to buy one of those fast-charging units. My bloody phone is always dying on me. Can I take you to Caprese tonight to make up for it?'

'I'm busy tonight.' She tapped her fingers rapidly on the table, a coping mechanism perhaps.

'Tomorrow then?'

'Fine. Check with Luca if he can fit us in.'

'Sorry again. You know what I'm like when I'm working. I was so immersed in this new genome editing project we have on the go that I didn't even think to check my phone or anything. We're so close to a breakthrough on it, it's all-consuming at the moment.'

'Text me the details,' she said curtly. 'I'll see you there.'

She hung up. It was difficult to figure out what was going through Ellie's mind. Anouska had noticed her squeeze and open her fists repeatedly whilst on the call, as if she was perhaps choking the life out of Scott.

Ellie gave a tight smile. 'Can you believe the nerve of him? Tied up? Really? Yes, what with, duct tape? I swear if he'd been in front of me, I might've strangled him.'

Anouska remained quiet. Ellie needed to get this out of her system, vent, rage at Scott.

'And he thought it was tonight? I mean, seriously? How dim does he think I am? God, I hate him!'

Yep, she definitely needed to vent.

'And all that crap about his phone being out of charge. Utter bollocks. I want to smash him to a pulp!'

Marion was approaching at that moment, and swiftly about-turned, clearly deciding to choose her moment later.

'Ha! It was so satisfying saying "Whatever" to him. I'm always so easy to please. He's not used to me being bolshie to him. Probably why he stuck around so long, albeit he was seeing other people.' Tears filled Ellie's eyes.

'Six years we dated. Six years! And does he honestly think twenty quid or so towards a pizza and a bottle of wine will cut it for standing me up? Do you know, we still go Dutch, except at my birthday. Well, he's in for a shock.'

Anouska murmured her agreement.

'I'd have held out and asked for something else, like concert tickets or a night at the theatre or something that would have hit him in his pocket, but that would mean spending more time with him and living a lie and I'm not prepared to do that. I want this over, and as soon as possible. I just couldn't do it tonight.'

'That's understandable. It's been a very stressful experience for you.'

Between clenched teeth, Ellie said, 'How easily the lies fell from his lips. He makes me sick.'

'I know it's hard to process right now, but you really are better off without him.' Anouska grimaced. 'And I'm sorry if that sounds like a platitude, it's not meant to.'

'Oh, don't you worry, I know I'm better off without him. And do you know what, just for the sheer hell of it, I'm going to end this relationship with a bang.'

Anouska looked at her quizzically and Ellie said, 'I'm going to dress to impress. I have the perfect figure-hugging red dress in my wardrobe. Very vixen. I want to show him what he'll be missing – forever.'

Chapter Seventeen

Ellie

Thursday 6 February

Next morning, Ellie woke to the sound of voices in the kitchen. Rosie was babbling away excitedly and a rush of love for her niece swept over her. She didn't see enough of her. That would have to change. Rosie was growing up so fast. Fleetingly, she thought of her promotion and what might change if she was successful at interview. Right now, though, she didn't have the headspace to deal with that. She'd have to park that for a while. First she needed to sort out this mess.

The doorbell rang. Someone went to answer it. What time was it? The clock on the bedside cabinet showed twenty past eight. Maybe it was the postman. She ought to go down. Rosie would be leaving for nursery soon, and she wanted to kiss her goodbye.

She met her brother-in-law on the landing as he came out of the main bathroom.

'Do you want me to go beat him up?' Mitchell drew himself up to his full height. 'I could take him, you know.'

Ellie bit back a smirk. Mitchell was one of the gentlest people she knew. He probably would beat Scott in a fight, but he would never initiate a confrontation.

Mitchell, like Chloe, had been there for her through every crisis she'd had in the past decade. She was so glad she'd introduced them. He was a good person to have in your corner.

Downstairs, Rosie, who had been eating toast with jam, ran to Ellie and buried her face deep in her stomach. 'Auntie Ell, I'm going to nursery. Why did you not come sleep in my bed last night?' She pouted, her eyebrows scrunching up.

Ellie ruffled her niece's curls. 'It was late, sweetie, and I didn't want to disturb you. Anyway, I'm here now. Tell me, did you dream about unicorns last night?'

Rosie clambered up on Ellie's lap and regaled her with more tales of her dreams, which was exactly what Ellie needed right now – to be removed from reality. Chloe mouthed 'You OK?' and Ellie gave a brief nod.

Once Rosie had left for nursery, Chloe asked, 'How are you really doing, sis? You've had quite the thirty-six hours.'

Ellie sighed at this. She had that right. 'Actually, I'm feeling really positive, apart from being totally pissed off that he took me in so completely.' She shook her head. 'He was just attentive enough for me not to suspect anything. He cooked me nice meals, we had great sex…'

'TMI, little sis,' Chloe said, screwing up her face in distaste.

Ellie smiled. 'Well, you know what I mean. The only warning sign should have perhaps been his inability to commit, but then he did, by asking me to move in.' She sighed. 'Anyway, that's all water under the bridge now, and

I'm feeling more positive than I have in ages. A few more pieces are falling into place though.'

'Oh?' Chloe tilted her head.

'Yeah, he went into work for a bit the day the estate agent came. We'd put in for holidays off work that day, yet he had to go in to work, at a university. I should have sussed something was up.'

'Hmm.' Chloe's response was noncommittal.

'So even the day he asked me to move in with him, I reckon he was actually seeing someone else that morning. *Her* probably.'

Chloe continued to remain silent. She must just be letting her vent. It was cathartic, after all.

'The one thing I didn't understand in all of this was why ask me to move in with him? That really made me mad. But the answer was staring me in the face.'

Chloe frowned. 'It was?'

Ellie nodded. 'Yes. He was so interested when I was talking to the estate agent, so enthusiastic and then gobsmacked when he found out how much the flat was worth. It doesn't take a genius to work out that his impromptu offer to move in with me was more calculating than romantic.'

'I'm not following,' Chloe said.

'C'mon, Chloe. You're usually more switched-on than this.' Ellie threw her hands out. 'Scott, not known for his altruism, clearly thought he could profit somehow from the capital I'd be injecting into the house we'd buy together.'

When Chloe's eyes bulged, Ellie continued, 'You know me, I wouldn't have thought to have an agreement drawn up, stipulating that if we parted ways, I'd get back what I put in. He probably planned to move in with me, then when it no longer suited, break up with me and take half of the profit from the house. My deposit would have been much greater than his. That much I do know.'

Chloe shook her head. 'He's even more of a scumbag than I thought, and even more deserving of the Scumbag nickname.'

Ellie zoned out for a moment, lost in her own thoughts.

'I know that look.' Chloe's eyes narrowed.

'What?' asked Ellie, feigning innocence.

'You've done something, and you know I'm not going to be happy about it. Spill.'

A tad sheepishly, Ellie said, 'Well, you know how you urged caution with regards to the proposal?'

'Yes, I must have felt something in my waters.'

'I don't know about that, but, whatever, you were right about the fact I should be careful.'

'Uh-huh. I'm still waiting, Ellie.'

'Oh, all right. This is the problem with having a sibling who knows you too well.' She blew out a breath. 'Well, I kinda booked a speedboat to take us to Eilean Donan Castle for the proposal.'

Chloe rolled her eyes.

'I know, I know.' Ellie held her hands up as if to ward off criticism. 'I should have waited. You warned me.'

'I did, but anyway, no biggie, you can cancel it.'

Ellie's eyes darted around. Chloe was going to kill her. She knew she was too impulsive, but Chloe had warned her and she hadn't taken any notice. Now she was for it.

Chloe's face fell. 'You haven't paid for it, have you?'

'It was a good deal!'

Chloe raised her clenched fists in the air then spread her fingers, waving her hands at Ellie. 'Ellie! That is not exercising caution!'

'Well, lesson learned.'

'How much are you out?'

'About three hundred and fifty pounds, plus a dent to my pride the size of Ireland.'

Chloe blew out a breath. 'Oh, Ellie, what am I going to do with you?'

'Put up with me?'

'Do I have a choice?'

'No.' Ellie shot her a grin.

'Did you tell Jess and Anouska?'

Ellie sighed again. 'I had a heart-to-heart with Anouska yesterday, but I couldn't cope with also having to explain it to Jess, so I asked Anouska if she'd let her know and tell her that I wouldn't be able to meet them at Cirque tonight.'

Chloe nodded. 'And have you heard from Jess since?'

'Oh, yeah. She texted saying she didn't want to bother me, but wanted me to know she was thinking about me and that I should get in touch, no matter what time of the day or night, if I needed her.'

Chloe nodded again. 'Sounds like a good friend.'

'Yeah, she is. And Anouska,' said Ellie. 'I'm lucky to have them.'

Her sister nudged her arm with her elbow. 'They're lucky to have you too.'

Ellie laughed. 'Ha! Here we all were, thinking we'd be supporting each other in our proposal strategies, and they've ended up supporting me in a break-up instead. The irony.'

'True, but you'd do the same for them,' Chloe said, her eyes fixed on Ellie's. 'Wouldn't you?'

'In a heartbeat. Right, I need to go home and get some

clothes for tonight. I'll come back afterwards and give you the post-mortem.'

'Giving me his post-mortem results would make me happier. The actual post-mortem, not the metaphorical one.' Chloe grinned. 'Anyway, you're not going anywhere just yet.'

'Oh?' Ellie asked, her brows knitting.

'Nope. Grab a cuppa and I'll tell you what I've booked for you today.'

'Now I'm intrigued.' Ellie picked up a Denby cup from the countertop.

The spa experience Chloe had treated her to at Le Meridien had been wonderful, and Ellie once again was grateful for how fantastic her family were. Chloe had insisted she stay with them again overnight, in case she needed moral support, a shoulder to cry on, or a group of people to celebrate with.

Chloe had also called Trish, Ellie's boss, the day before, and explained what had happened with Scott, and Trish had been both appalled and sympathetic. She'd even offered to go round and show him why he shouldn't mess with the friend of the scrum half on the women's rugby team.

Ellie's face was all plumped and dewy. As she put on her makeup and slipped into her red dress ready for the 'fun' evening ahead, she could only be pleased with her appearance. Hopefully, Scott would appreciate it one last time. After that she never wanted to see him again.

Ellie arrived at Caprese to find Scott already seated. Perhaps he was feeling duly chastised by her reaction to Tuesday's no-show and was trying to act contrite. Pity then it wouldn't have any effect on her. Ellie's heart had turned to granite. In less than forty-eight hours she had gone from wanting to marry this man to wondering why she had put up with him for so long. Not usual bedfellows those ideas.

Scott rose from his seat and kissed her on the cheek. Not for her the smooch he had afforded Tuesday night's conquest, although it was just as well, as she might have brained him. He was as handsome as ever but somehow the attraction she'd felt for him had already dissipated. He had opted for a royal blue Paul Smith shirt she'd bought him for his birthday and a pair of black jeans. She'd probably bought those too.

'Hi.' He gave her a bashful smile.

She smiled tightly at him and sat down. She hadn't quite decided when to tell him, but she'd at least let them order so he could be stuck with the bill. Then he could debate whether to sit like a plonker and eat the meal with all the other restaurant-goers glaring daggers at him, or have it boxed to take home.

Even when face to face, he didn't bother apologising. The nerve of him. He tried to make small talk with her and she trotted out stock responses. Then she said, 'Perhaps we should order then chat. I'm starving.' She wasn't. She wasn't remotely hungry, but she wanted to be able to think and she couldn't do that whilst he was wittering on.

Once they'd ordered, she would let the small talk dry up, Scott would have to mention the 'misunderstanding' again and she could launch into her spiel. It wasn't long and she could adapt it for whatever situation presented itself, whatever 'in' he gave her. If there was one thing Ellie hated, it was someone making a fool of her, and Scott had done that with bells on.

Luca came to take their order then retreated to the kitchen to pass it to the chef.

'So how's work?' Scott asked.

'I don't know.'

Scott raised an eyebrow. 'What do you mean you don't know? You're always on top of everything. Is anything wrong?'

'Not with work.'

'With what then? You're not ill, are you?' He frowned and Ellie figured that was something in his favour – he did seem to care about her wellbeing.

'I haven't been feeling great the past few days.'

'Oh? You don't mean…' His face turned pale.

'No, I'm not pregnant before you put two and two together and get five.'

He exhaled heavily, his relief apparent. 'So what's wrong then?'

'You really want to know what's wrong?' It was hard not to shout, but she managed only to let her voice creep up a couple of decibels.

'Yes.' Scott was beginning to look a little hacked-off. Too bad. She had first dibs on that sentiment.

'OK then. Let's see. One – on Tuesday you stood me up and left me sitting here on my own.' She paused for effect and to gauge the other restaurant-goers' reaction. She was still seated and her voice had only risen a little in pitch, but there was enough of a difference to make the other diners turn in their direction.

'I explained about that–' began Scott, but Ellie

interrupted him.

'That's right. You explained you were busy at work and forgot to check the messages on your phone, which was dead anyway and you didn't have a fast charger. How am I doing so far?'

'That's right.'

'Except when I couldn't get you, I was worried, and I couldn't drive because I'd had a Bellini whilst I was here waiting for you. But Chloe could drive, and I was so worried about you, that rather than start calling all the hospitals, and after I phoned your house and got no reply, Chloe drove me to yours.' Ellie paused again to allow time for that information to sink in.

The horror-stricken look on Scott's face told her she'd hit the target. 'Imagine my surprise when we arrived outside your house to find your car in the drive, another car next to it, the lights on...oh, but you were working late, weren't you? So, as you were working late, it must have been your identical twin, whom you conveniently forgot to mention up until now, who was snogging some blonde woman on your doorstep.'

'Els...'

'Don't talk. You have nothing to say I want to hear.'

'Els, it wasn't like that. It was only a peck. She's a colleague.'

'Scott, don't lie to me! You make me sick!' She screeched back her chair. 'Caught in the act and you still can't tell the truth, or do the decent thing.' Her lip curled in disgust. 'It wasn't a peck. Chloe and I both *saw* you. You're a cheat. A miser. A liar. I'm not going to waste another ounce of time or energy on you. This conversation is over, and so is this relationship. Don't contact me ever again.' Ellie stood up, slung her bag over her shoulder and strode out of the restaurant, not even bothering to look behind her. She did, however, hear the round of applause that broke out before the door shut behind her. Now she had closure and it felt bloody marvellous.

'I can tell from your face that it went well.' Chloe hugged Ellie to her. 'Mitchell, fetch the champagne, please.'

'We have champagne?' Mitchell gawped. 'Since when did we become a champagne-quaffing household? I thought the best we had was a light beer.'

'Since my sister dumped that lying piece of shit, that's when.' Chloe turned her attention back to Ellie. 'So, go on. Dish the goss.'

Ellie was relaying to Chloe the evening's events when her mobile rang. Anouska. 'How did it go?'

'Well, since I'm in the middle of telling Chloe, and soon Mitchell, when he comes back with the champagne, let's message Jess so she can join the group chat, too, and I can tell you all at the same time.'

'Good plan.' Anouska smiled.

By the time Jess had joined the call, Mitchell had returned from the kitchen with three champagne flutes and a bottle of Veuve Clicquot.

'Wow, bringing out the big guns,' remarked Ellie.

'This was worth going all out for,' said Chloe.

'Right, everyone, prepare yourselves to learn of Scott's undignified exit from my life.'

When she'd finished relating the scene in the restaurant, she raised her glass. 'Thank you, all of you. You're the best support network a girl could ever have.

Who needs men? Sorry, Mitchell, you don't count, you're an honorary girl!'

Her brother-in-law's eyes creased at the corners. 'Thanks, I think.'

'Cheers!' Ellie said, her eyes scanning those of her family and friends as her words echoed around her.

Now she definitely had closure.

Chapter Eighteen

Jess

Monday 10 February

Jess bounced along the street, lead in hand, ready to pick up Baxter, Nathan's Golden Retriever puppy. Baxter was adorable. Yes, Jess was biased, she thought all dogs were adorable, but Baxter was such fun. She'd always loved big dogs and Baxter was a *big* dog. Well, big puppy, since he was only just over a year old.

In the past few weeks, Jess had spent quite a bit of time with Nathan. Nothing untoward – a latte in the gym café, or a drink at the juice bar. Sometimes it was just Nathan, sometimes other gym-goers joined them. She'd even gone to the pub on Friday. Then there were the dog walks. As he'd walked back with her to drop off Betsy Boo, Teddy and Bella the day Bella had bolted, Nathan had told her he'd been looking for someone to walk his dog since his last dog walker moved out of the area the previous month. He'd had a woman lined up but then she'd broken her ankle, so he was still between dog walkers and now he hoped he'd found one. Jess.

Jess had laughed and asked why he'd want her to walk his dog when he'd caught her at her worst, having lost one, even if it wasn't exactly her fault. She'd told him about the young boy who'd hit her with the skateboard, sending her flying, and assured him that usually she had no problem keeping dogs under control. She'd also told him of her one dog at a time rule, and how she'd really regretted allowing herself to be in the position of handling three dogs that day.

Nathan was a nice guy, good company and he made her laugh and he certainly dedicated plenty of time to her – something Mark hadn't been doing for a while. She enjoyed talking with him and he listened, really listened. Apart from Kelsea, who was interested in everything, and Ellie and Anouska, it had been a long time since anyone had paid that much attention to what she said. They were simply a guy and a girl enjoying each other's company.

Her phone rang, breaking into her thoughts. Ellie.

'Hi, Ellie, how are you?'

'Still a bit dazed, to be honest, but I'm back to work today. Just thought I'd give you a call between meetings. It's tea break.'

'Ah. On a completely unrelated matter, have you heard anything about your interview yet?'

'Funnily enough, no, but someone else in the department has gone for the job, and they've been given an interview date of early March.'

'Well, that's good. It means you'll get your date in soon too.'

'I guess so.'

Ellie sounded so flat, Jess couldn't help herself. 'What's up? You don't sound remotely enthused at the prospect.'

Ellie sighed. 'It's just...when I stayed over with Chloe last week, I realised how much I'll miss them all if I move to Manchester. I'll miss seeing Rosie grow up. She's already changing so much every day.'

'Hmm. Yeah, that is definitely a consideration, but I'm sure Chloe and Rosie would come to visit you. And, ultimately, you have to do what you think is best for you. So, if it's the job, particularly now you no longer have the Scott complication, then go for it. But if taking the job won't make you happy, because you'll miss your family too much, don't do it.'

Ellie exhaled noisily. 'Oh, I wish I knew what to do.'

Jess could envisage Ellie putting her head in her hands in despair.

'Listen, you don't need to decide now. Go for the interview. Trish already knows you're not in a great place. Is she part of the interview process?'

There was a slight pause before Ellie said, 'I'm not sure. I suppose I'll be in a better position to know that once I receive my email. But doesn't that show my lack of commitment to the promotion if I don't even know who's on the panel? Usually I'd have all this info colour-coded!'

Jess laughed. 'Seriously, stop beating yourself up. Go for the interview, and if you get the job and change your mind, so what? People change their minds all the time, for a multitude of reasons. I bet no one's giving Trish hassle over leaving, are they?'

'No,' conceded Ellie. 'Thanks, Jess. I feel a bit better now. And thanks for agreeing to meet tomorrow night instead of Thursday.'

'No problem, I'm looking forward to it.'

As Jess ended the call, she reflected on Ellie and how her priorities had changed in a matter of days. Her mind then turned to her upcoming trip to Sicily. She hadn't even thought of her proposal recently. Now that the trip was booked, she should have been honing the details, especially with it now only being three weeks away, but she hadn't arranged anything apart from travel insurance.

Was that telling in itself? The state of Ellie's relationship and its subsequent falling apart had put the idea in her head. Was she doing the right thing? She knew Ellie and Anouska would tell her not to be silly, that she and Mark were totally different from Ellie and Scott, but she couldn't help the niggling doubts. Could you have pre-proposal nerves as well as pre-wedding nerves? Because if so, she was definitely having them. And could any of these doubts be attributed to the sudden appearance of Nathan in her life? Nothing had happened between them and nothing would, but was his effortless interaction with her showing her that men could actively engage in conversation and contribute instead of muttering and pretending to listen, or saying they were busy marking English homework or going off to play rugby?

It made Jess' anxiety levels spike, and she wasn't generally an anxious sort of person. So why did she feel as if she were doing something wrong when she wasn't?

As she walked up Nathan's driveway and took out the key, she could already hear Baxter's deep excited bark from the other side of the door, and she smiled. Why did dogs make her happier than most humans? She'd rarely met a dog she didn't like, yet she'd met plenty of humans whom she didn't gel with, even though she considered herself easy-going and non-judgemental, and she didn't gossip. Whatever the reason for her affinity with dogs, she was glad of it. Not only did it guarantee her an occupation, it meant she spent a great deal of her time doing what she loved with those she loved – her furry friends.

Baxter launched himself at her as she opened the door. It was only as she separated herself from the enormous puppy whose paws reached her shoulders that she became aware of a presence in her peripheral vision. She glanced up to see Nathan, halfway down the stairs, gawping at her. She stood frozen to the spot as Nathan finally collected himself, stuttering, 'I-I was looking for a towel. Give me a minute.'

Jess was so shocked at the sight of a completely naked Nathan – a rather pleasing sight, she might add – that she couldn't even look away. She stood, her mouth hanging open, as he raced back upstairs.

By the time he came back down a few minutes later in a T-shirt and joggers, her heart had almost, but not quite, returned to normal. She certainly hadn't been expecting such an adventurous start to the morning, and from the shock on his face, neither had he.

His dark hair curled at the nape of his neck and droplets of water still clung to the edges. For some reason that's what she fixated on. It was all too easy to recall the detail of his six-pack, now hidden under his plain white T-shirt, although it couldn't hide the definition in his arms. Jess wondered if she'd visibly gulped, because it certainly felt like she had.

She was relieved beyond measure that he had seen fit to throw on a pair of joggers and not just shorts, as she didn't think the memory of what she'd seen below the waist would ever leave her. She hoped her face wasn't as crimson as she thought.

'I'm so sorry about that,' Nathan said. 'I assumed it was the postman when Baxter barked.'

Jess lifted an eyebrow. 'You usually greet your postman naked?'

He laughed, a rich, melodious sound. 'No, of course not. I meant, I thought he'd delivered letters and gone, and that I was safe to come find the towel I'd left downstairs.' He gestured behind her. 'My airing cupboard's behind you.'

'Would you like me to pass you one?'

Nathan's face scrunched up in puzzlement.

'Your hair's still wet.' The urge to reach out and show him where exactly was strong, but she resisted, although it was almost like a magnetic pull was dragging her towards him. What the heck was wrong with her this morning? Or maybe she was just a hot-blooded woman with needs. Yes, she liked that idea.

'Sure. Thanks.'

Jess turned round, grateful for a few seconds to compose herself again, opened the cupboard and threw him a towel.

'Thanks.'

'Poor Baxter's champing at the bit here. I'd better take him out. See you later.'

'Yeah, bye, and sorry again.'

'No worries.' She stopped herself just in time from trotting out 'Anytime.' That was almost as bad as 'My pleasure.' She closed the door behind her thinking she wouldn't be seeing so much of him next time, or she hoped not for her heart's sake.

An hour later, Jess' heart rate picked up again as she approached Nathan's door, a tired and happy Baxter at her side. Her arm ached from having thrown the tennis ball so many times for Baxter, but he had a lot of energy to burn, and quite frankly, Jess had needed an outlet today too. During the entire walk and play session with Baxter, she'd thought of nothing but her earlier encounter with Nathan. It was hard not to as she couldn't shake the vision from her mind, plus she was playing with his dog. No matter how hard she tried, Baxter was there as a constant reminder.

This time she knocked at the door. She wasn't taking any chances, despite the improbability of Nathan deciding to take another shower today. She didn't think she'd ever again use the key he'd given her, quite so freely; instead, she'd pound on the door first to ensure he wasn't home.

She let Baxter back in, gave him a treat, refilled his water bowl and glanced around Nathan's kitchen with renewed interest. It was tidy, although not scarily so – a dirty cereal bowl stood in the sink, with some soapy bubbles in it – but there was no dirty laundry around, the worktop was immaculate and the floor was free of dog hair. Keeping that clean must have been a nightmare with Baxter. So Nathan knew how to use a dustpan and brush or a hoover. Bonus points.

Right, she'd better get out of there, before she engaged in proper snooping. An itch was growing underneath her skin. An itch to know, just for curiosity's sake, if Nathan was single. Her devil side would love to be able to know the answer to the question many of the women in her classes kept speculating about. But although she'd been keeping a keen eye open, she hadn't detected a female presence or a feminine touch to either the items in the kitchen or in the choice of décor.

Baxter circled her legs, trying to jump up, clearly having had his fill of water. A noise in the hall startled her. Oh no, had he come back? She didn't know if she could handle this much embarrassment in one day. She needed to get out of here before her mind returned to what he looked like naked. Too late. Her face flushed as the image indelibly imprinted on her mind resurfaced.

She braced for having to make small talk, but was relieved when a few seconds later, no sound came. She peered into the hall and breathed out as she saw the stack of letters on the doormat. Postman. Thank God.

'Bye, Baxter.' She patted him and didn't dally any further.

That evening, Jess came home a little later than usual, due to heavy traffic on the route back from the gym. As she opened the front door, a combination of delicious aromas wafted in her direction.

'What's all this?' Jess almost had to physically lift her jaw off the ground, such was her surprise.

'What? Can't I cook a delicious yet nutritious meal for my beloved?' asked Mark with a cheeky grin.

'Daily, if you like, but since you never do, I have to wonder if you're looking for me to donate one of my kidneys to you or something.'

'Oi, you, it's not that infrequent an occurrence.' Mark pointed his wooden spoon at her.

Jess put her hands on her hips. 'You think?'

'OK, OK, I'll admit I've been neglecting you, neglecting us, recently, but I'm here to make amends.' He pointed to the oven. 'What do you think?'

A dish was bubbling away invitingly. Its very proximity proved too much for Jess' taste buds and her stomach rumbled in response.

'Ah, that's what I like, a sign of encouragement. Baked feta with burst tomatoes and a chilli honey glaze.'

Jess smiled. Mark didn't know how to cook, so for him to do so was nothing short of amazing. And the meal sounded incredible.

'But that's not all, m'lady,' said Mark. 'Oh, no. Then we have souvlaki with tzatziki.'

Jess licked her lips. She was so hungry. She wished Mark would stop talking so she could just eat.

'I decided to go with a Greek theme,' Mark added. 'No dessert, though. I thought that was enough.'

'More than,' said Jess. 'Mark, this sounds and smells marvellous, but what's the occasion?'

'There isn't one, although it is Valentine's Day in a few days, so I thought we'd celebrate a little early.'

'Right.' The cogs in Jess' brain whirred, wondering why he couldn't just have prepared this fantastic meal on Valentine's Day itself then, although in many respects she was glad he hadn't waited, as she was ravenous.

The meal was fabulous. Mark had truly excelled himself. Afterwards, as they reclined on the sofa, replete, Jess promising to do the dishes later since she could barely move, a wave of contentment washed over her. Then another emotion replaced it – guilt. Whilst Mark had been planning to slave away over a hot stove, literally, she'd encountered Nathan naked – albeit by accident – and been unable to shake that image from her head all day. Even now it had re-entered her psyche and was taking up more space than it should be.

Time to redress the balance. She cuddled into Mark and they put on an action movie.

'Oh, Jess, on Friday, there's a leaving-do for Neil at

work. You have any objection to me going?'

'Objection? Why would I–?' She threw a cushion at him, scoring a direct hit to the head, despite him ducking, as a laugh burst from Mark's throat.

Valentine's Day. She'd been played.

Chapter Nineteen

Anouska

Tuesday 11 February

Anouska was enjoying travelling less for work, and was now taking her pregnancy in her stride, particularly since she'd decided not to present Zach with the facts yet and instead wait until she proposed. Plus, now she'd dispatched her mother back to Sweden, she didn't have her well-meaning running commentary on what she ought to do with regards to Zach. Maura had made her promise to ring her within an hour of proposing to let her know all had gone well and to describe Zach's reaction both to the proposal and impending fatherhood. Fortunately, that was still a few weeks off.

She was also enjoying her weekly meeting with the girls, although last week it had just been her and Jess because Ellie was having her showdown with Scott. Still, she was glad she'd been there for Ellie the day after her discovery, and they'd been in touch by phone and text most days since.

Telling Zach of his impending fatherhood aside, overall, she felt she was more in control of her life again. She had also managed, thank goodness, to secure a competent temp and both she and Leigh-Ann were training her up. Leigh-Ann did look a bit askance at some of the things Anouska was covering with the temp, which were usually more in Leigh-Ann's remit, but she couldn't explain without telling her she was pregnant, and she wouldn't do that to Zach. It was bad enough that her mum knew before he did, even though, she reasoned, she hadn't told Maura, her mother had simply worked it out.

So, she made a point of delegating more senior tasks to Leigh-Ann, things that she herself would normally take care of. Leigh-Ann frowned a few times at this, but Anouska pretended not to notice as she didn't know how to talk her way out of the situation.

As she parked her car and headed for Cirque, Anouska considered the deepening special bond she felt with her child. She was glad she'd nicknamed her baby Bean. Calling Bean 'it' seemed so impersonal. She'd had second thoughts about her original idea of proposing over a nice meal at home, but still hadn't worked out the details of an alternative, so she was hoping the girls might have some advice or be able to brainstorm with her tonight. And that brought her back to feeling uneasy at not having shared with the girls the fact she was pregnant, especially given they'd shared so much with her, particularly Ellie, with all the lurid details of her dramatic break-up with Scott.

Anouska spotted Ellie and Jess as soon as she entered Cirque. 'Hi, ladies.' She hugged them both, aware she was hugging Ellie more fiercely than usual, perhaps somehow trying to convey via the additional pressure that she was there for her whenever she needed the support.

She was surprised to see Ellie already there. So far, Ellie had earned a reputation for being the one who was always last to arrive, despite living less than ten minutes away.

Ellie looked well, all things considered, although last time they'd met, her face had been blotchy and puffy with the incessant tears she'd shed, not because of Scott's departure from her life, but the manner in which it had occurred and the years she'd wasted on him.

'The usual?' Marion appeared at her shoulder with the stealth of a ninja on a mission. Either that or some supernatural being had taught her how to glide silently. The woman had two modes – noisiest person for miles around or discretion itself.

'Latte, thanks, Marion.' They exchanged pleasantries and then Marion retreated to fix her order.

'So, how is everyone?' Anouska looked between Ellie and Jess.

'I'm doing really well,' Ellie said, her voice more chipper than Anouska had expected.

Anouska appraised her and thought that apart from her improved physical appearance, she genuinely did look so much happier.

'That's great. Any reason in particular?' She quirked an eyebrow.

'Well, as is always the case with these things, you never hear about something then when you discuss it, up it pops.'

'Sorry, you've lost me,' Anouska said. 'What do you mean?'

'You know how I've been waiting to hear about the promotion?' At Anouska's nod, Ellie continued, 'My letter came in today's post.'

'That's brilliant news. When is it?'

'Second of March. So I still have plenty of time to prepare.'

'What's to prepare? You've virtually been doing the job the past month or so anyway,' Jess put in.

'I have, and I've been shadowing Trish, which has been wonderful, such an insight. Hope the interview panel don't get wind of the fact I've had extra help or hands-on experience, direct from my mentor.'

'We all have to do what we can in business to get by,' said Anouska. 'It was Trish who suggested it, not you. Shadowing her is just a natural progression of your current job anyway.'

'True, but I'm not sure the other candidates would see it like that.'

'There are other candidates then,' Jess said.

'Yeah, like I told Anouska the other day, someone else in my department applied and has an interview, but I don't know who else is up for it, or how many other candidates there are in total. I've heard rumours there's at least two external, but you've got to hope it goes internally. I wouldn't mind if it went to my colleague, but it'll feel like a bit of a slap in the face if someone external gets it.'

'I see your point,' Jess said sagely.

'And have you heard anything from Scott?' asked Anouska tentatively.

'Yeah, he's been to the house a couple of times. I haven't answered the door, and fortunately he hasn't been shouting at the top of his voice or anything. Trish threatened to go sort him out.'

'Trish?' Jess' bemusement was clear from her tone.

'Yes, she plays rugby. You would not want to mess with her, believe me. That's why I'm always glad to have her in my corner.'

'So, what else have you been up to?' Anouska asked.

'I went rock climbing at the weekend with one of my friends, just to get away from it all. Weather was decent. That doesn't happen often in February.'

Jess rolled her eyes. 'Tell me about it. I've either been freezing or soaked the past few weeks when I've been dog walking. Not my favourite season, winter.'

'And what about you, Jess? What's new with you?' Anouska asked.

'Not a great deal. I haven't nailed down any of the proposal details, although obviously the trip's booked and everything, but I haven't figured out what I'm going to wear, or if I'm getting him a ring before the proposal or once we get back, or anything.'

'Haribo?' suggested Ellie.

They all laughed.

'Didn't you go shopping with Kelsea and Lauren last month for a new wardrobe?' Anouska asked.

Jess made a face. 'Yeah, but half the time we were having lunch and drinking Prosecco, so not much shopping actually got done.'

'That is a problem with those two.' Anouska laughed.

'I did have a very weird, but funny, thing happen the other day, though. It was embarrassing, actually.'

'Oh, pray tell.' Ellie leant forward. 'We do love a good embarrassing story.'

'Well, I went to pick up Nathan's dog. You remember I've not long started walking him?' They nodded. 'Anyway, I open the door and Nathan is coming down the stairs bollock naked.'

'Oh my God, I'd have died!' Ellie's hand covered her mouth. 'What did you do?'

Jess fidgeted. 'Well, I, er, I froze.'

'You froze?' A smile played on Anouska's lips.

'Yes, I couldn't move at all. And he sort of did the same and then seemed to finally come out of his daze and bounded upstairs to get dressed.'

'Please tell me you looked away then,' said Ellie, bursting out laughing.

'I couldn't! I froze.'

'So you watched as he raced upstairs? Hopefully, no dangly bits were visible.' Anouska waggled her eyebrows.

'I wasn't concentrating on that,' Jess said, in mock outrage.

'I would have been,' Ellie had no problem admitting.

'Well, he did have a nice–'

'Jess!' Anouska cut her off.

'I was going to say butt.' Jess turned a deeper shade of crimson. 'Butt. Anyway, enough torturing me, how's things going with your proposal ideas, Anouska?'

'Let me get us some fresh drinks and then I'll fill you in.'

As Anouska walked towards the counter to speak to Marion, she could hear Jess and Ellie chattering behind her. Marion wasn't at the counter. *She must be in the storeroom.*

Something was niggling at Anouska's brain. Something about the story Jess had just told. It was funny, but Anouska had the feeling there was more to it. If she didn't know better, she'd have thought Jess liked Nathan, and not just in an I-walk-his-dog capacity.

Marion reappeared, interrupting her thought process, and took her order.

When Anouska returned to the table, Jess reminded her she was to provide an update on her proposal.

Anouska sighed. 'Honestly, I don't know how to

propose to Zach. Usually, I'm the ideas person but I feel as if my creative well has dried up,' she said wistfully.

'Well, what's Zach interested in?' Ellie asked.

'He likes music, travel, architecture. Restaurants, obviously. Cooking.'

Jess scribbled notes on a napkin. 'That's plenty to work with. How about proposing at a favourite landmark, or one he has always wanted to go to?'

'I don't know. He's a very private person. I'm not sure he'd like others watching our intimate moment.'

'Anouska,' Jess said hesitantly. 'Excuse me if I'm overstepping, but are you sure you definitely want to get married, or propose on the twenty-ninth?'

Anouska gave a sharp intake of breath before Jess continued. 'Sorry, I'm honestly not trying to pressure you in any way, exactly the opposite in fact. It's just I have this sense something's going on in the background, like we're missing a piece of the puzzle.' Jess bit her lip and looked at Anouska, worry lines etching her forehead. She was obviously concerned in case Anouska took offence.

The irony of her having had a similar thought about Jess only five minutes before wasn't lost on her, and Anouska wanted to tell them what was going on, but she couldn't. How could she tell the girls without being disloyal to Zach? What to do?

'There is, and I promise I will tell you at some point, but it's complicated, and I can't tell you tonight. You see, it's tied up with the proposal and might be a dealbreaker. Sorry, I'm probably not making much sense. The bottom line is I need to propose to Zach before I can give you any more information. Apologies if that's cryptic.'

'Sorry, I didn't mean to pry,' Jess said.

'Not at all. We've shared so much of ourselves with each other the past few weeks, and been there for each other, it's only natural you'd notice if something felt off.'

'It must be lovely sitting out here in summer,' mused Jess.

Anouska wondered if she was changing the subject intentionally.

'Oh, it is. You must come back then. It's gorgeous here, busy, especially during the festival, but it feels like being on the Continent, people sitting in Princes Street Gardens in the evening sun, the street performers, the buzz, the tourists.' Ellie was clearly proud of the capital.

'I'm not great with crowds to be honest,' said Jess. 'Having to wait four deep to get to the bar panics me.'

'Really? Do you have some sort of phobia or something?' asked Ellie.

'Not as such, but I have had some panic attacks in large crowds.'

'That must be quite scary.' Anouska empathised with her, having her own issues with panic attacks. 'I don't like going in tunnels. I drive the long way around to avoid them.'

'That's funny, one of my friends is the same with bridges. Makes journeys with her so much longer, but a lot more interesting,' Ellie said.

By the time they left, with promises to meet again the following week and text with any updates, the ground was frosty underfoot.

'Brr, it's freezing.' Ellie took her gloves out of her pockets and put them on. 'The temperature's really dropped since we came in.'

'It hasn't half. Watch yourself, it's slippery,' Anouska said, just as her feet went out from under her and she landed heavily on her back. 'Ow, ow, ow!'

'Anouska, are you all right?' asked Jess.

'Yes. No. Oh God!' she mumbled.

'Sorry?' Jess bent down to try to help her up.

'I think I'm bleeding.'

'Where? Your leg, your arm?'

Anouska gritted her teeth at the pain in her back and said, 'Please God let the baby be OK.'

Both Ellie and Jess put an arm under Anouska and helped her to her feet, but not before Anouska registered the alarm on their faces. Jess took her phone out. 'I'll call an ambulance.'

'No, no, it will take too long for it to get here. I need a cab,' Anouska managed through her tears.

Anouska barely registered the Triage sign. This couldn't be happening. She couldn't lose the baby. She didn't know much about pregnancy yet, but she knew that bleeding was bad. Why was it taking so long? She knew she was being unreasonable, she knew the NHS was stretched beyond belief and she was in an overflowing waiting room, but she didn't care. All she cared about was making sure the baby was OK.

She wanted this baby. She wanted it with a fierceness she had never felt about anything. Bean had to be all right. And she couldn't even call Zach as he didn't know. God, what a fool she'd been. She could really use his support right now. The girls had been amazing, but she'd only known them for just over a month. She needed a familiar face and reassurance from the man she loved, the man whose baby she was carrying. She needed Zach.

Chapter Twenty

Ellie

Tuesday 11 February

Ellie couldn't believe what she was hearing, or seeing. Blood was staining Anouska's pink dress. Then she took in what Anouska said about a baby and she went on autopilot. They'd had no time to deal with the shock of Anouska's unexpected announcement, before Jess had flagged down a cab, taken off her coat and laid it on the seat for Anouska to sit on. As soon as Anouska had mentioned bleeding and the baby, she had swung into action. Ellie had to confess to being temporarily rooted to the spot in disbelief. It could only have been a few seconds, but then she was helping Anouska up and into the taxi. Her pale, haunted face sent shivers down Ellie's spine. *Please let the baby be all right.*

Ellie wheedled out of Anouska that she was about ten weeks pregnant. She prayed she wouldn't lose the baby. Ellie knew miscarriages happened to more women than you would expect, but she didn't want Anouska to be part of that statistic. Although they hadn't known each other that long, she already felt strongly protective of her.

The taxi ride to the hospital felt like the longest Ellie had ever endured. Fifteen minutes later, the cab drew up in front of the hospital. They'd already ascertained which hospital was the closest, and Ellie had phoned ahead to advise them of the situation and that they'd be coming in so they could arrange a wheelchair or whatever, and be on hand to deal with her as soon as she arrived – at least she hoped it worked that way. Meanwhile, Jess comforted a sobbing Anouska and asked her for her boyfriend's number, but Anouska kept whispering, 'He doesn't know, he doesn't know. Oh, please let the baby be OK.' She gripped Jess' arm as if she would never let go.

Ellie wondered why Zach didn't know. So many scenarios flitted through her mind but none made sense.

The porter hastened towards them with a wheelchair as soon as they arrived. The NHS got a bad press sometimes, Ellie thought, but they were here waiting for them with very little notice.

'Hi, love, I'm Mike. Let's take you on a wee trip,' he told Anouska, who was still openly sobbing. Jess' cream wool coat was ruined, but she didn't seem to notice or care.

'The baby, the baby,' Anouska kept repeating. 'There's so much blood.'

'Ah, blood always looks more than it is, love. A little goes a long way. Let's get you up to Triage. They'll sort you out in no time.'

It was hard not to take heart from Mike's cheeriness and it buoyed Ellie's spirits. She hoped it had a similar effect on Anouska.

When they arrived at Triage, they were met by an equally friendly but exhausted-looking nurse. She put them in the Triage waiting room, which was packed, and said she'd be back in five minutes. Ellie had so many questions, but she knew now wasn't the time. Jess had her arm round

Anouska, who was almost catatonic, and Ellie rested her hand on Anouska's knee in a gesture of support. The nurse's five minutes proved to be ten. Ellie knew. She'd been watching the second hand go round. Every tick felt like a blow to the head. When would they know if the baby was all right?

The nurse returned, clipboard in hand. 'Anouska Bennett?'

Anouska's eyes, which had momentarily closed, fluttered open.

'Can I call you Anouska?'

Anouska was so distraught she couldn't even formulate a verbal response, so simply nodded.

'Could you wheel the chair after me?' the nurse asked the girls as she headed through a set of swing doors. A sharp left after the doors took them to a cubicle, where the nurse pulled the curtain round the four of them.

'I'm Elaine, one of the midwives here. Are you Anouska's sisters then?'

Ellie wondered if she was trying to gauge if they should be in the room or not. Before either she or Jess could answer, Anouska managed, 'No, they're friends, but I'd like them to stay.' She turned to Ellie and Jess. 'As long as that's fine with you?'

'Absolutely,' said Ellie.

'Of course.' Jess held her hand.

'They can stay then. Let's get a few questions out of the way, then we'll have a little look-see. Girls, can you come and stand at the top of the bed, please?'

Ellie and Jess did as they were bid, and Ellie placed her hand on Anouska's shoulder, whilst Jess returned to holding her hand.

The midwife ran through her questions, checking how far along Anouska was, asking what brought on the bleeding, if anything, and finally, she said she'd examine her.

Ellie and Jess averted their eyes, as although Anouska was covered by a hospital gown, it wasn't the most dignified of positions to be in.

'We'll have to wait a little bit longer to be sure, but the signs are positive. Let me go and arrange a scan so we can be certain.' The midwife popped off her gloves, threw them in the clinical waste bin and exited the room.

The girls looked at each other.

'Anouska, it's going to be OK,' Jess promised.

'Jess is right. The midwife wouldn't have been so upbeat if the news was bad,' Ellie agreed.

Despite her words, and her and Jess trying to be strong for Anouska, until she heard the baby's heartbeat or saw it on the scan, she imagined Anouska would still worry. *She* was worrying. In fact, she felt physically sick. Poor Anouska. Ellie felt seriously under-equipped to deal with a situation of this magnitude and gravity. It all felt rather unreal to her. Now she knew what people meant when they talked of out-of-body experiences. How could they be sitting chatting in a café one minute and the next minute a life hung in the balance?

She told herself she was being overdramatic, but inside she knew that it was a very real possibility. Now was not the time to catastrophise and think of every possible thing that could go wrong. She had to stay positive and strong. Anouska needed her, and Jess.

Anouska sobbed again and Ellie tried to hug her, but it was awkward with her sitting on the bed.

'What's causing the bleeding? What if it's an ectopic pregnancy? I can't deliver the baby if that happens. I'm sure of it. Oh God, why didn't I tell Zach?'

Ellie struggled to keep up with Anouska's train of thought and outpouring of emotion. Her heart broke for her friend.

'How can I tell him about the baby now? And even if everything is OK, I won't be able to keep *this* from him. I've been such a fool. I should have followed Mum's advice.'

Anouska was babbling now. Sometimes she was almost incoherent, or she muttered so softly under her breath, Ellie couldn't make out what she was saying.

Anouska gave a wan half-smile. 'Mum would be delighted at me agreeing with her for once.' She burst into sobs again as Ellie exchanged a worried glance with Jess, and they both did their best to comfort her.

Ellie felt they'd been thrown overboard without a life raft. She had no idea how to deal with a situation like this. It felt bigger than her and made her own problems seem trivial by comparison. She held Anouska's hand and did something she hadn't done in a long time. She prayed.

It was an hour before Anouska was able to have a scan. The midwife rubbed cold jelly on her stomach, then swept the imaging scanner over her abdomen. The scan took only minutes, but it felt like hours. Ellie tried not to hold her breath.

Finally, the midwife smiled. 'Your baby's fine.' She turned her monitor so they could see the baby's outline. 'Now all we have to do is calm Mum down.'

Anouska let out a breath, then cried, this time tears of joy, as she looked at the monitor.

The baby was going to be all right. Ellie, too, exhaled.

She and Jess stood either side of Anouska, each of them gripping one of her hands.

'We're going to admit you for observation. Your blood pressure's a bit high, so we'd like to keep you in overnight,' said the midwife. 'You've had a bit of a shock and now we need to make sure you're OK.'

'No, I can't stay in overnight!' Panic laced Anouska's tone.

'Why not?' asked Ellie.

'Zach,' croaked Anouska. 'He'll wonder where I am.'

'Don't you think we should call him?' Ellie said.

'I don't know what to do,' she flapped. 'How can I let Zach find out about his baby in these circumstances? Nothing's going to plan. I needed time to get used to the baby idea and then I was so convinced proposing on the twenty-ninth was the right thing to do, then I'd tell him afterwards that I was pregnant, that I've been blinded to everything else.'

And Ellie didn't think now was the best time to make life-changing decisions.

Anouska rubbed her temples. 'I can't think straight right now.'

'Why don't we give you some time to yourself?' suggested Jess.

'We could go and get a coffee,' Ellie added.

Absent-mindedly, Anouska nodded. 'Yes…yes, thanks.'

'Would you like anything?' Ellie asked.

'No, I have water here, thanks.'

Jess poured her some water from the jug at the side of

the bed and then, after telling Anouska they wouldn't be long, she followed Ellie out of the room.

'I can't believe it.' Ellie touched a hand to her forehead in bewilderment.

'Me neither.' Jess placed her coffee cup on the table in front of her. 'Poor Anouska.'

'In more ways than one. We can't leave her overnight without anyone from her family knowing, and we won't be allowed to stay.'

'I know. I wonder how long it'll be before Anouska's moved to a ward.'

'Don't know. It could be half an hour, three hours, depends what's available,' said Ellie.

'We'll stay until they throw us out then. I don't like the idea of leaving her on her own even then. I wish she'd let us call Zach.'

'I know, but I can sort of understand her logic. Imagine how terrified Zach would be to hear his girlfriend, who hasn't told him she's pregnant, has been admitted to hospital, pregnant, bleeding, in another city.' Ellie tapped her foot repeatedly on the ground as if doing so would help her think of a solution.

Silence hung in the air between them as they tried to absorb everything. Finally, Jess said, 'Let's see how she is when we return. We'll let her know we'll come back first thing in the morning, or as soon as the staff will let us in. She'll need someone to collect her before she's allowed to leave.'

Ellie nodded. 'I'd assume so, and it goes without saying, you're welcome to stay at mine tonight.'

'Thanks. Hopefully, Anouska will feel better knowing we're both here for her.'

Ellie drained her coffee, threw the cup in the bin and then they headed back to discuss it with Anouska.

'No, I don't want Zach to know. Not like this.' Anouska was almost frenzied.

'OK, OK. Why don't we text him then and tell him you're staying at mine tonight and you'll see him tomorrow?'

Anouska's features relaxed at that and she gave a small smile. 'Thanks. I know it's complicated, but I feel better now I know the baby is all right. They'll be transferring me to the ward soon. You guys should go home, it's late. Oh God, Jess, what time is it? Have you missed the last train?'

'Don't worry about me. I'm staying at Ellie's. You just need to concentrate on relaxing,' Jess reassured her.

'I'm so sorry about tonight,' Anouska said, doing the exact opposite of relaxing.

'Don't be silly. You have absolutely nothing to apologise for,' Jess said.

'Jess is right. It's not your fault. I'm just glad we were there and you weren't on your own when it happened. You gave us a right scare, though,' Ellie admitted.

'This little one gave us all a scare.' Anouska stroked her stomach.

She fired off a text to Zach. *Having so much fun with the girls, have decided to stay in the hotel with them tonight as I'm a bit squiffy. See you tomorrow. A x*

'There. Done. Now, you two should get going. Are you able to come back in the morning? I know it's a big ask, but

I don't know if they'll discharge me if I'm on my own.'

'Of course we'll be back tomorrow.' Jess patted Anouska's shoulder. 'Won't we, Ellie?'

'Absolutely. We want to check you're all right and see you safely home. Now get some rest.'

Jess kissed Anouska goodbye and turned to leave at the same time as the midwife came back into the room.

'We'll have you up in the ward in five minutes. You're in luck. Things have quietened down a little. If you'd been here earlier, you'd have had to wait hours to be moved.'

Ellie sighed with relief that Anouska was already being transferred to the ward, shot her a final smile and she and Jess left her in the care of the midwives.

Chapter Twenty-one

Jess

Wednesday 12 February

Jess spent a fitful night's sleep and was almost grateful when the alarm went off at seven o'clock. Breakfast was a rather subdued affair. She and Ellie ate more out of necessity than from having an appetite, then called the hospital for an update. Jess lied and told them they were family as she knew they wouldn't give out the information otherwise. The midwife checked then told them Anouska was waiting to see the consultant, but had had a decent night. Jess thanked her, hung up and relayed the information to Ellie. Now they could only wait.

After Jess had made a couple of calls to her clients and the gym to apologise for cancelling at such short notice and to arrange cover, for want of anything else to do, she and Ellie took a walk up towards the city centre. It was a crisp morning and the sun gave off a little warmth, slowly melting the ice of the night before. They walked for around forty minutes, appreciating the views, the wildlife and the unaccustomed relative silence in Central Edinburgh.

'This is possibly the best thing we could have done,' said Jess as they strolled through Princes Street Gardens.

'I know. Glad I brought my hat and gloves with me, though. It's not exactly toasty.'

'I'll drink to that. Thank goodness you could lend me a puffy jacket, or I would've had to buy one. Oh look, there's a little café. Why don't we grab a hot chocolate or something in there?'

'Good idea.' Ellie pushed open the door and Jess sighed as the welcome heat from the café enveloped her.

Once they'd settled in and had their hands around steaming hot drinks, Jess exhaled heavily. 'We can't leave her today with no one knowing what's happened. What if something happens again? The baby's not due until August.'

'I know. I can't believe she has kept this to herself all this time. It must be absolutely exhausting keeping a secret like that.'

'I couldn't do it,' said Jess. 'I wonder why she hasn't told Zach.'

'She'll have her reasons. The question is, will she share them with us?'

'If she's ready to share why, she knows we're here for her, and if she's not sure that we are, we can underline that point.' Jess tapped her index finger forcefully on the table.

'Yeah, with a sledgehammer.' Ellie grinned.

They went back and forth over what to do about Anouska's situation and her refusal to tell Zach.

'I know. We have to convince her she can't hold off telling Zach about the baby until the twenty-ninth when she's going to propose. She needs to tell him about the baby now. The proposal can come later,' Ellie said.

'I wonder if anyone else knows.'

'What do you mean?' Ellie scrunched up her forehead.

'She didn't say no one knew, she just said that Zach didn't know. She must have a best friend she told surely.'

'No, I don't think so. Otherwise, why wouldn't she have asked us to call them last night? Right, I think we have to be firm with her. She's had a shock and isn't thinking straight. It's up to us to get some answers out of her,' Ellie decided.

'Softly, softly, though,' Jess reminded her. 'She *has* just spent the night in hospital and had the scare of potentially losing her baby.'

'Soft but firm,' Ellie insisted. 'She needs to understand how serious it is that she looks after herself now. And she'll be going home today. What then?'

Jess had to admit she didn't know and that Ellie was probably right.

Anouska was sitting on a chair gazing out the window when the nurse showed Jess and Ellie in.

'You look much better,' Jess said. 'How did you sleep?'

'Surprisingly well, given the circumstances and the amount of light they have in here all through the night, and the number of times people come in and out. I must have been exhausted to sleep like that.'

'Or maybe it's the baby,' suggested Ellie.

Anouska smiled. 'Yes, the baby definitely contributed.'

'So, how are you feeling and have you had the definitive all-clear?' Jess asked.

'Baby's fine, I'm fine. Doc said I'm good to go, but they want my midwife to monitor me in a few days, then a week later, and after that, if they feel the need, every two weeks until the birth.'

'I'm so glad you're both OK.' Jess hugged her.

'Me too. Thanks for everything last night, you two. I can't tell you how much I appreciate it.'

'You don't need to thank us. We're just glad it's all turned out well. Anyway, sorry for the subject change, and I know you haven't told Zach yet, but have you told anyone else?' Ellie said.

'We-ell, my mum guessed when she came to visit me.'

'OK. Anyone else?' Jess asked.

Anouska shook her head.

That put paid to that then. Jess knew Anouska's mum had returned to Stockholm only the week before, so she wasn't exactly handy for helping her out over the next few days.

Ellie looked at Jess, as if willing her to continue. 'Anouska, you must tell Zach about this. We'll even come with you for moral support if you want. I know you told him a little white lie last night,' Jess hurried on, 'but you need someone close to you, and who lives nearby, to know what happened and keep an eye on you, or at least be there for you in case anything happens again. I don't mean to be patronising, but you have to think of you and the baby now.'

Anouska sighed. 'I know. I've been thinking about it since I woke up. I just don't know how to tell Zach. And thanks for the offer of coming with me, but it's time to put on my big- girl pants and get on with it.'

Jess placed her hand on Anouska's arm in a gesture of solidarity. 'Look, why don't we go grab a nice pub lunch somewhere and have a chat, about how to tell Zach, or we can talk about something else if you wish, then we'll take you home? Unless you'd rather go straight there?'

'No, there will be no one home. Zach's at Bean There. Pub lunch sounds good. But you're not driving me back to Aberdeen.'

'It's not up for debate. Ellie and I've already discussed it. You'd do the same for us.'

Anouska mulled this over for a second then said, 'Fine, and thank you.'

'You're welcome,' said Ellie. 'We wouldn't have it any other way.'

'And Zach?' Jess wasn't letting up.

Anouska blew out through her mouth then said, 'I'll tell him tonight.'

They stopped at the Travellers' Rest just outside Kinross before starting the journey north to Aberdeen. It was nothing fancy but the food was reputed to be excellent.

'That was just what I needed,' Anouska said after she'd polished off sausage and mash. 'I don't usually eat this kind of food, but that hit the spot. Cold toast in hospital didn't quite do it for me.'

'Yeah, my Hunter's chicken was delicious too.' Jess rubbed her belly. 'That'll keep me going until I get home again.'

'Well, it'll save me having to cook tonight, at least,' said Anouska, who was already yawning.

'Definitely a bonus.' Ellie popped the final piece of her chicken wrap in her mouth.

'So, apart from congratulating you, we haven't actually talked much about the baby. You're having a baby!'

'I know! I'm sorry I didn't tell you before. It was only because I hadn't told Zach. No other reason. And I wanted to tell you so much, you have no idea,' Anouska finished.

'Don't worry about that,' Ellie reassured her. 'But Jess is right, this is huge. I know you still have to tell Zach, but take a moment, especially now you know everything's OK, to simply enjoy the fact you're having a baby!'

A smile slowly spread across Anouska's face. 'I am, aren't I? Oh my God, I'm going to be a mum. A tiny life is growing inside me as we speak.'

'Does it kick yet?' Jess asked.

'No, Bean doesn't kick yet, too early.'

Jess looked at her quizzically. 'Bean?'

'Yes.' Anouska smiled. 'I nicknamed the baby "Bean" as when I was reading one of the pregnancy books, the baby was the size of a kidney bean.'

'Aw, that's so sweet.' Jess crossed her hands over her chest. How lovely was that?

'And I can't wait until Bean does kick, although it may feel a little like being possessed by an alien, but I'm looking forward to it, alien or not.'

It was heartening to see Anouska smiling and joking after the ordeal she'd just gone through.

'And what about names? When I was younger, and played with my dolls, I used to think what my kids' names would be and called all my dolls those names,' Jess said.

The other two stared at her. Oversharing. Now she looked like a right nerd.

'Didn't you ever do that?' she asked, her voice coming out as a squeak.

Anouska's brows knitted and Ellie gave a vigorous headshake.

Jess prattled on, 'But anyway, name trends have changed considerably since then. Fashions go, well, out of fashion.'

Still the same blank stares.

'C'mon, Anouska, you must have some inkling of a name or the type of name you like.' At Anouska's hesitation, Jess went on, 'Or on the flip side, some you really don't like and could rule out in a heartbeat.'

Eventually, Anouska said, 'Well, I do like foreign names, like Aurelie, Anastascia, Brigita, Claudia. Perhaps because my own name is so unusual, although ironically Anouska is English. I also like Giovanna, Mercedes and Katerina. Actually, now you've got me started, I could go on forever.'

'Oh, I love those,' Jess breathed. 'Particularly Aurelie. So French, so pretty.'

Ellie leant forward on the table. 'And what if it's a boy?'

Anouska bit her lip and appeared lost in thought for a second then ticked off on her fingers. 'Leo, Julian, Maxim, Dmitry and Pavel are amongst the first to spring to mind.'

'Well, baby Bean certainly won't have a boring name.' Ellie grinned.

'Unless Zach has different ideas,' Anouska mused sadly.

The cogs were turning in Jess' brain. Her vision of the landscape of Anouska and Zach's relationship seemed to vary greatly from the picture Anouska was painting in her reluctance to tell Zach about her pregnancy. What was she so afraid of?

Although she hadn't met Zach, everything she'd heard about him sounded wonderful, so why the reticence? She simply didn't get it.

'Anouska, excuse me if I'm being too forward, but can I ask why you haven't told Zach about the baby? You said the proposal was complicated. Was this why?'

Anouska's eyes widened and she opened her mouth as if to speak, but no words came out. Finally, she said, 'He doesn't want kids. I do. I always have, but I was so happy with Zach, I didn't want to spoil things by telling him so, when I knew how he felt, so I suppressed my desire to be a mum, thinking we could be enough for each other. And we were. Until now.'

This time it was Jess' eyes that widened. She hadn't been expecting that.

'And Zach has so many hang-ups about marriage, as I told you before.' She turned to Ellie. 'Sorry, Ellie, I think you might have missed that conversation. He had a bad experience with an ex, and it has put him off marriage for life.'

Ellie frowned. 'But you're not his ex. Your relationship with Zach is totally different to theirs.'

'I know, but try telling Zach that. He's happy as we are. And I was, for the most part, but now I'm not. And even if I was, life has changed for me – dramatically.' She eyed her stomach pointedly.

Jess thought for a second then said, 'Anouska, Zach loves you. Yes, he'll likely be shocked you're pregnant, but human beings cope with shocks all the time. We just get on with it. This may be the best thing that has ever happened to you as a couple. I can already see how much you're looking forward to being a mum in the way you talk about Bean, the way you cover your stomach protectively. Believe in Zach. I really think you'll be pleasantly surprised.'

Anouska gave a deep sigh. 'I hope so, Jess, I really hope so.'

Two hours later, Ellie's car pulled up outside Anouska's flat. Jess and Ellie helped Anouska upstairs then Ellie made her a cup of tea whilst Jess made her comfortable on the couch.

'Now, listen, rest, I mean it. We'll be checking.' Jess pointed a finger at her.

Anouska smiled. 'Are you going to install a nanny cam or something?'

Jess smirked. 'Don't tempt me.'

They chatted for ten minutes or so whilst they drank the tea, then Anouska told them they should go as they had a long journey back.

'And you're positive you don't want us to stay, or at least remain in the vicinity? We could go to a nearby café or something and you could phone us if you need us,' Jess said, although she was wondering how she'd explain to Mark, the gym and her dog owners why she wasn't back yet. But some things were more important.

Anouska smiled. 'Thanks, Jess, but this is something I really need to do on my own.'

Chapter Twenty-two

Anouska

Wednesday 12 February

Anouska lay on the sofa, her phone in her hand. It had been twenty-three minutes since she'd waved the girls off. They'd stayed to ensure she was well enough and mentally able to do what she intended to that night. But she still didn't know how to do it. She didn't feel up to it one bit. She wasn't sure if she had it in her any longer. In fact, she knew it. She couldn't do it. Couldn't go through with the proposal. But she needed to tell Zach he was going to be a father. She picked up her phone and dialled his number.

Anouska frowned when Zach's phone went to voicemail. She couldn't leave him a message – she didn't trust her voice not to give her away. It was different when you were having an actual conversation. She sighed and clicked end. It would have to keep. In the meantime she'd potter around and figure out what to say.

When two hours later Zach still hadn't called, Anouska's patience began to wane. She knew it was irrational. He was busy, at work, no doubt inundated, even though it was a weeknight. He didn't seem to have many quiet periods, which was good for business, she supposed, less so for their relationship. She knew he had no idea why she was calling, but she needed him. And she didn't like that. Anouska rarely needed anyone. Normally, she was the epitome of self-sufficiency. She was happy to *want* to be with someone but not to *need* to be with them, or need them. Now things had changed, and how. And she couldn't get hold of Zach. How would it be when the baby came? What on earth would she say when she saw him, because this time there was no hiding. Zach knew her well enough to be able to tell from her face that something was amiss.

She must have fallen asleep, as she woke when a key turned in the lock. Disoriented, she glanced at the clock. Ten past ten. She had slept the evening away.

Zach came into the living room, hair sticking up, a sheen of sweat on his forehead and his trousers covered in what looked like splodges of ragu. Anouska had never loved him more. But how could they have a family life when they both worked all the hours they did? She wasn't being fair to him, hadn't been fair to him, and now wasn't a good moment to lay this on him, but when would be? Exhausted herself, especially given the events of the past twenty-four hours, Anouska drew on her inner strength, pulled herself up and said, 'You look like you could use a glass of wine.'

'Thanks, sweetheart.'

He took off his trousers, explaining as he did so that he had been preparing some ragu for the freezer, slipped on the kitchen floor and upended the container all over himself, his chef's whites only managing to catch the majority of it.

'I don't want to imagine what your whites are like then,' Anouska joked.

'Soaking in bleach.' He gave a wry smile.

Anouska passed him his wine, which he accepted with a sigh.

'Zach.'

Zach turned to face her, and spurred on, Anouska continued. 'I have something to tell you. I've been trying to find the right moment, but there hasn't been one, and I know right now is possibly one of the worst moments, but we rarely see each other and this can't wait any longer.'

Zach spilled some of his wine as he set it down. 'Anouska, you're scaring me. What is it? You're not ill, are you?'

'No, Zach, I'm not ill. I'm pregnant.'

'What?' A multitude of emotions crossed Zach's features – shock, disbelief, then horror. Anouska bit back a sob. She knew it. She knew he would be shocked, but how could they come back from this? The final expression on his face said it all.

'But how?'

'I think you know how, Zach,' she said dryly.

'No, I mean, we're always so careful, and you're on the pill. Oh my God, you were throwing up a few weeks ago. Was that morning sickness?'

'It turned out to be, yes. I didn't know then.'

'So, how pregnant are you?'

'Ten weeks.'

'Ten weeks? How long have you known?'

'A few weeks,' she fudged. He didn't have to know absolutely everything.

'I can't believe you kept this from me.' He ran his hands through his hair and looked so distraught, Anouska wanted to take him in her arms and comfort him. She also needed him to reassure her.

'And does it have like bits and everything? Can you see it yet?'

'I suppose it depends what bits you're referring to, but yes, you'd be able to make out its outline.' Again, he didn't need to know yet she'd already seen the baby, already had a scan. She struggled to swallow, fighting back tears.

'I do-do-don't know what to say,' said Zach. 'We're going to be parents!'

'Are you pleased?' Anouska was almost too scared to ask, but she had to.

'Honestly, I'm shocked more than anything, but I-I-I, yes, I'm pleased.'

Anouska's breath left her in a whoosh, then she let Zach embrace her and she hugged him back.

'Oh my goodness, Anouska, this is huge. I wonder if it will be a boy or a girl. What will we call it? I didn't think I wanted kids, but now you've presented me with a fait accompli, it seems right.'

Relief flooded through Anouska. 'Oh, Zach, I'm so glad you feel that way. We've always said we wouldn't have kids. I was worried how you'd react. It's going to change our lives in a big way. Like ninety-five per cent of our lives.'

'What about your work?' Zach appeared to suddenly realise the impact their child would have on their, and more pertinently Anouska's, day-to-day life.

'I don't know yet. The travelling is out for sure. I can't fly after seven months anyway. I'll probably need to get a manager in, or promote one of my managers in one of the territories.'

Zach snuggled into her. 'I can't take it in. We're going to have a baby.'

'Yep.'

They sat on the sofa chatting and cuddling, until the phone rang, interrupting them. Anouska picked up, but inadvertently hit speakerphone.

'Anouska,' boomed her mother's voice. 'It's me. Have you told him yet? Have you asked him yet?'

Shit! Anouska jabbed at the phone, trying to click off the speakerphone.

'Anouska, have you told him about the baby yet?' her mother insisted.

Dreading turning around, and still stabbing at the phone to turn off the speakerphone, Anouska twisted and saw Zach's horror-stricken face. It was almost as if the words 'You told her before you told me?' were coming out of a speech bubble at his mouth. The situation couldn't have been any more hideous.

'Mum, I need to call you back.' Anouska clattered the handset back in its cradle and walked over to Zach, who now had his face in his hands as if trying to blot out what he'd heard.

'You told her?' Zach whispered.

'Yes, no, she knows.' Anouska's tear-stained face appeared to have little impact on Zach, who rounded on her. 'And how come she knew and I didn't? Has she...she's known since she was here, hasn't she?'

Anouska nodded, unable to make a sound.

'But that was over a week ago. Why didn't you tell me?'

'There...there never seemed a good time.' Anouska knew it sounded feeble but it hadn't felt like an excuse at the time.

'A good time? But your mother knew, and you still didn't think I might like to know about the existence of my child?' Zach's face contorted into a grimace. Then, as if something had dawned on him, he asked, 'Does anyone else know?'

For once Anouska considered lying, but she was a terrible liar and knew it. 'I'm not sure.'

'What do you mean you're not sure? You've either told someone or not.'

'Well, I haven't told anyone, but Mum knows. She guessed.' She shrugged. 'It's a mum thing, apparently.' She hesitated. 'And I think Leigh-Ann might know.'

Zach's mouth fell open. 'What? How does Leigh-Ann know?'

'I didn't say she definitely did, but she has been giving me funny looks. I think she may suspect but she hasn't challenged me on it.' She paused for a second to collect her thoughts. 'She sees me most days, and she's not stupid.'

'What? But I am? You should have called me before you took the test,' Zach said, his voice rising. Anouska could see he was trying to keep his cool, but she realised it couldn't be easy for him.

'Anyone else?' he asked, clearly expecting her to say no. 'Or is there a long list of clients, other family members, people at the airports you pass through that you might have told before me?'

Anouska sighed. 'Ellie and Jess know.'

At Zach's incredulous expression, she said, 'I didn't have a choice. They only found out yesterday.'

Zach ran his hands through his hair, tension flowing off him in waves. 'You told two complete strangers that you're pregnant with my child before you told me. Do you hear yourself?'

'Zach, I'm sorry. You and I had never planned to have kids and then bang, I'm pregnant. I didn't know how to tell you and when I've tried to bring it up, something has got in the way, or you've been late home, or exhausted.'

'Oh, so it's my fault now, is it?'

'No, it's nobody's fault. It just is.'

'What about trust, Anouska? Do you have any idea how much it hurts that you couldn't trust me with this?'

The phone rang. They let it ring. It stopped.

'Zach,' Anouska began, 'I...I need to know that everything is going to be OK. I...I need to tell you something else too.'

'What else could you possibly have to tell me? You're secretly an assassin? You've won the lottery but that slipped your mind, too?'

He was cut short by Anouska's mobile ringing. Anouska glanced at it. Mum.

She left it unanswered and turned her attention back to Zach, whose train of thought fortunately seemed to have been broken.

'Zach,' Anouska started again. 'The reason the girls know is because I've been in hospital.'

'You've what?'

'The baby.' She wrung her hands then scratched her neck.

'Is something wrong with the baby?' Zach's tone gave away his concern.

'No, I—'

Zach's mobile rang.

'Jesus. Does your mother never learn? Three phones.' Zach picked up. 'Yes, Maura.'

'Yes? You said yes. Oh, I knew it. I told her she should propose.'

'What? Propose? Anouska didn't propose. Propose?

Why would she propose?' He glared daggers at Anouska, certainly not the response she was hoping for at the prospect of her proposing.

Silence came from the other end of the phone.

Zach passed the phone to Anouska. 'Here, talk to your mother. You can have a good old chat about all the important things in our life before you discuss them with me. I can't do this. I'm going out.'

'Zach, don't.' She held out an arm to stop him passing her, but he pushed her arm down and strode past. 'You're being unreasonable. I didn't *tell* anyone…' she called as he yanked the door open.

'Don't wait up.'

He slammed the door. Anouska stared at it for a long moment before coming to and realising her mother was still talking to her from Zach's mobile. Now she didn't even have any way to contact him.

'Anouska, I'm sorry. I thought you'd asked him early. What's he so upset about?'

And to delay thinking about the events that had just occurred and rehashing them, and to put off thinking about the possible negative outcome, Anouska let her mother give her advice and comfort her, after she apologised about forty times.

When she finally concluded the call, Anouska collapsed into bed, dragging the duvet over her, spent. Now Zach knew he was going to have a son or daughter, but the question was, would their baby have a father?

Chapter Twenty-three

Ellie

Friday 14 February
Valentine's Day

Surprisingly, the most romantic day of the year flew by, and before long, Ellie headed to the Ladies' to get changed into the little purple dress she'd thrown into a suit carrier that morning. Lauren and Kelsea had suggested after her break-up with Scott that she accompany them to a supper club event that evening. Their other halves were going to a gig, so they'd decided to do something together.

It was guaranteed to be bereft of loved-up couples, there were to be no hearts and flowers, nor was it to be one of those ghastly anti-Valentine's events that seemed to have sprung up in recent years. Rather, it was a collection of people who wanted to mark Valentine's Day with nice food, good friends, great music and some live comedy. The fact they would mainly be single people was immaterial. She figured what the hell and had allowed them to sign her up for it too.

The event was being held at Cuisine, which wasn't far from where she worked. She would have walked but it was tipping it down and the sun had been sadly absent all day.

She checked her phone messages and voicemail again, her WhatsApp, her Facebook Messenger, but there was still nothing from Anouska, although Jess had sent a message, two hours ago, asking if she had heard from her. She quickly typed back that she hadn't, then fired off a text to Anouska.

How are you feeling – physically? How did it go with Zach?

Straightaway a message pinged back from Jess. *Do you think we should contact her?*

Already done so. Will let you know if she replies.

Thanks.

How are you?

Settling back in. Feeling a bit more zen after some yoga classes, understandably.

I can only imagine – seriously, I can ONLY imagine!

What are you up to?

Off to that supper club event. The food is meant to be good and that comedian, Freddy Finlay, is doing a stint. Looking forward to it.

Have fun. Catch up later. Jess x

Hope you have a nice evening. Ellie x

Ellie took the lift down to the ground floor and walked outside to hail a taxi. It didn't feel like Valentine's Day. She couldn't remember the last time she hadn't been part of a couple on this usually happy day. Time for a fresh start. To think ten days ago she had wanted to marry Scott. What a lucky escape.

Deposited outside Cuisine, Ellie gawped. The queue to get in snaked around the block and the evening chill seeped into her bones. Damn the taxi driver for having his heating on full blast. Now she felt even colder.

Fifteen minutes later, she was in a huge hall devoid of any hearts, flowers or any of the other paraphernalia that surrounded Valentine's Day. She scanned the room, finally spotting table eight.

Ellie weaved her way to her table, where many of the seats were already occupied. She found her name card, sat down and began perusing the menu. It was unusually good fare for such a large event; she hadn't expected such a fine-dining experience.

'Hello, my darling,' an exceedingly posh voice said.

Ellie turned to see Kelsea grinning at her, then Lauren appeared from behind her.

Ellie stood and hugged each of them in turn, then they all sat down and had a five-minute catch-up.

'I'm starving,' Kelsea said. 'When are they feeding us?'

Ellie smirked. Kelsea was as bad as her, if not worse, for liking her food and lots of it.

'Hopefully soon.' Lauren looked at her watch. 'I had a roll and sausage at eleven o'clock this morning and a packet of Polo mints on the train, so I could eat right now.'

No wonder she was rake thin.

'Check out the menu. It looks amazing. I'm sure they'll be round to take our orders soon,' Ellie consoled them.

The organisers had surpassed themselves in offering food just as good if not better than if the attendees had been out having a regular Valentine's Day dinner with a loved one. Scallops, bouillabaisse, goat's cheese and caramelised onion tartlets to start; dorado, fillet steak or mushroom Wellington for mains, with grilled peppers and asparagus; and for dessert, Prosecco panna cotta, Gianduja bread and butter pudding or pistachio and hazelnut tart.

Ellie's stomach rumbled. She hadn't eaten anything apart from crackers since she had wolfed down a slice of toast that morning. As Lauren and Kelsea chatted, Ellie realised the two seats to her right were still empty. It was quite late, and she wondered if they would be no-shows.

'Would you like something to drink?' A waitress stood over her, iPad in hand, ready to take her order, and Ellie turned to face her.

'Prosecco, please.'

As she slid round to face the table again, the missing guests arrived. A man and a woman. She was a mass of blonde curls and oozed bubbliness. The man towered over his companion. Six foot plus? Sandy-blonde hair. Nice eyes. He flashed her a smile. Mortified that she'd been caught checking him out, she gave a nod and focused her attention on the menu to cover her embarrassment.

Ellie spent the next few minutes talking to Lauren and Kelsea, enthusing over the menu choices with them. In the end, she opted for scallops, mushroom Wellington and the pistachio and hazelnut tart. She turned around in her seat, unsure if it was because she felt she could no longer politely ignore the man to her right, or more likely, that she wanted an opportunity to appraise him further. Disappointment coursed through her when she saw his empty place.

The woman smiled at her. 'Hi, I'm Courtney. Lovely menu, isn't it?'

Ellie agreed that it was, and for a few minutes they discussed how they had never been to one of these events before but how fabulous it was to have an alternative to a romantic Valentine's Day dinner. As Courtney sipped her wine and became distracted by the person to her right, it struck Ellie that she was here with – she squinted at his name card as subtly as she could – Spencer, and even if he was easy on the eye, he was spoken for. Not that she'd be thinking of doing anything about men at the moment, but he had a nice smile. And the cerulean eyes hadn't been lost on her. Rather, they'd held a teasing quality, almost as if he'd known he'd caught her out, and was calling her on it. Anyway, it was irrelevant. He was here with his date. Ellie gave herself a shake and turned her attention back to Kelsea and Lauren's conversation.

'Enjoying your scallops?' came a voice to Ellie's right ten minutes later.

She turned her head to see Spencer smiling at her. Wow, that was a killer smile, and those eyes. No adjective could do them justice.

He pointed a finger to himself, his eyes brimming with amusement. 'Spencer.'

Ellie became aware she hadn't answered his question yet and managed to respond, 'Yes, delicious. Yours?'

Spencer indicated his bouillabaisse with his spoon, nodding. 'Pretty good. Not as good as mine, mind you, but not bad at all.'

Ellie made a mental note that he could cook. *What am I doing? He's attached. Stop it! Stop it!* She shook her head as if to eradicate unwanted thoughts about him.

'Sorry? No, what?'

Crikey. Had she shaken her head? That was nearly as bad as talking out loud without realising it.

'Oh, nothing. I was thinking about work. I forgot to do something.'

Well-recovered. She breathed a sigh of relief.

'So, what is it you do…? Sorry, I don't know your

name.'

'Ellie. I work in Marketing.'

'Marketing…?'

'Yes, I know, everyone seems to work in Marketing. It doesn't really tell you what I do. I work for a travel company. How about you?'

Spencer took a sip of his wine then said, 'I'm a graphic designer. I project-manage, working with the clients and the art director to come up with a concept they're happy with, then I create it.'

'Oh, we use a graphic design team obviously. Who do you work for?'

'Myself.'

Confusion crossed Ellie's face. 'But…didn't you say you work with the art director? Aren't they your boss?'

'No, although I do take direction from her sometimes. It's an odd setup. I work as a graphic designer but I also own the company.'

Ellie was warming to Spencer more by the minute. A creative type with a business head, but who liked to get involved in the day-to-day tasks. She could think of a few tasks she'd like to give him, but they weren't work ones. Where had that thought come from? Appalled and flustered for a moment, she finally said, 'That must be an interesting story.'

His eyes crinkled at the corners. 'I don't know about that. I just wanted to follow my passion, so I started out, then the company became bigger than I expected, and I needed help, but I didn't want to lose sight of what was important to me. I love to design, not manage, so I brought a management team in. That way, I could keep doing what I'm passionate about.'

Head screwed on, principled, sexy. What was wrong with her tonight? She felt as if Cupid had trained his sights on her and had no intention of letting her go. And it wasn't appropriate. Spencer was here with his date, Courtney, who had seemed lovely when Ellie exchanged a few words with her earlier. She resolved to keep unwelcome thoughts of him out of her head, but it was difficult when she was talking to him and he was smiling at her, and those eyes. *Heaven help me.*

'That's very admirable.' She hadn't meant her response to sound so clipped, but she didn't want to give away even the tiniest notion that she was attracted to him.

He grinned. 'Fortunately Courtney's good at all that management stuff.' He nodded over his shoulder at her. She was mid-conversation with another guest, but winked at him.

Another reminder of him being part of a couple. It did make her wonder though why they were at this event. Maybe they simply disliked the Hallmark holiday, or the over-the-top falseness of it.

At that moment, the waitress arrived with her main course and Ellie was grateful for the distraction. She cut into her mushroom Wellington with gusto; it was sublime. Whilst she ate, her thoughts wandered. How could she feel so attracted to someone when she had only split up ten days ago from her long-standing, useless ex-boyfriend? And to top it all, it was someone unattainable – aargh!

Ellie chewed her food, sometimes able to relish its flavour, other times it tasted of nothing as she broached the dilemma in her mind. Typical, just typical. The first person she'd seen in years who had raised her pulse rate and he was spoken for. Someone up there evidently didn't like her. She glanced heavenward subconsciously and as she looked back down to her plate, her eyes met Spencer's again. He smiled and said, 'You seem to be enjoying that.'

'Delicious,' Ellie managed, wondering if she could acquit herself well with one word, without appearing rude, whilst not inviting further conversation. It turned out she couldn't. Either that or he was a talker.

'Yes, I was torn between the mushroom Wellington and the fillet steak, but I was having a macho moment.' His eyes twinkled as she took in his fillet steak covered in peppercorn sauce. Was he flirting with her? Surely he wouldn't do that in front of his girlfriend, fiancée, wife, whatever Courtney was. Her eyes widened.

'Look.' He leant in towards her, his aftershave sending her senses into overdrive. 'I know we've only just met, but could I take you out for dinner sometime?'

The blood drained from Ellie's face.

'Sorry, have I said something wrong? Too soon? I knew it. I should have waited until dessert,' he joked. He was still trying to rescue the situation, but how could he sit there so calmly and callously ask her out when his other half was two feet away? She'd underestimated him. And she thought she had been badly off with Scott. At least he hadn't tried to wangle – that she knew of – a date with someone whilst she was in the room.

Ellie opened and closed her mouth but no words came out. She didn't know what to say.

'Sorry to butt in. Spencer, that's Mum on the phone. She's asking if you can walk Jasper tomorrow.'

Giving Ellie an apologetic look, Spencer excused himself, took the phone from Courtney and left his seat for a few moments.

Courtney smiled at Ellie. 'Food's lovely, isn't it?'

Ellie nodded, still unable to form a coherent sentence.

'Mum's always on at Spencer to walk Jasper. She takes advantage a bit since he lives round the corner from her.'

'Oh, where do you live?' Ellie asked.

'Me? Oh, I live in Morningside, converted church. Share with three others. Spencer lives in the west end.'

'Ah,' Ellie said sagely. For want of something to say, she asked, 'So, where did you two meet then?'

Courtney's forehead scrunched up. 'Meet?' Then she smiled. 'Ha ha ha, did you think we were a couple?'

Ellie's silence told her all she needed to know.

'He's my big brother, by four years. My boyfriend's doing a gap year in South America.'

Ellie was sure her sigh of relief must be audible. And she'd been having all those uncharitable thoughts about him too. Courtney continued to chatter on and Ellie tried her best not to zone her out entirely, but she couldn't help but hope Spencer would resume their earlier topic of conversation when he returned.

'Sorry about that. My mother doesn't stop once she gets going.' Spencer sat down and passed Courtney's phone back to her. 'I told her I'd walk Jasper.'

Courtney rolled her eyes at him then looked from her brother to Ellie and back again. 'I'm going to the loo. Back in a sec.'

She wasn't sure but Ellie had the distinct impression Courtney was leaving them alone together intentionally.

'So,' said Spencer, turning to Ellie, a smile tugging at the corners of his mouth. 'Did I crash and burn or is there any chance of that date?'

Chapter Twenty-four

Jess

Saturday 15 February

Jess stretched and yawned. It had been a long day. She had stepped in to help out another yoga instructor whose three children had gone down with chickenpox. Fearful of losing her job, the instructor, Gaynor, had asked Jess if she could plug the gap whilst she tried to sort out childcare for the next two weeks. Concerned at the stress in her friend's voice, Jess had told her not to worry, she'd take care of it.

So she had spent the day flitting between the two sites – her own in the south side and the other in Glasgow city centre. Her car was getting an unscheduled outing. She had forgotten how chaotic the traffic was in the middle of the day, particularly on a Saturday, and she remembered why she hated driving in the city.

She missed lunch as she had no time to eat the pre-prepared feta cheese and sun-blushed tomato panini she'd managed to pick up after queuing for almost fifteen minutes at the café near the leisure centre.

It had been just as well she'd already been in her yoga kit as she barely had time to sign in at the desk, nip to the loo and introduce herself to the power yoga class before it started at two o'clock. She'd followed that with the Les Mills body balance class, by which time even she was exhausted. A quick energy drink at the café in the leisure centre and she'd struggled her way through the nose-to-tail traffic all the way back to Gaynor's class in Bath Street. Again, she made it to her class with minutes to spare. Fortunately, it was yoga as it helped her wind down, and she didn't think she'd have had the energy for anything more taxing.

It was tempting to forgo a shower and head home, but it played havoc with her skin if she went too long without a shower after exercising and she felt grubby. Her hair was sticking to her head, she was an attractive shade of tomato and she was sure she ponged. OK, shower it was.

Jess let the water stream over her tired limbs, relishing the cleansing both physically and mentally. She prayed Gaynor had planned ahead for tomorrow as she didn't think she could manage so many classes again in one day. She was wrecked. And she felt awful. Gobbling down a panini at five o'clock in her car whilst waiting at traffic lights wasn't at one with her zen lifestyle.

Organised and methodical to a fault, having her schedule interrupted had more than upset her routine, it had upended her internal body clock. She dressed in jeans and a chunky cream knitted jumper with star-shaped lace cut-outs, aware the temperature was hovering around zero, and stifled a yawn.

She needed to grab something to drink, but first she'd text Mark. He'd be watching TV or marking papers anyway as he'd said he had no plans tonight. She'd reminded him he had promised to repair the faulty lamp in the living room, and that he was to pick up the new rug from Argos.

Apart from that, as far as she knew, he was vegging, his body making a dent in the cushions in her absence.

Once she'd packed away her gym clothes, she slung her gym bag over her shoulder, smiled a greeting at one of her regulars and left the changing rooms.

'Bloody machine.' Jess groaned in frustration. Could this day get any worse? All she wanted was an energy drink. And of course the machine kept regurgitating her money.

'Giving you problems, is it?'

Jess spun around to see Nathan standing in front of her, a smile twitching the corners of his mouth. Despite her grumpy mood and the tiredness she was feeling, she managed an eye roll and a small smile.

'I think it's out of order. It won't give me the drink I paid for.'

'Do you mind if I try?'

Jess raised an eyebrow. 'Be my guest.'

Nathan inserted a few different coins. The machine didn't work for him either. Then finally he tried putting in ten-pence pieces. It accepted them and allowed him to make a selection. Yay! Except then it hovered over the collection tray without letting go of the item.

'Aargh!' said Jess. 'Thanks for trying anyway.'

'It's no trouble. Look, why don't I buy you a drink in the café?'

Defeated and struggling to stay awake, Jess accepted. If she could just drink something, she would feel much better. Didn't matter if it was Lucozade, cranberry juice, green tea or Red Bull, anything would do. Heck, she was at the stage of putting her head under the tap in the Ladies' and taking her chances. OK, that was perhaps going too far and the gym had water fonts after all, but no, she needed something with sugar in it.

'Sorry, guys, the fridges have gone off, so we've had to close early tonight. Watch your step – floor's wet,' the café assistant said when Nathan and Jess approached the counter.

'I don't believe it,' Jess said under her breath.

Nathan tapped her on the arm. 'Don't worry. That new coffee shop round the corner, Slice of Pie, is still open. I think it shuts at ten. We can grab something there.'

Jess was in no position to argue. Nathan had found a solution and she was too tired to think any more. It was refreshing for someone else to come up with the answers for once.

'So, were you in the gym tonight, or doing one of the other classes?' Jess asked Nathan as she stirred her latte. Coffee and sugar. She knew it was crazy at this time of night, but she would need it to enable her to drive home without falling asleep. Nathan had also talked her into ordering a plate of pasta as he'd eaten there a few nights before and professed it to be restaurant quality.

'In the gym. Kris gave me a new cardio workout. I'm training for a couple of marathons I'm doing this year and want to make sure I'm in the best shape.'

It was on the tip of Jess' tongue to say he'd looked in good shape to her when she'd caught him naked, but she stopped herself in time.

'Oh, I've thought about doing a marathon. In fact, I already signed up for the half-marathon in April to see if I can go the distance. I haven't started my training though.'

'I wouldn't have thought yoga and Pilates went hand in hand with running.' Nathan took a sip of his Americano then placed his cup back on the table.

'Perhaps not, but remember I cover the full range of classes – spin, high-intensity interval training, cardio. And yoga is about stamina as well as balance.'

Nathan held his hands up in a placatory gesture. 'Point taken.'

Their food arrived and they tucked in with relish.

'You weren't kidding this place was good.' Jess sighed. 'I needed this. I've been surviving off a limp panini all day.'

'I'm sure there's a story in that statement.' Nathan's smile was warm and his eyes showed an interest in her that Jess hadn't witnessed in Mark of late.

Jess regaled him with the exploits of the day.

'No wonder you're shattered. You're not doing double classes again tomorrow, are you?'

'I don't know. She didn't ask me. I'm assuming she's arranged childcare for tomorrow. I meant to text her earlier. Sorry, do you mind if I do it now? That way I'll know sooner rather than later what tomorrow holds.'

'Of course not.' Nathan spooned another mouthful of fettuccine Alfredo into his mouth as Jess bashed out her message to Gaynor.

'I didn't even know this place was opening. I must walk about with my eyes shut,' Jess said.

'It was all quite sudden. The previous place had been closed for a good few months, but once Arlene was given the go-ahead, she set the ball in motion quickly.'

'Arlene?' Jess smiled at him. She could guess how he knew her name.

'Yes, Arlene, the owner. She insisted on giving me the low-down on how the café had sprung up so fast.'

I bet she did, thought Jess, glancing in as covert a manner as possible towards the counter where Arlene was busy taking in everything they were saying and making no pretence of the fact. It was clear she fancied Nathan, and well, Jess could understand that. He was pretty hot.

'So, when are you starting your training?' Nathan asked.

Jess exhaled. 'You'd think working my own hours, I'd manage to fit everything in, and I have been doing plenty of indoor running, but it's simply too dark by the time I get home from work to train outdoors, and you know yourself, it's not the same. It feels different and it takes a different type of stamina.'

Nathan nodded. 'Yeah, you're right there.' He appeared to think for a minute then said, 'When do you usually finish work?'

Jess smiled. 'I don't have a usual. I work different hours every day.'

'In that case, are there any days you finish earlier than others? Or do you have free time during the day?'

'Well, on a Tuesday I have some time early afternoon and on a Thursday morning too, and on a Friday I finish at seven.'

'OK.' Nathan paused. 'So, assuming your friend doesn't need you to cover her classes, how about you and me going for a run next Thursday then? I could meet you at the gym.'

Jess was about to protest, but Nathan cut in with, 'I need to get marathon ready and the sooner I start taking it seriously, the better.' When she hesitated, he said, 'You'd be doing me a favour, really.'

Well, when he put it like that. She hadn't worked out how she'd fit in those outdoor runs and it looked like Nathan had solved her problem.

'Fine then, you're on.'

They ate the rest of the food in relative silence and although they got into a 'No, I'll pay', 'No, put your money away, I've got it' contest, Nathan won, swiping his contactless card against the machine and not brooking any argument.

Jess' mobile pinged a text alert. Gaynor. She breathed a sigh of relief. She was off the hook, although she would happily have done six back-to-back classes she felt so elated. She didn't know quite why, but she was looking forward to her training run. It didn't even faze her that Nathan would have to run slowly so she could keep pace. He'd obviously considered that and didn't care. She'd managed to put something positive in place today and she left the café on a high.

'What are you smiling at?' Jess asked as she walked into the living room.

Mark looked the picture of guilt. 'Nothing.'

Jess wasn't convinced. She'd wheedle it out of him later. 'How was your day?' She leant down to give him a kiss.

He twisted on the sofa and kissed her full on the lips. Mmm. Interesting. Unexpected.

'Come here and have a snuggle.' He patted the sofa beside him.

Jess didn't need to be asked twice. She hoped he wasn't

looking for anything energetic as she was exhausted. She was pretty sure within about ten minutes she'd be fast asleep, catching flies.

'Cup of tea?' Mark asked. Jess didn't know if he was offering her one or asking her to make him one, so since she had no energy, she said, 'Only if you're having one.'

'Back in a tic.' Mark bounced off the sofa with an unusual jauntiness and Jess sat down heavily, idly flicking through TV channels as she awaited his return.

She glanced up to see Mark standing over her, beaming – a kind of manic, scary smile, to be honest – holding a tray with two mugs on it and some biscuits.

He was behaving very strangely tonight. She had no patience nor headspace for oddness right now.

He knelt down in front of her, and for one heart-stopping moment she thought he was going to propose. He put the cups onto their little side tables and handed her what she now saw was a white envelope.

Her brows knitted, then Mark said, 'Go on, open it. You've been working really hard recently, and doing almost all of the housework, and I've not been around much. This is just my way of saying how much I appreciate you, even if I don't always show it, or as often as I should.'

Jess opened the envelope to find a ticket and itinerary for a week's meditation retreat in Devon in July.

'Oh my God, Mark, I've always wanted to go to this.' She knew she was smiling literally from ear to ear. This was nearly as good as winning the lottery. Well, not quite, but it was a pretty close second.

He grinned. 'I know. I do listen, even if it sometimes seems I don't. And that's not all. I spoke to Gaynor. Her mum's bought her a ticket for her birthday, and she's watching the kids that week as it's during the summer holidays, so you'll have someone you know on the retreat too.'

Jess was so touched she almost couldn't express her gratitude. Recently, she had felt that Mark was somewhat detached, but this showed he was still capable of considering her, properly considering her and her needs, and doing something about it. He had no idea how much this meant to her.

She knelt down on the rug and hugged him, then they kissed and then somehow, from somewhere, her energy reserves replenished themselves and their lovemaking on the rug was worthy of one of their sessions in their first years together.

It was only as she lay there, sated, that the gnawing thought of her dinner with Nathan crept over her. She tried to banish it to the back of her mind, but it wouldn't let go. As Mark stroked her arm, Nathan's face kept superimposing itself over Mark's.

This wasn't right. What was she going to do?

Chapter Twenty-five

Anouska

Saturday 15 February

'I'm sorry, Nush, I really am. He told me what happened, but he isn't here. To be honest, I'm a little pissed at him, as he's left me in the lurch with the bistro too. I've had to get a temp in.'

Anouska gave him a look.

'Not that that's his biggest offence, of course. It's so unlike him. He's usually so responsible.'

Anouska couldn't disagree with that. It wasn't like Zach to let people down, nor put his business under pressure. He had two babies now, Bean There and Bean. Except he didn't even know she'd nicknamed the baby that. A lump rose in her throat at the thought that he might never find out.

'Has he not been back to the flat?' Todd asked.

'Not since he collected his phone when I was at work.' Anouska exhaled slowly. 'Anyone else he might have gone to?'

'I've tried everyone I can think of, for both your sake and mine.'

'You don't know of a way to track someone's credit

card usage, do you?' Anouska asked, only half kidding.

'If I did, I would have called upon my sources by now, as I want to find him too. All he told me was he'd had a shock, and that the two of you had a huge argument.'

Anouska's eyes were wide.

'But he didn't say what about exactly. Do you want to tell me? I'm not prying, but if it would help, or if you need someone to talk to, I'm here.'

'I know, and thanks, Todd, but right now, I need to focus on finding him.' A thought struck her. 'Does he have any meetings scheduled?'

'Hmm, he took his diary, but I might be able to find something on the computer calendar.'

Hope surged in Anouska. If she could only see him. Surely he must have some compassion. She had loved this man for years. She knew every inch of him and he her. He was the father of her unborn child, for goodness' sake. That must bind them together somehow. She was certain he wouldn't shirk his responsibilities towards their baby, but would he still want a relationship with her? Right now, she had no idea, and she wasn't likely to find out until she located him.

'Here. He has a meeting at Dyce Vintners.'

'When's that?' Anouska tried but failed to keep the excitement from her voice.

'Monday at four.'

'What's the address?' Anouska was already opening up the notes app on her phone.

Todd read it off and said, 'Let me know how you get on, will you? And if you need anything, anything at all, please call me, day or night. I mean it.'

Anouska clasped his arm. 'Thanks, Todd, you don't

know how much that means to me, especially right now.'

Sending her off with two dishes of freshly made pasta and quiche to keep her going over the next few days, Todd hugged her. 'Good luck.'

'I'm hoping I don't need it and he'll see sense.'

'I have everything crossed for you,' Todd said, 'and when I see him, I'll be giving him a piece of my mind.'

The problem was Anouska didn't know if even that would work, but she had to pray that she could catch up with Zach at the vintner's on Monday and talk some sense into him. She just hoped he would hear her out.

The phone rang eight times. Anouska didn't know why she let it ring so many times before hanging up. She wasn't usually that patient. However, she was glad she did as on the eighth ring, Ellie picked up.

'Hi, Ellie.'

'Oh, Anouska, how are you? Jess and I have been so worried.'

'I've been better.' Anouska said, her voice cracking. Then she burst into noisy sobs, stopped only by a bout of hiccoughing.

'Anouska, what's wrong? Is Zach there?'

'No. He's gone.'

'Gone?' Ellie asked, her voice rising an octave.

'Zach found out that Mum knew I was pregnant before I told him.' Anouska tried not to nibble at her once perfectly manicured nails, now almost bitten to shreds. She'd never been a nervous person but the last few days had taken their toll on her. And it couldn't be good for the baby, so she was trying to calm down, but it was so hard, and much easier said than done.

'Oh shit. I take it that wasn't well-received.' Ellie exhaled.

'No, and Zach's furious. When I told him about the baby, initially he was shocked but happy, but then Mum called whilst we were still discussing it and I accidentally hit speakerphone and she asked me if I'd told him I was pregnant yet.'

'Hmm, I see why he'd be pissed off, but even so.'

Anouska burst into noisy tears again. 'Sorry, it's the hormones. I can't help it.' That's what she kept telling herself anyway.

'Right, I don't care that he's pissed off at you, he has to see that swanning off isn't good for your state of mind, particularly in your condition.'

'I agree, but I need to see him to tell him that.'

'And you haven't seen him?' Ellie seemed either furious or concerned, she couldn't quite tell.

'No. He said he was "going out" when he left after our "talk". When he didn't come home, I assumed he'd gone to Todd's, and I haven't heard from him or seen him since.'

'You've been to see Todd, I take it,' Ellie said after a pause.

'Yes, but he didn't stay at Todd's, even though that's what I thought he'd do. He told Todd he was going away for a few days to do some thinking, and that we'd had a falling-out.'

'Can I assume you've filled Todd in now?'

'I think Zach told him bits and pieces,' Anouska said. 'He didn't seem to know everything, but he knows the gist. He also offered support.'

'It's Zach who needs to offer support.' The note of

anger in Ellie's voice didn't escape her.

'I know.' She sighed. 'I'm hoping to see him on Monday. He has a meeting with a supplier here in Aberdeen. My plan is to ambush him before he goes in, or wait until he comes out if I somehow miss him.'

'Do you want me to come up?'

'No, Ellie, you have your own life to lead. It's up to me to sort this mess out.'

'If you're sure.' Ellie didn't sound convinced.

'I am. Right, I'm exhausted. I'm going to heat up one of these dinners Todd gave me and have a bath. I need to rest.'

'You do that. What are you doing about your work?'

'I've had Leigh-Ann cover as much as she can, and I brought a temp in anyway because of the pregnancy, but I'm finding it hard to concentrate on the company at the moment.'

'You've done the right thing. At the moment your priority has to be you and the baby.'

'Quite. I'll let you know what happens on Monday. Thanks for listening, Ellie.'

'Anytime. Call me if you need me, doesn't matter if it's three in the morning. Understand?'

'Got it.' Anouska rang off, feeling a little better that there were people on her side. The trouble was it made her less charitable towards Zach for doing a runner. He had responsibilities, which he seemed to have forgotten.

Monday 17 February

'Zach! Zach!' Anouska shouted to his retreating back as the door closed. Damn it. She'd made sure she was at the vintner's for three thirty in case he arrived early and he'd still beaten her to it. He was known for being punctual but he was half an hour early. He must have pulled the meeting forward. At least he hadn't seen her. She'd just have to wait until the meeting was over. Hopefully, she wasn't in for a long wait.

It was freezing, so she had the heating on full blast in the car. She yawned. She'd barely slept for days. Her eyes fluttered closed as all the events of the past week went round and round in her head.

She woke to a rat-tat-tat at the car window. A man was staring in at her. No, a police officer in a reflective yellow vest.

She frowned. Why was a policeman knocking on her window? She rolled the window down. 'Can I help you, officer?'

'Step out of the vehicle, please.'

'Sorry?' Anouska tried to blink the sleep from her eyes.

'I said, step out of the vehicle.'

'Why?'

'Just step out of the vehicle.'

'I'm pregnant.'

'Does that mean you can't step out of the vehicle?' the police officer said.

His attitude was really beginning to grate on her.

'No, but it does mean I wouldn't mind knowing why before I haul my exhausted body out of the car.'

'We've had a complaint.'

'A complaint?' Anouska screwed up her face.

'Of a suspicious person in a car outside this building.'

'I'm pregnant, not suspicious.' Anouska couldn't believe what she was hearing. 'And I was asleep.'

'Well, the owner would like you to leave. This is a secure facility.'

Anouska fought the temptation to say it wasn't that secure since she'd been able to drive in undetected. 'I'm waiting for someone.'

'Oh really?' Disbelief was etched upon the police officer's face.

'My boyfriend.'

'Your boyfriend?'

'Yes. He's inside.'

'Does he work here? Shall we go and ask for him?'

'No, no, it's complicated.'

'In that case, I think you need to make it a little simpler.'

Having had just about enough of her current run of bad luck, as well as the injustice of it all, Anouska finally snapped.

'Right, since you asked, I'm pregnant, I didn't tell my boyfriend as we hadn't planned on having kids and I wasn't sure how to tell him, then I told him and after the initial shock, he seemed happy, but in the middle of all that my mother rang. She knew I was pregnant and asked me how he took the news. Unfortunately, I accidentally hit speakerphone and he heard and so found out that she knew before him, and he left "to think things through", and I haven't seen him since. I found out he had a meeting with his supplier, here, today, and I've come to see if I can talk some sense into him. I called out to him just as I arrived, early, but he didn't hear me and went into his meeting, and I fell asleep.' She gulped in a huge breath. 'Sorry, it's called mental exhaustion.'

'I know how you feel.' The police officer looked

drained and a tad more sympathetic. After remaining silent for a while, he said, 'Look, I'll have a chat with the owner, tell him there's a simple explanation and that you'll be gone shortly. How about that? But you need to promise not to cause a scene when your boyfriend does come out.'

'Guides' honour.'

'Excuse me,' interrupted a familiar voice.

Anouska cringed.

The officer turned around. 'Yes, sir?'

'Is something wrong? I only ask as that's my girlfriend's car.'

Anouska knew the officer's body was shielding her from view.

'Ah,' said the police officer. 'Well, maybe now would be a good time to talk to her.' The officer shifted to the side and Anouska saw Zach staring at her, open-mouthed. He had huge bags under his battleship grey eyes and his five o'clock shadow appeared days old.

'Anouska!'

'Hi, Zach.' This so wasn't how she'd envisaged this playing out.

'What are you…? How did you…? What are you…?'

'I'll leave you to chat, shall I?' The police officer turned towards Anouska and winked.

Once he'd gone, Zach bent down so he was level with Anouska at the driver's window.

'Why was that policeman talking to you?'

Choosing to ignore Zach's comments so as not to antagonise him, Anouska said, 'Can we talk?'

Zach frowned. 'We are talking.'

'I meant properly.' Anouska's pleading look must have melted something in Zach's heart as he said, 'Fine, there's a coffee shop round the corner. We can go there.'

By unspoken agreement and since Anouska was already in her car, Zach got in. The journey there, whilst only minutes, seemed to last an inordinate amount of time. At the back of Anouska's mind was the fact Zach hadn't immediately asked after her or the baby; he was more concerned about why the police were there. She hoped that wasn't an omen.

'So, how have you been?' Zach asked, once they were ensconced in the coffee shop.

She decided to be brutally honest. 'Worried sick, scared, confused, terrified.'

'That good then?' Zach's mouth upturned a smidge.

'Yep. So…' Anouska struggled with the words as he hadn't made one single gesture towards her or embraced her and it hurt like hell. She fought down the tears that threatened to surface and folded the napkin in front of her into triangles, something she only did when she was nervous.

Zach, for his part, didn't look in any hurry to help her out with the conversation. So finally Anouska plumped for, 'Where do we go from here?'

Zach leant forwards, hands clasped, elbows on the table, and said, 'I don't know, Anouska, I really don't. I trusted you, and you betrayed that trust.'

Anouska gritted her teeth and tried to keep her voice as calm and neutral as possible, but her patience was wearing thin. 'Zach, I didn't *break* your trust. I didn't actually tell anyone. Mum guessed. I can't keep saying this. And the girls wouldn't have known had I not started bleeding and they had to take me to hospital.'

Zach sat mutely staring at the table. If she didn't love him so much, and now need him so much, she'd have happily strangled him. Why was he being so pigheaded? Couldn't he see the bigger picture here? It wasn't all about his ego. He was going to be a father. They were going to be parents, whether he liked it or not. He needed to sort his priorities out – and fast.

Suppressing the urge to sigh, she decided the best course of action was to let him talk. Finally, he said, 'I never thought I'd say this about us, but I don't know if we have a future. Trust is everything to me. You know that I had issues with Marcie before. I always said I'd never go through that again. It broke me.' He paused, took a sip of his milky tea, grimaced and set it down on the table again.

Anouska knew his ex-fiancée had almost destroyed Zach, but Marcie had slept with an ex-colleague of his, someone he'd gone to football training with for years. And everyone else had known except him. He'd felt so humiliated, and she couldn't have cared less when he confronted her. This was hardly comparable. All Anouska had done was discuss with her mother, erroneously perhaps, the fact she was pregnant, after her mother guessing. She hadn't cheated. She hadn't wronged him. And there was the simple fact that a child was on the way, no matter how irked Zach was, or how slighted he felt. Yes, it had been a mistake not to confide in him at the outset, but she'd been scared. Any rational person would recognise that, especially in a hormonal woman carrying their baby. But here was Zach now talking about them potentially not having a future.

'You don't need to worry about money or anything.

Obviously I'll contribute towards the baby. And I'm not saying no to us, just, I need some time.'

A lump rose in Anouska's throat and try as she might she couldn't make it go away. She started to heave, her breathing coming in thick gasps. She needed air. Oh God, not now. Struggling to get her scarf off, she stood up from the table, gulping air into her lungs, as her legs gave way.

'Anouska,' called Zach, grabbing her as she slumped forwards, his eyes wide. 'Stay with me.' The last thing she remembered was wishing he had meant that literally.

'She's coming round.'

'Thank God.' Zach's voice. 'Anouska, can you hear me?'

Anouska tried to move her tongue away from her teeth – blood. She must have bitten her tongue. Did she fall? The baby! She tried to sit up but the blood rushed to her head and she wavered again.

'Whoa. Steady.' Zach.

She cracked one eye open. It was so bright. A man was standing over her with a kitchen knife. She screamed.

'Sorry, I didn't mean to scare you,' said the man, who she now saw was wearing chef's whites. 'I was peeling onions when I heard your husband calling for help.'

Husband. Chance would be a fine thing.

Two hands were under her armpits, lifting her to a standing position. They then lowered her to a seat. She hated her panic attacks, and they were usually stress-induced.

'Anouska, are you all right?' Zach's face, worry evident in the creases around his eyes.

'Wh-a-a-a-t?' He seemed so far away. She didn't feel good. Maybe her blood sugar was low. At least that inability to get a breath appeared to have gone. She blinked several times, then focused on first Zach's and then the chef's face.

'Water, please,' she finally managed, and the chef scurried behind the counter and filled a glass at the sink.

Zach held her hands. 'Look, we don't need to decide anything right now. Let's just get you home.'

Still feeling woozy, Anouska's thought before the chef handed her the water was: *But I want us to decide right now. I need to know we're OK.*

Chapter Twenty-six

Ellie

Saturday 22 February

'Hey, sis!'

'Hi, Ellie. Check you. What time did you get into the city this morning to have so many shopping bags already? I was going to ask you to come shopping with me after lunch.'

'I've been in since early,' Ellie said as Chloe shrugged herself out of her coat and cast off her gloves and scarf. 'Perks of being on holiday.'

'Lucky you. Brr, it's freezing out there.'

'Yes, roll on spring. Anyway, how's my darling niece?' Ellie asked after giving her sister a peck on the cheek and a brief hug.

'Causing havoc as ever. I asked her what she was building today with her Duplo and she said "a care home".'

Ellie burst out laughing. 'At least it's original.'

'Last week it was an orphanage. She's going to have social services at my door shortly if she tells anyone at nursery. Can you imagine the conversation?'

Ellie grinned then picked up the menu and flipped it over, then turned it back. 'New menu?'

'Yep, out today,' said Chloe. 'That's why we're here.'

'You get fed up with eating the same things after a while,' Ellie said as her phone pinged with a message.

Her eyes flitted to the screen and her lips curved upwards.

'What?' asked Chloe.

'What?' said Ellie, one of her dark curls falling across her eye.

'Well, I may need pliers to prise that smile off your face, so what's causing it?'

'Oh, a message from a friend, that's all.'

'Which friend? Not that I'm being nosy or anything, but that's the kind of smile usually associated with the opposite sex.'

'Is it?' Ellie asked nonchalantly.

'Els.' There was no mistaking the warning tone in Chloe's voice. She was pulling the elder sister card.

'OK, OK, I was going to tell you. That's why I suggested lunch today.' She paused for effect then shrieked, 'I have a date!' Realising too late how loudly she'd spoken, she then ducked under the table.

'Els, get out from under there. You're making a spectacle of yourself. And me,' Chloe hissed.

Ellie slid back up. 'I dropped my spoon.'

'Liar,' said Chloe good-naturedly. 'So, c'mon, spill. You have a date? That was fast work.'

'Yes, and I was hoping for some advice.' Ellie gave Chloe her best puppy eyes.

'Right, right. What do you want?' Chloe knew her well.

'The little black dress you got from Whistles, the one with the mesh panel.'

'You mean, my favourite dress, the one that I have

never lent to anyone, because I've only worn it three times and it cost the equivalent of a month's mortgage?'

'Well, I suppose it's all relative as it depends how much your mortgage is, doesn't it?' Ellie said.

That warning glare again.

'OK. Yes, that dress.'

'Wow, you must be really into him, and think I'm a sucker.'

'I do.'

Chloe's eyes were wide.

'Like him. Obviously, you aren't a sucker.'

Chloe sniffed dramatically. 'OK, you can have it, but on one condition.'

'Anything.'

'The Eagles.'

'No, no way. I hate that stuff.'

Chloe folded her arms. 'That's my offer.'

'I can't believe you are asking me to go and listen to a band whose music I'm not remotely interested in. Can't you take someone else? Someone who can name one of their songs?'

'Nope. That's the deal.'

'What about babysitting? I could babysit and you guys could go out for a meal?'

'No can do. You love babysitting.' Chloe smirked.

Damn, she was right. She loved Rosie. Chloe could be so infuriating.

'Fine. But you're buying the tickets.'

'Already have done.' That smirk again.

Ellie's mouth fell open.

Chloe said, 'I knew you'd need a favour at some point.

So, shall we order, then you can come back to mine for the dress?'

Three minutes to seven. Ellie was starting to get nervous. She smoothed down Chloe's dress for the hundredth time, fluffed up her curls for the thousandth time and spritzed herself with her favourite perfume. Not too much. She didn't want him to suffocate in a cloud of Joy.

A car door closed outside. Careful not to be seen, Ellie peeped through the curtains. Moment of truth. Giving herself the once-over, she deemed herself ready, grabbed her handbag and hoped she appeared less nervous than she felt.

Ding-dong.

'Hi,' she said shyly on opening the door.

'You look incredible.'

Ellie considered saying 'What, this old thing?' then thought better of it, as it was, after all, a gorgeous dress and perhaps now was the time to start accepting compliments graciously rather than batting them away.

'Thanks. You don't look too bad yourself.'

What an understatement. He looked breathtaking in a long black coat, kind of like those you saw lawyers wearing over their suits, with a pale pink shirt underneath, no tie. Phew. Ties had their place, but not on dates. She remembered then that she didn't know where they were going, but guessed her choice of attire would pass muster given Spencer's classy outfit.

Spencer opened the passenger door of his Mercedes for her, waited till she was inside then gently closed the door. Ellie couldn't remember the last time a guy had done that for her, if ever. Clearly she had been moving in the wrong circles, and equally clearly she was now moving in the right ones. No, she was getting ahead of herself. Let's see where he was taking her first of all, and how they got on.

Twenty minutes later, they parked on one of the side streets off Princes Street. Spencer took her arm and they walked companionably together, chatting about inconsequential things. Apprehension bubbled in Ellie. She cast a sidelong glance at Spencer as he spoke with the manager at Monteiths, for he'd brought her to Monteiths, only the hot ticket of the moment, known for its extravagant cocktails and extensive list of whiskies. Part of her was terrified as this wasn't her usual haunt, the other part was elated. What was she worrying about?

Spencer evidently thought she would fit in. Ellie absorbed the cocktail bar atmosphere, the high stuccoed ceilings, the ornate rose centrepieces and cornicing. Yet she felt oddly at home here. It was her sort of place, albeit with a bit more class than she was used to. She had frequented bars like this with Chloe, just never with a date, and much of that she knew was down to Scott being tight.

At that moment, a server appeared, interrupting her musings as she showed them to their table. Ellie was delighted to see it was the very table she would have chosen, at the window, overlooking Princes Street, with the imposing backdrop of the castle. She was glad they weren't tucked away in a cosy little spot. It was too soon for that and her nerves were already jangling. That was a good sign, right? If she was nervous, she cared. Spencer seemed like one of the good guys and she could definitely do with one of those after her abject failure with Scott.

'It's lovely here,' Ellie said once they sat down. 'I was almost too afraid to wipe my shoes on the mat when I came in, in case I dirtied it.'

'Ha ha, it's not that fancy. I like it here, though. It's central and does good cocktails.'

Ellie's radar went on alert. If he drank and drove he was a no-no.

'What do you fancy?'

She guessed 'you' was not what he was expecting as an answer, so restricted herself to saying, 'I don't know. I'll need to have a look first, but I do like mojitos.'

'Ah, the mojitos here are fantastic. That's what I'm having.'

Before Ellie could raise an eyebrow, or give him a black mark, he clarified, 'A virgin mojito.'

Trying not to exhale with relief, nor blush at the use of the word 'virgin', Ellie applied herself to the task of choosing a cocktail, conscious of Spencer's eyes on her.

Finally she declared, 'I'll have a rosehip gimlet.'

'A what? That sounds like a turkey needing surgery,' Spencer said. It was marginally funny but Ellie, whose nerves had kicked in, overdid the joining in laughing thing, until people at nearby tables started to give her strange looks.

Mortified, she tried to rearrange her curls so they covered her face. Spencer leant over and his fingertips grazed her forehead, sending a zing to parts of her that hadn't zinged in a while as he brushed back the lock which was dangling in front of her eye. 'Relax. We're just two people getting to know each other. I can tell you're nervous. Don't be. Seriously, I don't bite. It's more of a nibble.'

Ellie rolled her eyes and Spencer said, 'OK, that was a terrible pun. I'm nervous too, which is why I'm talking absolute nonsense. So, what do you say we ditch this nervousness and simply enjoy ourselves?'

Ellie couldn't argue with that. And recognising that she wasn't the only nervous one made it so much easier. She was a girl, he was a guy, they appeared to like each other, be attracted to each other. There had been a spark at the supper club event, and here they were. Now to see where it took them, if anywhere, and if it didn't, well that would be that, but if it did. If it did…

Half an hour later, nerves firmly cast aside, starting on their second cocktail each, they moved through to the restaurant. Ellie noted the luxurious cream leather-bound menus with their stiff scalloped card insert. The place oozed sophistication. The dishes were mainly seafood and steaks, with the occasional nod to vegetarians with an appropriate pasta or risotto dish. It would be slim pickings for them and she was glad she wasn't vegetarian or vegan as her mouth watered at the many offerings available.

Ten minutes later, she had made her choices. It had been no easy task as there were so many things she liked and even more she wanted to try. She opted for halloumi, carrot and orange salad to start, and baked cod with tarragon jus and a side order of rustic fries for her main. She salivated at the thought of it. Her lunch with Chloe seemed a long time ago. At least she didn't have to worry about her dress not fitting her afterwards. When she'd tried it on at Chloe's, she'd been pleasantly surprised to discover it was a little roomy. The break-up diet had its advantages.

Spencer chose the smoked salmon with capers and the halibut to follow. Once they had ordered, he placed his clasped hands on the table. 'So, Ellie, tell me about yourself. So far, all I know is you like mojitos.'

Agreeing that was a pretty dismal CV, Ellie then said, 'Well, I've lived in Edinburgh all my life, give or take some time out for travelling. I have family here.'

At Spencer's quizzical expression, she clarified, 'Parents, sister, brother-in-law, niece.'

She couldn't help but note the audible sigh Spencer gave. Hopefully, that was of relief that he didn't appear to have a rival for her affections.

'And do you like what you do?'

'I love it. I've been doing it for about eight years now. I love Scotland, love Edinburgh, and love painting them in their best light, as well as helping our many B&B and guest house clients to market their properties so they appeal to tourists. I help them find their USP.'

'Sounds satisfying,' Spencer agreed.

'What about you? I already know a little about your work, and of course I met Courtney, and almost met your mum.' Ellie smiled. 'But what do you like doing? Is this where you'd normally hang out on a Saturday night?'

'Ha, not at all. I'd usually be under a blanket on the sofa watching a quiz show. Sorry, did I say that out loud?'

''Fraid so.' Ellie grinned. She quite liked the idea of being under a blanket with Spencer, although she'd happily forgo the quiz show. Perhaps his comment held a hidden message. No, she had to stop reading into things.

Spencer said, 'Unfortunately I'm often travelling for work, so I don't get much time to socialise. One of those decisions you make when you don't have much going on in your life and then when you do, it's not something you can get out of.'

Ellie let her thoughts catch up then looked at him, a question on her lips.

'I said that out loud too, didn't I?'

Ellie was beginning to suspect he was doing this on purpose, but she found it endearing nonetheless. There was a lot to like about Spencer Delaney. Before she had time to reflect upon it further, their starters arrived and silence reigned.

'That was delicious,' Ellie said as they left the restaurant. She was a little unsure of what to do now. It was so long since she'd been on a first date, she didn't know how to act. She and Scott had only had two proper dates and then they had just been together.

When she thought back on it, their relationship had been more akin to friends with benefits. He hadn't treated her much, that was for sure, although she had forked out plenty on him, and his miserliness had always been a sore point, particularly given he had no mortgage, maintained his lifestyle through a substantial trust fund his parents had set up for him years ago, and had no responsibilities. She couldn't believe the relief she felt that they were no longer together, and that wasn't only because she was here with Spencer right now.

They drove back to Ellie's, and during the drive, they took the opportunity to find out more about each other. At one point Spencer suggested that in a few weeks they could arrange a quiz to see who had the best recall, who could remember the most of the other's answers. At mention of the future, Ellie flushed. Maybe they'd have that second date then.

Spencer pulled the car up in front of Ellie's flat, hopped out and opened her door before escorting her to the main door to her building. She liked that he performed these little courtesies.

He stood facing her, a smile playing on his lips. She studied the contours of his face, as if trying to commit it to memory.

'Thanks, Ellie. I really enjoyed your company. Could we do this again next week?'

Next week? She knew he'd said he was going away, but a whole week. Her heart had been trashed by Scumbag Scott. She had to be careful with it.

'That sounds good,' she said as butterflies did a jig in her stomach. 'Which day were you thinking and I'll check if I'm free?'

Spencer's eyes searched hers. 'I was hoping Saturday. Can I pick you up at seven?'

Saturday was the twenty-ninth, the day she'd been going to propose to Scumbag Scott, before she knew he was a scumbag. The irony of going on a second date with someone else the day she had been set to propose to Scott wasn't lost on her. In fact, she decided to deliver one final kick in the balls to Scott. 'Saturday's good for me.'

'Fantastic, see you then.' He started to head towards his car, then seemed to debate something with himself, turned and loped back towards her.

Ellie's brows knitted.

'I forgot something.'

'Oh?'

'This.' He gently cupped her face in his hands then kissed her ever so lightly on the lips. Seconds later, she rested her arms on his shoulders and when they finally broke apart, she gazed up at him, her bottom lip held between her teeth.

Wow.

Chapter Twenty-seven

Jess

Thursday 27 February

Jess slammed her case shut, picked up her gym bag and headed for the door. She was running late. The irony wasn't lost on her. Running late for running. Did her subconscious somehow know that although her friendship with Nathan was purely platonic she found him attractive? It would be hard not to. He was very handsome, toned but not buff and to cap it all, he was lovely, and he listened. They were only going for a run, her internal voice reasoned. It wasn't as if they were booking into a boutique hotel to get down and dirty. But a small voice at the back of her mind told her Mark wouldn't be happy if he could see his girlfriend getting so close to another guy.

In the end, Jess took the moral high ground as she knew nothing untoward would happen. She'd just finished packing for a trip to Sicily to propose to Mark for goodness' sake, but it didn't stop her curiosity wondering again whether Nathan was single.

She rounded the corner and saw him outside the gym doing stretches. He was obviously serious about his warm-up.

'So sorry I'm late,' she huffed. 'Give me a second to drop this bag off and I'm all yours.'

Nathan grinned at her, revealing those pearly whites again, making her heart go all aflutter for a moment. What was wrong with her? Plus she was blushing now, given her inappropriate 'all yours' remark. She wished her brain would engage.

'No problem,' he called after her.

Jess stowed her bag in a locker and headed back outside, breathless, although she wasn't sure from what: seeing Nathan or rushing around. *Get a grip.*

'So, I thought we could run from here up to Pollok Park and back into Shawlands. Do you think you could manage that?' Nathan's eyes shone as he watched her.

'Let's hope so.' Jess gripped her running water bottle. She'd unearthed it in a cupboard late last night. Personally, even though she was fit, she wasn't sure she would be able to match him for speed, but she was determined to try.

'Let's go then, and remember we shouldn't be going so fast we can't talk comfortably.'

Jess was a whirl of emotions. She didn't think she'd be able to talk for two reasons. One, she was feeling a little tongue-tied, and two, she would probably be exhausted, gasping for air.

They chatted as they ran.

'Baxter really seems to be enjoying your walks together.'

'He's a great dog,' Jess huffed. 'Full of energy. So sweet too.'

'Oh, he's full of energy all right. That's why I needed another dog walker. He was starting to chew stuff again as he was being left home alone too long.'

'Don't you have any family who could have walked

him?' Here was the way to find out, for research purposes only, of course, whether he was attached.

'No, my family are all back home in South Island.'

She'd pegged him as a Kiwi, although sometimes she'd thought his accent was South African. She found it hard to distinguish them. Funny how his nationality hadn't come up in their conversations until now.

He fitted her idea of what a Kiwi looked like, now she thought about it. Tall, broad, rugby player – idly she wondered if he played and if he'd ever met Mark – and he was a physio, the kind of occupation she'd equated with someone who fitted that profile.

Now she was overthinking it.

Soon Jess' conversation dried up as she found the pace tough-going. She should have done those lunges and stretches Nathan did before they started. No doubt she'd pay for it later. She drew parallels between Nathan and Mark, unfairly so, but then apart from the meal he'd sprung upon her, and the thoughtful retreat gift, Mark hadn't been present much lately, emotionally or physically, even though they lived in the same house. She'd go so far as to say he was more than a little distracted, but then he had a lot on his plate with rugby, extracurricular school activities, parents' nights, coaching the school team, as well as his catch-ups with his mates. She wasn't contemplating doing anything with Nathan, except running and enjoying the occasional coffee, or meal, she reminded herself, but it was refreshing to have someone to talk to about things that were of interest to her and not just 'There's the gas bill in', 'Have you seen my rugby shirt?', 'Do you know where my Cross pen is?', 'Sorry, was the visit to your mum's today?'

She realised she'd zoned out when Nathan's gaze fell on

her, a smile upon his lips. 'So, are you game then?'

Oh Lord, I wasn't listening. Jess tried to dig herself out of the hole she'd created, saying, 'What does it involve?'

Again that amused smile, as if he knew she hadn't been giving him her full attention. Should she fess up?

'Well, meeting me at the club twice a week to go for a run, slightly longer than this one.'

He must have been talking about training together and she'd asked him a banal question that showed she hadn't been listening. Right, there was nothing for it. 'Sorry, I was miles away.'

Nathan looked unfazed, simply giving her a lopsided smile and saying, 'I'll have to make my chat more interesting then, but what do you think?'

She was on dangerous territory here. On the one hand, it would be good to have a regular training buddy, as it would spur her on. She would actually go running instead of procrastinating and telling herself she did exercise all day every day, and that was enough. She knew it wasn't – running used different muscles.

On the other hand, she was aware of the dangers involved in being so close to Nathan so often. And she didn't want to send him the wrong signals. Maybe she could say yes and then drop into the conversation later that she was off to Sicily that night with her boyfriend. He had never asked if she was attached – why would he? They had only drunk coffee, eaten pasta and gone running together.

'OK, you're on, although it depends what times and days you can do.'

'Don't worry, we'll work something out.'

That smile again. It really would melt your heart…or set it racing.

'You ready to pick up the pace a little?'

Er, no. Can't you see I'm barely able to keep this pace? 'Sure.' *At least he won't find me attractive as I'll be a sweaty mess every time he sees me.*

Nathan was great company. Even though he did most of the talking, often out of necessity as Jess was too out of breath to utter more than a grunt or a one-word answer, he asked her about herself. He didn't show off or offer many details of his life, apart from when there was common ground with one of Jess' answers. She wondered again if he was single. He certainly seemed like someone who should be in a relationship, yet there was no wedding ring, but then again so many couples bypassed the marriage stage – hopefully not her – and just lived with each other. She was done with that.

She really needed to stop thinking about him. He was a mate. She cut herself some slack by attributing some of her conflicting feelings and inappropriate thoughts about Nathan to the fact she was a little hacked-off with Mark's lacklustre efforts the past few months.

They passed people out walking their dogs, as well as friends and couples enjoying a stroll, taking advantage of the unusually mild weather. You could never tell when it would change again. Jess stumbled a few times, but between her catching herself and Nathan righting her, she remained unscathed.

They'd run about another quarter of a mile, when she had to dart to the side unexpectedly as a cyclist coming towards them took up more than his fair share of the path.

'Aargh,' yelped Jess.

Nathan pulled up. 'You OK?'

She gestured with her right hand. 'My hair's stuck.'

Her hair had snagged on a low-hanging branch.

'Here, let me. You can't see properly from that angle.' With great care, Nathan untangled the strands of her hair from the branch.

'Thanks.' Relief flooded through her. She must have looked a right idiot. A nanosecond later, she became aware of Nathan's eyes on hers and saw he was still holding a lock of her hair. Trying to drag her gaze away, she said, 'Sorry, I'm such a klutz. I should have been paying more attention to where I was going.'

Nathan didn't seem to have heard her, or if he did, her clumsiness didn't bother him. His eyes didn't leave hers and his voice dropped to a whisper. 'I like you, Jess.'

Jess smiled. 'I like you too. You're so easy to talk to.'

He shook his head and his lips curved in amusement. 'No, Jess, I *like* you.'

Oh God.

Nathan touched his fingertips to Jess' cheek, her hair still held in his other hand, and brought his mouth down on hers. *Zing!*

Oh sweet Jesus, that mouth tasted as good as it promised. Jess couldn't help herself. She returned the kiss, reciprocating when he deepened it. When they finally pulled apart, she was breathing hard, Nathan's eyes were dark and they were both panting as if they'd run a marathon.

Jess' head was too much of a mess to compute anything right now. The delicious sensation of Nathan's mouth on hers had drowned out all rational thought. Nathan interrupted her reverie by saying, 'Can I see you tomorrow?'

What am I doing? Jess burst into tears before blurting

out, 'I can't. I'm flying to Sicily tonight to propose to my boyfriend.'

Jess chattered away almost incessantly to Mark as they waited in the departure lounge at Glasgow Airport that afternoon. She hoped he wouldn't notice anything was amiss and instead presume she was nervous about the flight. She loved travelling but was often a little unsettled when flying.

Would passengers travelling with British Airways to London Gatwick, please board now through gate number ten.

'That's us,' Jess trilled, her voice overbright.

Mark frowned. 'You OK? You seem a little on edge. You've not rediscovered a fear of flying without telling me, have you?'

'No, nothing like that. I'll just feel better when we're on our way. You know how excited I get in airports.'

'More like at the duty-free shops.'

'Yes, that too.' Jess once again tried to convey an outward sense of calm. Inside, she was a roiling mass of jumbled thoughts. Her brain felt like it was about to detonate. Why had she let Nathan kiss her? It was her fault. She hadn't clarified her situation. She'd fooled herself into thinking men and women could be platonic friends. She wouldn't be making that mistake again. But then, she reminded herself, he hadn't made his relationship status known either, although as it turned out, that was because he wasn't in one. He'd assumed that because Jess hadn't told him otherwise and didn't wear a wedding ring, she was single.

He had been so nice about it all, so understanding,

which made her feel even worse. He said it was timing, he wished he'd met her earlier and hoped she and Mark would be happy together. He also said that much as he'd like to have her as a training partner, he thought there might be too much chemistry between them, so that might not be the best way forward. He had one question for her: Did she enjoy the kiss? She'd admitted she had, then they'd walked back to the gym, her a little subdued, him telling her not to worry about it, he was a big boy and would get over it, but to let her know if they got divorced. Then he'd told her Mark was a lucky guy, flashed her that smile again and said, 'Kidding!'

Mark couldn't have been more attentive on the flight from Glasgow to London, stowing her cabin bag for her and letting her have the window seat then taking out a snack he'd prepared for them both. It reminded her how endearing he could be when they made the effort to spend time together, and that made her feel even worse. Should she tell him what had happened between her and Nathan? No, that would only ruin the holiday, certainly the proposal. The proposal. How could she propose now? She could hardly propose two days after she'd kissed another man. What sort of woman was she?

The flight to Catania from Gatwick had left on time, which Jess took as a good omen. Villa Azzurra was every bit as picture perfect as it had seemed in the brochure, with fairy lights accentuating the orange groves and the sea below, or rather, what she could see of it, given the hour.

'Looks nice,' said Mark. 'Just what we need. A few days of R&R in a luxury hotel. C'mon, let's go sample the delights of our room.' He winked at her, and she couldn't help smiling. He was incorrigible.

As Jess trailed Mark to the elevator bank, she only hoped the following day would be simpler and she'd be able to sort out the mess in her head. It would, after all, leave only one more day before she intended to ask the love of her life to marry her. But was he still the love of her life? And did she still have the courage to propose?

Chapter Twenty-eight

Anouska

Thursday 27 February

Anouska sat down heavily on the sofa and imagined for the millionth time what it would be like to be a single mother. It was hard enough to take on board in many ways the concept of being a parent, but being a single parent? Sure, Zach had said he would help with the baby and be in Bean's life, even if he didn't yet know if he wanted to be in hers, but without any family support network around her, how could she possibly look after a baby? She worked so much that she had little time for making new friendships. As a result, she had few real friends. It was all becoming a bit too much for her. She was feeling so stressed out and she knew that wasn't good for the baby. She was trying meditation to help her relax but it wasn't really working so far.

Gypsy purred next to her and Anouska gave a wan smile. Even she was missing Zach. Well, she was his cat after all. She wasn't normally known for being affectionate, not with Anouska at least, but she appeared to sense Anouska needed her, needed the presence of another living being, if not another human being, close to her.

Anouska smiled when she thought of Zach and how close he and Gypsy were. He'd brought her home as a rescue just after his brother died, before she and Zach were together. He sometimes said the cat's mannerisms reminded him of his brother. And when he'd had a few drinks, he'd been known to say it was his dead brother, come back as a cat.

Personally, Anouska didn't believe in reincarnation, but if it brought Zach a modicum of comfort, then who was she to disabuse him of the notion of it being possible?

Anouska didn't consider herself a cat person, although she did give a nod to the Nebelung's foibles by providing her with her two favourite things – tomato soup and cheese, although not together. She'd tried that once, and it hadn't gone down well.

Plus she always sided with the underdog, pun intended. When Zach had chosen Gypsy at the rescue centre, she'd been missing her tail. A pity, apparently, as Nebelungs are known for having fabulous tails. Unfortunately, Zach had no idea why Gypsy was tail-less, but whether she'd been in an accident or had been mistreated by someone, he'd made it his mission to ensure she had a safe and comfortable home with him. And now he wasn't here.

Anouska thought she'd had a safe and comfortable home with Zach too, but now even that was up in the air. What if Zach decided they shouldn't stay together? The flat was legally his, even though she'd contributed to it for years. She wasn't concerned about the money; she had plenty of that, and she knew Zach would do the right thing financially by her, but there was the very real possibility she might have to move out of the home she'd lived in for the last two years.

Moving whilst pregnant wasn't high on her wish list. It would be even more upheaval and uncertainty.

Zach still hadn't told her where he was staying. They kept in touch by infrequent text messages. He had told her he had returned to Bean There as he couldn't leave Todd on his own any longer, but what of leaving her on her own to cope? And their baby? Now she was close to being unable to forgive him. How could it have all gone so wrong? If she could turn the clock back, she would tell him straightaway and not tie herself in knots

about being able to tell him face to face. Who knows, maybe he would have picked her up and swung her round with joy. She tortured herself with this type of scenario, over and over. Her next scan was in eight days. He'd said he would go with her, but she wanted it to be a happy occasion. Her emotions were mixed about him being there if they weren't together as a couple. She was so tired all the time, had so many decisions to make and was incapable of making any.

Leigh-Ann had been tremendous, as ever. After Zach left to do his thinking, and the next time Anouska ventured into the office, she had blurted out the whole sorry tale to her. Although her assistant had been saddened at Anouska feeling unable to confide in her earlier, she had been flabbergasted at Zach's reaction, disappointed in him and had said men were stupid sometimes, even good ones like Zach, and that he'd come around. She'd then focused on Anouska and her wellbeing and made sure Anouska did the same. She'd also assured Anouska she would have her unwavering support, no matter what happened with Zach, and that she would also be there for her and the baby. She was a true friend indeed. Anouska had burst into tears at her kindness.

Leigh-Ann had tried to play things down, when Anouska repeatedly thanked her, telling Anouska she was simply delighted to be an auntie at last, even if it was an honorary one.

She took control, and Anouska let her as exhaustion threatened to overwhelm her. She rescheduled Anouska's appointments for a few weeks to give her some space. So now the business side of things was running as best as could be expected but her personal life was still in tatters. She woke every day to discover Zach's side of the bed empty, and it was as if she remembered it anew each time. She didn't know how much more time she could give him.

On impulse, Anouska picked up her phone and sent a WhatsApp message to the 'LYP' group, the irony of that not lost on her. At the moment there may only be one leap-year proposal, as hers appeared to have stalled before it could even get off the ground and poor Ellie's was history. That said, Ellie, from her messages, had bounced back with this new guy she had met. Spencer. Good on her.

Hi, girls, how are you? Is life still good with Spencer, Ellie? How about you, Jess? Flights on time?

Nothing. They were all busy with their own lives, of course. Although, they'd been each other's rocks recently, right now they had their own messy lives to fix. Anouska sighed and decided it was time to sort out her mess of a life. Starting today. She grabbed the notebook Todd had given her for Christmas and began outlining a strategy. Time to get her man back…before she no longer wanted him back.

As Anouska scribbled away in her pad, her phone pinged. A message in the LYP group chat. Ellie.

Hi, Anouska. Yes, all going well with Spencer. How are

you? Are you and the baby OK?

Without even knowing Ellie that well – although they had shared something that brought them closer together than many best friends – she could read the subtext in the message: Has Zach been in touch? Or maybe she was imagining things now. She had reached that point of having difficulty differentiating between fiction and reality.

We're good, thanks. Scan next week. Keeping in touch with Zach by text. I've decided I'm going to give him one more – and only one more – chance. I can't be in this constant state of limbo. I get that what I did was wrong, but I feel that the punishment doesn't fit the crime, and there's more at stake here. I just need to figure out how to get his attention since he appears to have no intention of seeing me.

Deciding to give Ellie time to compose her reply, Anouska went to put the kettle on. Simply Red's 'If You Don't Know Me By Now' was playing on the radio, in the background. Everywhere she turned, she felt as if she were being kicked in the teeth. Why did songs have so much more significance when you were going through a break-up?

She sat down with her tea and saw that she had two WhatsApp messages, one from Ellie, the other from Jess.

Jess: *Hi. Just at the airport now. Sorry to hear Zach hasn't seen sense yet. He will. For the record, I think it's right to give him one final chance. You can't stay like this forever. You must be shattered. Have you any thoughts yet on how to get his attention?*

Ellie: *I agree. The punishment doesn't fit the crime. Everybody makes mistakes, nobody's perfect, and your mum guessed, you didn't tell her. It's time for Zach to step up. Let me get my thinking head on – I am a marketing guru, you know!*

Anouska: *Thanks, girls. Sadly, nothing yet, Jess x*

When no further messages seemed forthcoming, Anouska decided to put her feet up with a book. It had been a while since she'd had so much free time. She only wished it was under different circumstances.

About an hour later, her phone rang. Ellie.

'Hi, Anouska. I hope you don't mind me calling instead of messaging, but I had some ideas I wanted to run past you – some might seem cheesy, but I have one that I think is a winner. Obviously I don't know Zach, but at this stage I think you need to think outside of your comfort zone.'

'I'm listening.'

Ellie ran through a whole host of options, many of which Anouska discounted as either being too out there or too ordinary. She needed something with oomph but that wasn't too radical. Zach hated fuss.

'Hang on, hang on, what did you say there?'

'How about proposing to him on the radio? Do you know what station he listens to in the bistro?'

'Yes, I do, but Zach's a very private person. I'm not sure if that's such a good idea, and it's not really me either.'

'But don't you think desperate times require desperate measures?'

Anouska considered this for a moment. 'Agreed, but we can't guarantee he'll be listening when the broadcast goes out.'

'No, we can't,' said Ellie, 'but don't you think it's worth a shot? You've tried what you've expected to work. How about trying the unexpected?'

'Hmm.' Anouska tapped a finger against her lips. 'I suppose we could figure out a time, and I could ensure

Todd knows that Zach needs to be near a radio then. He listens to Northsound 1. Let me work out what I want to say and then I'll contact them.'

'Excellent. Don't forget to tell me how you get on. Good luck.'

Anouska pulled up Northsound 1's contact details and fired off an email asking for a special favour. She explained that she and her boyfriend were having some difficulties, and to please not air that, but she would be so grateful if they could have her on Saturday morning's live show so she could propose to him as per the age-old twenty-ninth of February leap-year tradition.

She pressed send. Now all she could do was wait.

An hour later, her mobile rang.

'Hello, is that Anouska?'

'Speaking.'

'Hi, Anouska. This is Calvin Claridge from Northsound 1. I'm one of the producers here. We're very excited about your proposal. Here's what we're thinking.' Calvin then outlined in detail what would happen on the twenty-ninth. 'How does that sound for you?'

'That sounds perfect.'

'Fantastic. I'll send you some details over then we'll be good to go. Good luck!'

Anouska punched the air when she came off the phone. 'Yes!' She was taking back control of her life. This was make-or-break stuff, but at least at the end of it all, she'd know where she and Zach stood.

She immediately called Ellie, who was delighted. 'I'll be tuning in on Saturday at ten.'

Anouska had reckoned the busiest period for breakfast at Bean There would have passed by ten, so chose then as she thought it most likely Zach would be there and not off at a supplier, which he tended to leave until the afternoon. She hoped he didn't go to the cash and carry. He usually avoided going at the weekend, but sometimes he made an unscheduled visit to meet demand. She prayed the gods were with her on this one. She really could use all the luck she could get.

She messaged the LYP group chat, thus bringing Jess up to speed with recent events. She joked. *I might be proposing before you, or indeed at the same time as you. If you have any tips, we should trade.* She was aiming for lighthearted, but inside she felt wrung out. When had life become so complicated? She placed her hand over her non-existent bump and said, 'Let's hope Daddy wants to marry Mummy, Bean. But whatever happens, we both love you very, very much.' Then she kissed her fingertips and pressed them to where she reckoned Bean was.

Chapter Twenty-nine

Ellie

Thursday 27 February

Ellie gave a squeal of excitement. Spencer had texted her.

Hope you're having a good week. I really don't want to wait until Saturday to see you. Are you free tonight?

Not one for playing games, she fired back a quick text. *You're in luck. I was supposed to be washing my hair.*

He replied almost immediately. *Excellent. I thought we could go for a drink after work then dinner. How does that sound?*

Perfect.

Great. Text me your work address and what time you finish and I'll pick you up. Do you have any particular preference with regards to food? She liked that he'd asked. It was fine to take the lead on a first date but by the second date, it felt right that he should check she was on board with whatever cuisine he chose, or that he gave her the chance to choose. Since she wasn't a fussy eater, she told him she was happy to leave matters in his hands. She'd leave herself in his hands too, she thought, then laughed at herself. What was she like?

Ellie had texted Chloe to fill her in on the latest. She hadn't wanted to be all jollity with regards to her love life when poor Anouska had no idea what was happening with her own relationship, and Jess was probably on her way to the airport by now.

Chloe had suggested a meet-up at a child-friendly café in town since she would have Rosie in tow.

Ellie had blown in, late as usual, her curls tumbling around her face and plonked herself down on the chair opposite her sister. Once she'd greeted them both and stopped smiling, thoughts of Spencer ever-present in her mind, Chloe finally got a chance to grill her.

'So, what's he like?' Chloe asked as she bounced a tearful Rosie on her knee. Her niece was being a bit clingy, wouldn't even go to Auntie Ell.

'He's nice, really nice.'

'Nice? Seriously? Els, that's an insult not a compliment. You can't call the poor bloke "nice".'

'OK. He's gorgeous, a little over six foot, blonde hair, amazing blue eyes, lovely smile. Easy to talk to, down to earth, runs his own company, artistic. Has all his own teeth, as far as I know. Unattached.'

'Now, that's a better picture you've painted,' Chloe said.

'So glad to have met your expectation this time.'

Chloe made a face. 'So, when are you seeing him again?'

Unable to hold back the smile dancing on her lips, Ellie said, 'Tonight. He texted to say he couldn't wait until Saturday to see me! I can't wait. He's been away for work. Drawbacks of owning the company.'

'You know what they say, absence makes the heart grow

fonder.'

'Yes, but we've only just met. We haven't had time to fall madly in love and then miss each other when we're apart. What if he meets someone else? Or what if he has someone in every city he visits?'

Chloe shook her head. 'Oh my God, you've got it bad!'

'No, I don't,' Ellie protested.

'Yes you do, otherwise you wouldn't be making such wild, stupid accusations. Why would he fool around when he's only just met you and is obviously into you?'

'He wouldn't be the first,' Ellie muttered.

'C'mon, you're just scared because of what happened with Scumbag. I think you should let things take their course,' Chloe said. 'Don't get me wrong, don't take any crap from him, but don't spoil something that could turn out to be amazing by overthinking and overanalysing it, or tarring the luscious Spencer with the same brush as Scumbag.'

'Maybe you're right. Ooh, I have some good news, at least, I hope so.'

'Oh?' Chloe tilted her head to one side.

'I suggested to Anouska that she try to get Zach to come back by proposing on the radio on the twenty-ninth.'

'You did not!'

Ellie nodded. 'I did, and she's agreed to give it a try. I'm praying both Jess and Anouska's proposals go off without a hitch, even if my own was never meant to be.'

Chloe took Ellie's hand. 'You know something, Ellie Macpherson? You're a good soul.'

Ellie reddened and was fortunately saved by Rosie.

'Auntie Ell, can I sit on your knee, please?'

'Sure, poppet. Up you come.'

'Good, that means Mummy can go and get me some chocolate buttons.' Rosie shot her mother an angelic yet smug smile, then clambered down off Chloe and onto Ellie as the two adults shared an incredulous look.

'That one's too clever by half,' whispered Ellie.

'Oh, don't I know it. Would you like some chocolate buttons too?'

Giving Chloe a look as if to say, 'What am I, five?', Ellie then said, 'Of course. Can't believe you had to ask. Can you grab me a latte, too? I need to be back at work in half an hour.'

The afternoon passed surprisingly quickly. Ellie had been so embroiled in the work she was doing shadowing Trish that she had barely notice the hours go by. It was almost five o'clock when her desk phone rang.

'Ellie, there's someone in Reception for you,' the receptionist told her.

'He or she?'

'He.'

'Did he give a name?'

'No. He said you'd know who it was.'

Spencer.

Ellie thanked her and replaced the receiver, a skip in her step as she strode towards the elevator bank. Her body zinged with anticipation. It had been a long time since she'd felt like that.

As the lift doors opened, her jaw clenched and her fists involuntarily balled up.

Scott.

Why couldn't he leave her alone? She was doing fine

without him. Yes, she had the occasional pang when she thought back to the few positive memories of their relationship, but in retrospect those were so long ago, they were barely worth mentioning. She routinely asked herself why she had ever considered marrying him. Surely she deserved better. It must have been a case of not wanting to give up on the relationship, having already put so much into it.

She could about-turn, then call down from her office to ask the receptionist to deal with him, saying she wasn't available after all, but he'd only come back another time. She had to sort this once and for all.

'Scott. To what do I owe the pleasure?' Ellie's voice held a note of steel as she strode towards him.

He had the good grace to look shamefaced at least.

'Els,' he said, setting down on the reception desk the heart-shaped balloon he had been carrying and reaching his hands out towards Ellie's shoulders as if to pull her towards him.

'Don't *Els* me,' she spat, her voice dangerously soft. 'I only came down here to advise you not to come here again. Get it through your thick head. I don't want to see you ever again.'

'But Ellie–' for once he'd taken note of her insistence and not used her nickname '–I just want to explain.'

'There's no need to explain,' she hissed. 'I'm not blind. Nor is Chloe. I don't need someone like you in my life, and anyway, for what, two nights a week? We weren't going anywhere. That's clear now. It just took me a long time to realise it.' She leant in to him. 'Now. Don't. Come. Here. Again.' She glared at him for a long moment to hammer home her point then stalked back to the lift.

When she returned to her desk, the phone was ringing.

For goodness' sake, this had better not be him again.

'Hi, Ellie. Sorry, but I couldn't help overhearing. Well done. He looked right up himself, that one. Glad you put him in his place.'

Ellie grinned at the receptionist's comment. She had acquitted herself quite well. 'Thanks.'

'He left something for you, though.'

When Ellie didn't answer, she said, 'It's in a White Company bag.'

'Small mercies,' Ellie muttered under her breath. 'I'll pick it up on my way out.'

There was no point in whatever was in the bag going to waste and since she'd spent plenty of time, effort and money on Scott in the past, if he'd bought her a gift and she liked it, she'd keep it.

As Ellie sat back down at her desk, she received a message from Anouska, saying that the radio proposal was a go. Fantastic. She smiled, praying this would work.

It was a pity matters with Anouska and Zach were still unresolved. It had been going on for well over a week now, with Zach not quite able to forgive Anouska, yet saying he would one hundred per cent support the baby when it came. Personally, Ellie wanted to take Zach and shake him until he saw sense, but she didn't think telling Anouska so would be particularly productive. She just felt so sorry for Anouska and her situation. She needed to avoid undue stress. It was bad for the baby. Surely Zach must know that.

Fingers crossed, the proposal would do the trick.

She wondered how Jess was getting on. She hoped her

proposal would go well. For a moment her thoughts turned to Scott and the Eilean Donan Castle proposal that never was, then she mentally shook him from her head and replaced him with Spencer. He was far more deserving of featuring in her daydreams.

Twenty minutes later, Spencer was not featuring so much in her daydreams as her nightmares. He hadn't turned up. Surely she hadn't been stood up again.

This was ridiculous. The building would be closing soon, leaving only the security guard for company. Most people in the company tended to leave on time. They had lives to lead, or parties to go to.

Ten minutes later, Ellie had had enough of waiting around. She texted Spencer. *Pity you couldn't make it. I was looking forward to tonight, but I don't appreciate being messed about. Have a nice life.*

Hot tears pooled in her eyes and she brushed them away angrily, glad no one else was around to witness her pain. How had she been taken in again so soon? Half an hour late on a second date, with no message, nothing. No, she was done with being treated like crap. Spencer Delaney was history. As if to press home the point, she deleted his number, then ordered herself a cab. Since he'd suggested he pick her up, she had no transport to take her home.

Ellie sat in the toilet cubicle for a full ten minutes, willing herself not to cry. She'd come in here just in case Security could see her sobbing at her desk.

What was wrong with her? Why did she attract assholes? He'd seemed so genuine too, so into her. Clearly she had no idea how to read men. Well, she was done with them now – Scott, Spencer, all of them. She sobbed harder into her hands as she perched on the closed toilet lid, a tissue in her hand to wipe her dripping nose.

She finally came out and baulked at the sight in the mirror. Oh well, that mascara wasn't waterproof after all. She cleaned herself up as best she could, then returned to her office to pick up her bag and phone.

Three missed calls. One text. Unknown number.

In her foggy state, it took Ellie a minute before she realised this would be Spencer's number, which she'd deleted.

Tentatively, she opened the text.

Ellie, I'm sorry. I didn't mean to mess you about, but when I saw you with that guy earlier, it was clear there was something going on with you both. We've all got baggage, but I think yours might be too fresh still. I'm not sure you're ready to move on just yet, and honestly, I don't think I'm strong enough to unpack it all. For the record, I really like you, which is why I didn't want to wait until Saturday to see you. I wish you all the best. Spencer.

Shit! He saw me with Scott. Ellie groaned, and the sound was almost primeval. How could that two-timing, lying scumbag still be ruining her life? Aargh!

After a few minutes of trying, and failing, to calm down, she did her best to focus, then her heart soared. Spencer liked her. Ellie gritted her teeth. She was not letting Scott screw things up for her. He'd been doing that for quite long enough. She picked up her bag and flew down the stairs, two at a time, her final thought that Spencer was still up for grabs ... if she could only talk to him.

Her fingers flew over the keys of her phone as she stood outside her building, impervious to the cold.

If you really do like me, trust me. Yes, that was my ex,

emphasis on the ex. And our issues are most definitely resolved now. If you still want to see me, I'll be outside my building for the next fifteen minutes. If you're not here in that time, I'll take that as your answer. Ellie.

Ellie's toes went numb first, despite her hopping from foot to foot to try to keep warm. Why had she said she'd wait outside the building? That was a dumb move. In February, in Scotland. Her neck hurt from constantly craning to see if any of the cars coming were Spencer's. Ten minutes gone.

Her fingers were freezing. Whose idea were fingerless gloves anyway? She was only wearing them because she'd lost her other ones, and Chloe had gifted her these. Useless they were. Twelve minutes.

She tried to think warm thoughts in an attempt to forget how cold she was. Hot water bottle. Latte. Hot chocolate. Flames. Scalding shower. Nope, it wasn't helping.

Fourteen minutes. She sighed. The tears threatened to fall again. This was it. She'd made an even bigger fool of herself now, but not only that, she'd got it wrong – again. She checked her phone. No new messages.

The lights of an approaching car blinded her and she shielded her eyes as Spencer Delaney unfolded his long, lean body from the driver seat and loped towards her, his eyes twinkling.

She hadn't realised how much she'd missed him until he was standing there in front of her, all sexy and dishevelled.

'Hi.' He pulled on his gloves as he reached her, his eyes searching hers.

'Hi,' Ellie said, barely daring to speak. 'You came.'

'I did.' He smiled.

'Spencer, I can explain.'

He shook his head and held up his hands. 'No need. I've given myself a right talking-to since I left that message, knowing I'd messed up. I was actually talking to myself out loud in the street. I got some right funny looks, I can tell you.

'I had no right to assume or presume anything. The past is your business, and it's just that – the past. And we have to move on from it.' A soupçon of a smile escaped his lips. 'I probably don't deserve it, but can we start again?'

Ellie breathed a sigh of relief. 'I'd like that. Very much.'

'Good, because I think you might need me to heat you up. You look frozen.'

Ellie grinned. 'I am, and I do. Just one thing first.'

Spencer quirked an eyebrow, his cheeky smile disappearing into uncertainty for a second. 'Go ahead.'

'Don't ever stand me up again.' Her tone was playful, but her message was clear.

'Oh, don't worry, I won't. I couldn't be that stupid twice.' Then Spencer bent down, their bodies met and as they embraced, Ellie's soul fizzed with happiness.

Chapter Thirty

Jess

Friday 28 February

Jess lazed by the indoor pool, which had windows that gave onto the gardens, and drank in the magnificent scenery around her. Mark was happy to do likewise, chilling, fetching cocktails and mocktails every so often, occasionally having a swim. It had been so nice being alone together, with no work, no interruptions. The kiss with Nathan was fading into obscurity and she hoped that wasn't a case of out of sight, out of mind, and that she had simply succumbed to a temporary madness. It all seemed unreal now.

'I can't believe how sneaky you were at organising this trip,' Mark said, lying on his side and raising himself up on one elbow to talk with her more easily.

Jess smirked. 'I should be working for the Secret Service.'

Mark bit into a slice of pear and the juice dribbled down his chin, before he wiped it with a napkin. The sight was unbelievably sexy. Somehow Jess wondered if it would have seemed so if they were back home in their flat in Glasgow. She thought not. But here in Sicily, eating fresh fruit, relaxing by the pool, and being away from their usual humdrum existence, it did.

'I can't believe the trouble you went to just to plan our winter getaway. It was so thoughtful. Thank you.' He bent over and kissed her gently on the forehead, then when he drew back, his eyes met hers and he leant forward again and kissed her, this time on the lips.

'Mark…' Jess said in warning as things began to heat up between them.

'There's nobody here. We could make love right here, or in the pool and no one would know.'

He was right. They were alone. It was clearly out of season. But whilst the risk of being caught might have been a turn-on, the reality wouldn't be. It would be mortifying, they may be thrown out of the hotel, returning home in disgrace, and her plans would be in tatters. Plus, the hotel may well have CCTV.

No, if they wanted to indulge in any extracurricular activities, it would have to be in the confines of their room.

Discreetly, she disentangled herself from Mark, whose cry of 'Aw!' made her smile. 'Later,' she murmured as she fetched them each a mojito.

When she handed Mark his drink, he sat up and said, 'I can't believe you were able to pull this off because my deputy head goes to your yoga class.'

Jess burst out laughing. 'It wasn't only down to that, but it helped with getting you the time off.'

'You still haven't told me *exactly* how you managed that?' Mark searched her face as if it would provide the answers. Not a chance.

'If I told you, I'd need to kill you.'

'I think I can live without knowing.' Mark grinned.

'Anyway, since I haven't had any time to plan this trip, let me bore you with what the guide book I found in the room says about Etna.'

They had ordered an early lunch because of their upcoming Etna trip, and whilst they feasted on the most exquisite cold cuts and focaccia – a completely different beast to what passed for the real thing back home – Jess once again tortured herself with her dilemma over whether or not to tell Mark about the kiss she'd shared with Nathan.

She hadn't told the girls or Kelsea or Lauren. And she had specifically held back from telling Ellie because of what had happened with Scott. But was she any better, or was she a hypocrite? If she told Mark, was she doing it to appease her own conscience or because she honestly thought he should know? It wasn't as if she had slept with Nathan, although Mark might not believe that. Or was she simply making excuses not to tell him? Aargh, she was driving herself mad here.

'Are you going to eat that?' Mark pointed at the remaining pieces of mortadella on her plate.

Distractedly, she shook her head.

'Everything OK?'

'Sure, delightful.' Delightful? What was she, eighty?

Mark gave her a strange look then placed a piece of the mortadella on some focaccia and popped it in his mouth.

If she didn't start acting normally, Mark would get suspicious. She forced a smile and said, 'You ready for this trip to Etna?'

'Yep, we can't be so close but not visit it. We may never come back.'

Jess gave a sigh of relief and made a mental note to speak to Reception to change their dinner reservation to later, to give them plenty of time to get to the volcano and back. The staff had been so accommodating and had happily made the arrangements for them to go to Etna on the hotel's courtesy bus.

After lunch, Mark went to sort some camera equipment for the trip and Jess took the opportunity to message Anouska and Ellie.

Hi, ladies. Taormina is lovely. Villa Azzurra is amazing. I'm feeling really nervous about popping the question. Probably pre-proposal nerves, but I don't know if I can go through with it. Thank goodness I still have another day to work up the courage! Anouska, that's amazing. All the best for it x

She attached two photos showing Villa Azzurra at its best. The views were spectacular and the crystal-clear waters made you want to plunge yourself into their depths there and then, until you remembered it was February.

Fab photos, Jess. Ellie.

Absolutely you should propose to Mark! And not just so I'm not the only one proposing! It's natural to be nervous. I feel sick to my stomach, and it's nothing to do with pregnancy. What are your reservations?

How could she put into words how she was feeling? She certainly couldn't put it in the group chat, especially not when Scott had cheated on Ellie. Although technically she hadn't cheated on Mark – Nathan had kissed her – it felt like she had. Had she? Oh God, now she was even more confused.

Well, there was no way, even if Ellie hadn't been cheated on, she could commit her thoughts to writing.

It's probably just me being silly. Hopefully the butterflies will go away soon.

'You ready?' Mark asked as he reappeared with his camera bag. 'The driver's waiting for us in Reception.'

Jess pasted on a smile, took Mark's outstretched hand and headed for the minibus.

Two hours later, as she stood at the halfway point up Mount Etna, Jess gawped and said, 'It's incredible.'

They'd decided not to go all the way up as it took two hours to get up the mountain as well as another hour for the drive back. It really was breathtaking. She surveyed the landscape, imagining what it might be like when the volcano erupted. How did the emergency services evacuate people in time? Zafferana in particular was in grave danger from any lava flow.

'It's quite something, isn't it?' Mark said at her side, snapping away with his Nikon. 'Here, stand right there so I can get you with Etna in the background.' Jess adjusted her position and Mark took a few snaps.

'You look beautiful in this photo, Jess.' Mark showed her one of the pictures he'd just taken.

'You sound surprised,' Jess teased him.

'Not at all. You always look beautiful.' He kissed the top of her head.

Tears pricked Jess' eyes. He was being so sweet.

She returned her attention to the panorama around her. Snow-capped peaks, tiny villages, there were even some serious hikers out. She had no intention of doing that level of hiking today. Too cold. The summit was closed too, because of the amount of volcanic activity – nothing threatening, but enough that it was unsafe to approach the top.

They'd taken the cable car up to the mountain hut which doubled as a cafeteria and stopped in for some hot chocolate.

She took Mark's hand in hers, relishing the feel of it, the familiarity, how safe she felt when she was with him. They just needed to focus on each other more. Sicily was helping. It was a pity they couldn't stay longer, but she had no intention of procrastinating. She wanted to marry Mark. She knew it. One hundred per cent. He was her soulmate. Her safe haven. Her go-to person. He was the one she wanted to have adventures with, explore new places with, bore friends senseless with as they showed them the holiday snaps taken in faraway places. She couldn't imagine doing all that with anyone else, nor did she want to. Recently, they'd had a bumpy ride, life getting in the way, but their relationship was solid. They were meant to be. Jess inhaled a deep breath then blew it out slowly. They needed to talk.

Back at the hotel, they were dressing for dinner. It was now or never.

'Mark, have you got a sec?'

'Yep. Just let me put my trousers on.' He winked at her. 'Or not, depending on what you were about to say.' He indicated the bed with a smirk.

'Not that, maybe later.' Despite the gravity of the situation, her mouth turned up at the corners.

'You look nice,' he said, his eyes drinking her in.

Now wasn't the time to point out to him that a man should never tell a girl she looked 'nice'. Any other positive adjective was always preferable.

'Mark, put your trousers on and come and sit down. I

need to talk to you.'

His eyebrows furrowed. 'Sounds ominous.'

Jess said nothing but continued to look at him.

'Should I be worried?' He smiled, but it was a surface smile and didn't reach his eyes. He slumped down on the bed beside her like a condemned man reluctantly sitting in the electric chair.

It was harder to do this side-on, but at least she could hold his hands.

'Mark, you know I love you…'

His smile faltered. 'Why do I feel there's a but coming here?' There was an edge to his tone.

'There's no "but". I love you one hundred per cent. But–' Too late, Jess caught herself. She gave Mark an 'OK, you were right' lopsided smile. '–I do have to tell you something.'

Mark didn't break eye contact with her but he fidgeted, as if concerned over what was coming next.

'I didn't mean for it to happen. Sorry, that sounds as if it's something more serious than it is, but basically someone kissed me, and I kissed him back. It only happened once and it won't happen again, but it's been eating away at me, and we always tell each other the truth, and nothing else would ever have happened, but I couldn't not tell you.' She stopped, aware she was babbling.

'You kissed someone else?' Mark said.

'No, yes, but…' Jess couldn't formulate her thoughts never mind words.

Mark held up a finger. 'Did you enjoy it?' he asked, his voice dangerously soft.

Jess flushed. She was a terrible liar, and she didn't want to lie anyway, but neither did she want to hurt Mark any further. Her scratchy throat told her she was on the verge of tears, and unable to trust herself not to bawl her eyes out, she nodded mutely as misery overcame her.

'So, you've been seeing someone else.' It was a statement not a question.

'No! Not like that, at least,' Jess protested. 'I didn't realise he liked me like that. I promise.' She was breathing hard now.

Mark studied her in silence. Although it was torturous, Jess was too afraid to break it, terrified of what Mark might say.

Finally Mark said, 'I believe you.'

Jess let out the breath she'd been holding. 'Thank you, and I'm sorry I didn't read the situation properly, but I had to tell you. I couldn't have it between us.'

'I already knew.'

Jess' mouth fell open. 'You knew?'

'Well, I didn't know about the kiss, but Daz saw you with a guy in that new café, what is it – Piece of Pie?'

'Slice of Pie,' Jess said, wondering belatedly if she should have let the minor error slide; it wasn't important.

'That one. Yeah, Daz said he saw you having dinner there the other night.'

'It sounds worse than it was, I promise. I'd only had a soggy sandwich all day, and I tried to get a juice out of the machine, but it wasn't working, then the gym café was shut, so Nathan, that's the guy I had some pasta with–' she blanched when Mark winced '–he suggested that new café. There was nothing more sinister to it. And he helped me find Bella the day the boy hit me with the skateboard and she bolted. Then he asked me to walk his dog Baxter, which I've been doing. And he offered to be my running partner as I told him I needed to start training for the half-marathon. He's been attending my classes. I didn't think anything of it, and then the other day when we went running, he kissed me. I was so taken aback, I kissed him back. I'm so sorry. We hadn't discussed relationships. It was a misunderstanding. He liked me, and I hadn't realised it wasn't just in a platonic way.' She gasped for breath.

'Jess, I'm not being funny, but you're so naïve. Look at you, you're gorgeous, you're fit, you're sweet, you're kind, you're funny. Why wouldn't any guy be interested in you? Obviously, I'd rather you hadn't kissed, but as long as you can promise me it won't happen again, I can live with it. You and me, we're meant to be, aren't we?' He gave her a hopeful smile.

'Absolutely we are.' Jess wrapped her arms around Mark and hugged him. 'I love you, Mark. Don't ever forget it. And I won't see him again – not running, not walking his dog, nor the classes. He's a decent guy. He just misread the signals.' She hoped that was true. 'I don't think he'd even think of coming back to class.'

'I love you, too, Jess.' He kissed her forehead, leaving his lips against it for a few seconds. 'Anyway, I don't think I'm completely blameless. I know I haven't been spending very much time with you lately. It's taken us coming on holiday for me to realise that. I'm sorry. Relationships take work. Our relationship needs work, our attention. We're too important to take it for granted.'

'Agreed.' Jess smiled and said, 'Let's finish getting ready, then we can go sample some more of that incredible food.'

'Yeah, you can make it up to me later. But for now, lead on, Macduff.' Mark grinned. 'I'm starving.'

Chapter Thirty-one

Anouska

Saturday 29 February

On Saturday morning, Anouska was a quivering wreck. She'd hardly slept all night, tossing and turning, fearful of the outcome, terrified to go on live radio. Conducting all the meetings in the world couldn't have prepared her for this. Her voice felt hoarse, her mouth was dry and she tried over and over to make her tongue feel as if it wasn't coated in cotton wool, by drinking copious amounts of water, but all that achieved was to send her on countless trips to the toilet.

She'd been receiving messages of support all morning.

Ellie: *This will work. I know it. Good luck and text me later x*

Todd: *Inspired idea. You need to sort him out. Absolutely rooting for you. I'll make sure he picks up, not me. Love you both x*

Kelsea: *Ellie let slip about the proposals when we went to that supper club. Lauren just told me you're proposing this morning on air. Go you! Zach would be an idiot to say no. Good luck! X*

Lauren: *I'm going to kill my sister. I told her not to text you. Zach loves you. He'll do the right thing. Love you x*

It tickled Anouska that Lauren was going to have it out with Kelsea for being indiscreet, and it took her mind momentarily off the task at hand. And she needed distracting. The clock was counting down the minutes painfully slowly. She didn't know for how much longer she could hold back the nausea, nor if it would remain just nausea.

Five to ten. The moment of truth approached. Her stomach was churning, and she was sweating as Calvin from Northsound 1 called and asked her to stand by. She listened to the radio as she waited for her cue. Jamie Flaherty's show was playing the Bee Gees' "If I Can't Have You". She didn't know whether to laugh or cry at the aptness of the song choice. It also occurred to her that it could have been chosen intentionally, but perhaps it was just a general nod to today traditionally being the day women could propose.

That thought also had her speculating for a second on what all the hard-core feminists out there would think of her proposal. Stuff them. She was a high-flying, jet-setting, relatively wealthy woman with her own business. If she wanted to propose in an archaic way, to their mind, that was entirely up to her, and if they didn't like it, too bad. She'd do so. Surely feminism was about choice anyway.

She could faintly hear the show's presenter saying, 'This is Jamie Flaherty on Northsound 1. We have a woman on a mission this morning. Can we help her in her hour of need? Let's see. Anouska, how are you?'

Belatedly, Anouska realised she'd been patched through to Jamie. 'I-I'm fine, Jamie, thanks. You?'

'I'm good, thanks. Well, Anouska, what a story! Not

many people, I imagine, these days, propose on the twenty-ninth of February. I've never met anyone who has done so. Have you, Anouska?'

'I haven't, no.'

'So I'm curious. Why today then?'

There was no way she was telling him the real reason: her pregnancy and the chain of events that had sparked her decision to propose. Nor was she going to tell Jamie and the station's listeners about her friendship with Ellie and Jess; instead, she trotted out something she'd read online about the history behind it.

'Well, I've always thought it quite romantic. A little different. I love the history of it too. Or the legend, whichever you prefer,' Anouska corrected herself.

'Oh, and what's that?' said Jamie. 'I must confess I've never really thought about how the tradition started.'

Anouska tried to remember what she'd read. 'It's an old Irish tradition, where St Brigid, in effect, campaigned for women to be allowed to ask men to marry them as they were waiting far too long for their suitors, as they were known then, to ask them.'

'I *did* not know that.' Jamie's tone showed he was genuinely surprised.

'Yes, and St Patrick decreed that women could ask men, but only once every four years, and only on one day, the twenty-ninth of February.'

'Well, that's astonishing. I had no idea there were saints involved in this at all. Who knew? I feel quite uninformed now.' Jamie laughed. 'Right, Anouska, thanks for that. Now, are you ready to speak to Zach?'

'I am,' Anouska replied, her fingers digging into her palms. Or rather, she was as ready as she ever would be.

'You stay on the line whilst I call Zach. Can you also turn your radio down so there's no feedback from it?'

At Anouska's acknowledgement, Jamie continued, 'Right, everyone, let's find Anouska's prince. Time to call him.'

There was the sound of Jamie pressing buttons, then, 'Bean There, Zach speaking. How can I help you?'

'Hello, Zach, this is Jamie Flaherty at Northsound 1. How are you this morning?'

'Is this a wind-up?' Zach asked, and Anouska allowed herself a grin. Zach didn't cope well with time-wasters, despite being the most mild-mannered person she knew.

'No, Zach, it's not a wind-up. In fact, we're live on the radio right now, and we have someone who badly wants to speak to you.'

'Uh-huh.'

Not his finest response. Did he sound cagey?

'Is it OK if we put them on now, Zach?'

A short silence then, 'I suppose.'

'Excellent. Over to you, caller.'

'Hi, Zach, it's Anouska.' She let that sink in for a minute before adding, 'I know this might come as a bit of a surprise, it is to me too, but this was the only way I could get your attention. Zach, I love you, and what I'm trying to say, rather inelegantly, is, will you marry me?'

Anouska thought she would burst whilst she waited…and waited…and waited.

'Zach? Zach, mate, are you there?' Jamie asked. An awkward silence descended until Jamie finally broke it. 'Anouska. Sorry, I think we've lost him. Let me try and call him back.'

'No, don't bother,' Anouska said, tears coursing openly

down her face. 'I think we have his answer. Thanks for letting me come on the show.'

'I'm sorry it wasn't the outcome you were expecting, but you never know, he might just need some time.'

Anouska didn't tell Jamie he'd had plenty of time already. She simply thanked him again and hung up.

After a minute, she turned the radio back up a little, but already it was playing another song: The Beatles' "She Loves You". Now she knew someone was playing a cruel trick on her. No one could be that unlucky.

Within minutes of her coming off the phone, Ellie called. Anouska couldn't bear to speak to her, to anyone. She really was going to have this baby alone. It was almost impossible to take in – she was actually going to be a single mother. She didn't mean it in a bad way, but she had never envisaged herself ending up in this situation. How would she cope? Anouska sat on her sofa, pulled her knees up to her chin, glad she had no visible bump to encumber her yet, and wept until the tears ran dry.

After a couple of hours and having soaked in a long bath to relax, Anouska settled down with a Greek salad and a glass of sparkling water. At least now she could plan for the future, bleak as it might seem. Energised, she started making a list of the positives. She'd ignored the pings of her text message notifications, and decided to go off grid for the remainder of the day. Hard as it was, she needed to be alone with her thoughts.

The landline rang. Her landline never rang. She left it. Then it rang again. This time it seemed foolish not to answer it; it might be important.

'Hello, is that Anouska?'

Anouska instantly recognised the voice: 'Calvin here, the producer from Northsound 1.'

'Hi, Calvin. Yes, thanks for today, it was worth a try.'

'Well, actually, we have a caller on Thea Goode's show hoping to speak to you now.'

Could it possibly be? No, it must be someone calling in response to her call from this morning. She rather wished they hadn't put her through this torture and she was about to say as much when she heard a familiar voice.

'Anouska, it's me. I'm so sorry about earlier. I dropped the phone into a vat of ragu in shock. We did try calling earlier, but there was no answer.'

She'd been in the bath with music up loud. Anouska tried not to smile at the image of Zach dropping his phone in the ragu. She also sensed it was not the time for talking. She listened.

'Anouska, I've been an idiot, I'm so sorry. I know the listeners won't know why I'm sorry, but that's not important. I love you. Could you ask me the question again that you asked me earlier?'

'I don't know. It was a once-in-a-lifetime offer,' Anouska said, smiling.

'I'd really appreciate it if you did. I'll beg if you want me to.' And this time Anouska could hear the smile in his voice.

'OK, I suppose so then. Zach Bedford, will you marry me?'

'Yes, yes, and a thousand times yes!'

'We're getting married,' she shouted. Then she jumped up and down for joy, fist pumping the air. She knew no one could see her, which made it even more liberating.

Dear, sweet Zach, her Zach, had agreed to marry her. They were having a baby and getting married. They were going to be a little family. She'd have that secure family unit she'd craved so much over the past few weeks.

Happy tears ran down her face and she wiped them away with her sleeve.

'I think we have a success story here, folks. And, we at Northsound 1, being the generous people we are, are sending you on an all-expenses-paid honeymoon to a destination of your choice to the value of three thousand pounds. So Cornwall or Canada, Devon or Dominica, you choose, we pay. So pleased for you guys, all the very best for the future, and please can you let us know when you've set a date. For now, from all of us here at Northsound 1, congratulations!' And Thea's voice gave way to the chorus of The Proclaimers' 'Let's Get Married'.

'So, Zach, what are you waiting for? Go get the girl.'

'I'm on my way home,' Zach said. 'Thanks, Thea. You've no idea what this means to me. And thanks for the honeymoon too.'

Anouska offered her thanks as well, then the next song began to play. The Supremes' 'Baby Love'. This time Anouska smiled at how apt the song choice was and decided to get herself into something a little sexier than jeans and a sweater. Being twelve weeks pregnant didn't stop her indulging in certain things just yet.

The second she came off the phone, her mobile started blowing up with texts and calls, which this time she answered.

I knew he'd say yes. So happy for you both. Congratulations. Todd x

OMG, I just heard. I'm so happy for you. Lauren x

The girl gets her guy. Congrats, my love. Leigh-Ann x

Who told Leigh-Ann? She hadn't even remembered to tell her she would be on air. Everything had happened so fast. Maybe she'd simply been listening to the radio at the right time.

Her phone rang. Ellie.

'Congratulations! OMG, you're getting married! Anouska, I am so happy for you.'

Anouska grinned at Ellie's excitement. She wasn't embittered by her own negative experience with Scott, if anything the opposite. She genuinely wanted Anouska and Jess' proposals to go well, for her friends to get married.

'Thank you. Zach's on his way here.'

'I won't keep you then, I just wanted to congratulate you, well, both of you, actually, all of you. Bean, too, obviously.'

Anouska laughed. 'Yep, it'll never just be the two of us ever again. Oh wow, that's a scary thought.'

'Indeed. So make the most of your time on your own, just the two of you. Text me when you come back up for air.'

'Ha. Wait, how did your date go?'

'Now there's a story, but that'll keep for another day. Upshot is, we're going out again tonight.'

'Brilliant. Stick that to Scott.'

'Funny, that's how I felt initially. Right, I'm really going now. Don't do anything I wouldn't do.'

'I don't think I can get myself in any more trouble, do you?'

'Oh, yeah, you're already pregnant. Fair point. Bye!'

Anouska grinned. She was lucky to have Ellie, and Jess. They made quite the team.

Twenty minutes later, Zach burst into the flat. Anouska didn't know who gravitated towards who first. All she knew was she was in his arms, he in hers and they were kissing with a passion she hadn't noticed in either of them in quite a while. Possibly not since Bean's conception.

When they broke apart, Zach said, 'Anouska, I'm so sorry. Stupid male pride. And I, pardon the pun, usually pride myself on not being a stereotypical alpha male, but I reverted to type with the way I reacted.'

'Don't worry,' Anouska reassured him as she stroked his cheek, gazing into his beautiful gunmetal grey eyes.

'I bolted when you needed me most. I have no excuse. I know guys aren't meant to get emotional, but it was too big for me. I'd just learned about the baby and then your mother threw the proposal thing at me and I flipped. Two of the biggest events or decisions of my life, and your mum knew them before me. I saw red. I'm so sorry. I've been such an idiot. Can you ever forgive me?' His eyes looked so doleful she almost wanted to laugh.

'I already have, Zach. We–' she pointed to her stomach '–already have. Haven't we, Bean?'

Zach placed his hand on her stomach. 'Hello, Bean. Daddy's back.'

Chapter Thirty-two

Ellie

Saturday 29 February

'Wow.' Spencer gave Ellie the once-over then said, 'You look amazing.'

The grin on his face made it quite clear that he liked the new look. Ellie was wearing a navy skater dress with woolly tights, it was February after all, and a cream sheepskin gilet. She was aiming for stylish, and was glad he thought she was a knockout. One point to her.

It was also a vast improvement on the last time he'd seen her, straight from work, blotchy, tear-stained face, snotty nose and puffy eyes, after she thought Scott had ruined everything for them.

Spencer's outfit of dark blue jeans and a cream Hollister jumper meant they matched.

'Twins.' He grinned.

'Great minds,' chuckled Ellie.

'I thought we'd go down to Leith tonight,' Spencer said as he handed her a planter filled with snowdrops. They were so sweet and so much prettier and more thoughtful than the stereotypical roses.

'Thanks. They're gorgeous. Give me two minutes and

I'll put them inside.'

When she returned, she locked her front door and followed him to his car. 'Leith sounds good. Where did you have in mind?'

'Ventura.' Spencer once again opened her door before getting into his own side. Again, Ellie gave an internal nod to his manners, and she definitely approved of his choice of restaurant, although the Michelin-starred eatery was a bit outside of her price range. As if reading her mind, he said, 'This is my treat tonight.' Ellie began to protest, but he silenced her with a 'You can pay next time – at Gleneagles.'

She laughed at that, the renowned golf resort a little too far away and also a bit out of her budget, even if she did get the new job.

'OK, you're on.' She knew if they had a next date, and she was warming to that idea, it wouldn't be Gleneagles.

Ellie had a hard time dragging her gaze away from Spencer to the menu to make her choices, and she loved the fact she could see the chefs in the kitchen, which had a large viewing window overlooking the restaurant. Already impressed with the surroundings, she thought if the food was as good as its reputation suggested, she would be in heaven. *Although*, a little devil voice reminded her, *you're already in heaven, because you're with Spencer.*

'So, you're off to Kuala Lumpur next week,' Ellie said when they'd chosen their starters.

'Yes, four days. And it's quite a long flight.'

'I've always wanted to visit the Petronas Towers.'

'They are pretty special. I love the walkway that separates them.'

'Yeah, although I'm not sure I could walk across it,' Ellie admitted.

'Scared of heights?

'No, quite the contrary. I like extreme sports, and I love watching the base jumpers jumping from the Petronas Towers, but only the most skilled could do it. Way out of my league, but I would wish I could do it, and I'd be annoyed I couldn't manage it.'

'You are a woman full of surprises.'

With a little thrill, Ellie could see that she had intrigued him. 'I've always liked extreme sports. Finding people to do it with is more difficult.'

'What other extreme sports do you do then?' Spencer asked.

Ellie counted off on her fingers. 'White-water rafting, bungee jumping, parasailing, kite-surfing, off-piste skiing.'

'You're quite the daredevil.' The impressed look on Spencer's face made Ellie laugh. 'So, who is the usual unlucky victim? Who do you take with you to participate in these "feats"?'

'Well, none of my friends are into it, so I registered with a club, and about once a month I go and do one of the activities.'

'And how did you get into it all? Are you an adrenaline junkie?' Spencer probed, taking his napkin and smoothing it out on his lap.

'Guilty as charged.' She grinned. 'I can't help it. I just love the feeling, the freedom.'

'Hmm.'

Ellie could see he didn't quite get it, but that was OK. She wasn't expecting him to, nor did she kid herself he would offer to join her.

'Anyway, enough about me, what else can you tell me about Kuala Lumpur?'

Spencer spent a good ten minutes rhyming off the places he'd been and advising Ellie on where to go, as well as telling her of a few spots he hadn't yet visited but were on his wish list.

'I have a Rough Guide for Malaysia. I'll lend it to you if you like,' Spencer said as their starters arrived. Ellie had opted for the mackerel, finding the snails and bone marrow a stretch too far even for her adventurous palate. She wasn't sure if she'd like the texture of snails and decided it was best not to throw up the contents of her dinner later. Spencer, on the other hand, had no such qualms.

'I first got into snails in Spain, in Andalusia, to be precise. You should try one.' He held one up, but she shook her head.

He could keep his snails. She liked to experiment with food, but she drew the line at snails.

'How's the mackerel?'

'Delicious.' In reality it was pinker than she would normally have eaten it, but she was generally willing to try something new. 'So, I take it you've been here before?'

'Yeah, my dad used to bring me here all the time before he passed.'

Ellie's face fell. 'I'm sorry.'

'It's OK, it was a few years ago now, but he taught me a lot about good food, so it's quite a passion of mine now.'

At the mention of the word 'passion', Ellie blushed, then pretended to cough so he didn't catch on to why she was turning red.

'Water?' Spencer offered her.

Ellie nodded, accepting the glass and taking a sip.

'So, tell me, what have you been up to since I last saw you?'

Ellie relayed what had been happening at work, with Trish's mentoring, a few other candidates who had declared for the job, and the fact she was feeling more than a little stressed. She didn't mention the role was in Manchester. She didn't want to spoil such a potentially wonderful friendship from blossoming before it even got out of the starting gate.

'Now there's a bigger pool of candidates, I'm a bit concerned the promotion may go to someone else.'

'That's only natural,' Spencer said, 'but these days half the time bosses know who's getting the job before it's been advertised.'

'True. Hopefully this time that will go in my favour.'

The waiters removed their empty plates and replaced them with wagyu beef for Spencer and lobster for Ellie. She was thoroughly enjoying the restaurant experience, but she was enjoying even more being in the company of such an intelligent, interesting, kind and generous man. And he was handsome too, always a bonus.

He stopped her talking about him too much and asked her plenty about herself. He was particularly interested in her love of extreme sports, which although he didn't share, he found fascinating. His words.

The evening flew past and all too soon they had to leave.

'Compliments to the chef,' Spencer told the waitress as he paid by card then discreetly left a generous tip on the counter.

'Thanks, Mr Delaney.'

Ellie scrunched up her eyebrows. 'Deference?'

Spencer laughed. 'Not sure about that. Mutual respect. They give me good service, and I come back time after time.'

Ellie liked the fact he hadn't said it was because of the huge tip he left. Unpretentious.

As they walked back to the car, Spencer said, 'I had a really good time, Ellie.'

'Me too.'

'I'm so glad we gave this another chance.'

'So am I.'

What was wrong with her? Why was she monosyllabic all of a sudden? She liked this guy. She really liked this guy. *Get it together, Ellie.*

'Spencer, I…'

He quirked an eyebrow. 'Yes?'

Could she do this? Could she be this forward? 'I-I really like you,' she stammered.

Spencer seemed to grow even taller, if that were possible. If he'd been a peacock he'd have been primping his feathers.

'That's good, because I really like you too.' His eyes shone, whether with happiness, amusement or lust, she wasn't sure, but she was hoping it was a mix of all three.

'Good.' She stood directly in front of him, her back against the car, and looked up at him, her eyes never leaving his.

He leant down slightly, but it was she who closed the distance between them first. As their lips touched, she wanted to groan. This was how it was meant to feel. It had never even come close with Scott. Not even at the beginning. Every touch of Spencer's lips sent wonderful messages to her synapses. She heard a moan. She couldn't tell if it came from Spencer or her. She didn't care. Their lips touched again, ever so lightly. It was almost torture, but it was exquisite torture and it sent a thousand tingles to every part of her body.

They deepened their kiss until it would have been indecent to continue. When they broke apart, they were both breathing heavily, and Ellie noted Spencer's eyes were glazed over with lust.

Spencer grinned. 'I can't believe I nearly let you go. What an idiot.'

'True,' said Ellie, earning a playful punch on the arm from Spencer. 'I can't believe you thought I was still *with* Scott. Didn't our body language give anything away?'

'I was a little far away, but it looked like he'd brought you a gift. You were both sending out mixed signals from where I was standing.'

'Oh, they definitely weren't mixed from my side. I told him not to bother me again. And he had brought me a gift. White Company, too, if you please. I thought about keeping it, since his gifts were always uninspired. Sorry, probably shouldn't diss an ex this early with someone new. Anyway, I changed my mind and told the receptionist to keep it. Didn't want any reminders of him around.'

'So, I'm your someone new, am I?' Spencer grinned.

'Oh, I think so. I mean you're a bit rough around the edges, but I'm sure I could whip you into shape.'

She cringed inwardly and moved a couple of strands of hair out of her face in a bid to play for time. Her attempt at humour had probably set off another image in Spencer's mind. It certainly had in hers. She glanced at him and he was visibly shaking with laughter.

'That didn't quite come out how you meant it, did it?'

Ellie grinned. 'Not exactly.'

He held the lapels of her coat together as if to ward off the cold. 'Could we meet up when I get back from Kuala Lumpur?'

'I'd like that. Maybe we could go rock climbing.'

Spencer blanched then laughed and gently hit her on the arm. 'Stop winding me up. I nearly fell for that.'

'What?' asked Ellie, pretending confusion. 'Fell for what?'

'We're not going rock climbing on a date.'

'Why not?'

Now he looked wrong-footed. Ha. He clearly didn't know if she was joking or not.

'Yeah, right, like I'd do that to you!' Now it was her turn to give him a playful pat on the arm.

'Phew! Don't do that. You had me going there.' He held his hand over his heart and Ellie couldn't help noting the long, well-cared for fingernails, the strong hands. Her mind wondered what those strong hands could do with her. Oh God, she had it bad. She tore her thoughts away from Spencer's strong hands to focus.

'Of course I wouldn't take you rock climbing on a fourth date.'

'Thank goodness for that.' Spencer opened the car door for her.

'I keep that in reserve for the tenth.'

Spencer turned and shot her a look. 'There's a new bouldering place nearby. Will that do?'

Ellie laughed for a full minute. Wuss.

On the drive back to Ellie's, they chatted about music and

books, architecture and sport, and it was more like a continuation of their date than a journey. Or a journey of discovery of each other. What was she like? Everything was a metaphor these days. She needed to snap out of it.

Spencer stopped the car outside Ellie's. As before, he came round her side and opened the car door for her. She didn't want to act out the clichéd romcom moment of fiddling with her keys, so she simply said, 'Thanks for tonight.'

'No problem.' Spencer must have sensed he wasn't being invited up as he leant in and kissed her, the type of instinctive kiss she'd hoped to receive from him, where she wanted nothing more than to drag him inside her flat and have him stay until morning, but she kept her resolve.

When they broke away his eyes were full of regret. 'I guess I'll just have to wait for Gleneagles,' he said as he walked away, throwing her a cheeky grin over his shoulder as he did so. Heartened by his parting comment, Ellie watched him go. Try as she might not to, she was falling for him and hard.

As he reached his car, she called after him, 'You might want to check your pockets.'

His brow furrowed. 'Why, have you pickpocketed me? Seriously, the luck I have with dates these days.'

'No, quite the opposite.' She stood, her arms wrapped around herself, warding off the chill February night air. Could it really be the first day of spring tomorrow? Hopefully the new season heralded new beginnings for her, with Spencer.

Spencer felt in the pockets of his overcoat, his lips curving into a smile as he found what she'd left for him.

Slowly, he withdrew it from his pocket and held it up.

'A key?'

She nodded.

'Your front door key?'

She nodded again.

'Are you inviting me up?'

She tilted her head to one side as if considering this idea. 'I guess I must be,' then she shrieked as he sprinted towards her and lifted her off the ground, swinging her round and round until she felt the breath leave her body.

Finally, he set her down and she regained her composure, brushing her curls back from her face as she took a deep breath in.

'Shall we?' Spencer said, key poised in the lock.

Tentatively, she took his outstretched hand. 'Oh, I think we should.'

As the door swung open, she said, 'I'll race you,' and as they darted up the stairs, Ellie felt younger and lighter than she'd done in years.

Chapter Thirty-three

Jess

Saturday 29 February

'This is incredible, Jess.' Mark stood awestruck, taking snap after snap of the Teatro Antico of Taormina.

She'd known as soon as she'd booked Sicily that they'd have to go to Etna. That was an absolute must-see, but she hadn't really known at that point what else there was to do in the surrounding area, or quite frankly, in Sicily.

So when Mark had professed a desire to see the Greek amphitheatre, which dated from the third century B.C., she'd been delighted at the possibility of a distraction. It might help settle her nerves. At the very least it would give her something else to think about.

Now that they were actually here, she admitted to being gobsmacked. To be standing in the midst of something so old, so ancient, was humbling. To imagine those who had gone before them was mind-blowing.

She gazed at the pillars, absorbing every last detail. When she glanced at Mark, he was staring at her, an odd expression on his face.

'Mark,' she called. No response. 'Mark,' she tried again. Nope, he was lost in a wee world of his own. 'Mark!'

He started then said, 'Sorry. What?'

'You were miles away.'

'Yeah, just thinking about how old this place is.' He looked down and read from the guide book. 'The Romans rebuilt it a century after the Greeks constructed it.'

'You have to wonder why they needed to,' Jess said. 'It looks amazing. And let's face it, the Romans were pretty good at building stuff. Think of all those roads we've got back home that are still there today.'

Mark nodded. 'Indeed, and walls.'

'Walls too,' Jess agreed. One of the walls, the Antonine Wall wasn't so very far from where they lived.

Mark was in his element, clicking away, then flipping through the guide book as Jess walked amongst the amphitheatre's ruins, transported back in time.

Occasionally, she'd turn round and he'd be standing staring at her, or into space; it was difficult to tell. Clearly, he was as overwhelmed by this place as she was.

'Ten thousand spectators. Flipping 'eck.'

Jess turned to see Mark waving the book at her as if she needed to see the words for validation.

'I believe you.' As she wandered around the amphitheatre and took in the views from it, she thought of all the plays that must have been performed here, and wondered if any of those studied at universities and colleges around the world today had actually been performed here all those centuries ago.

Her mind drifted until finally she felt a sense of peace wash over her. Was this an omen? A portent for this evening's potentially life-changing event?

As the driver took them back to the hotel, Mark showed Jess all the photos he'd taken.

'I'd forgotten how much I enjoy photography. I really must get back into it,' he'd enthused. 'Let's definitely come back here someday.'

At Jess' raised eyebrow, Mark said, 'What?'

'It's so unlike you to want to return to a place you've visited. All those pastures new waiting to be explored,' she teased him.

'I know, but this place is magical.' His eyes shone and a wave of love for him swept over her. 'Thanks, Jess. I know I've already thanked you for arranging everything for this trip, you duplicitous little witch.'

Jess widened her eyes, pretending to be offended.

'That's a term of endearment in some cultures, my sweet,' he said, laughing. 'But seriously, I have no idea how you came up with Taormina, or Sicily, as a destination, but well done, you.'

'*Cinema Paradiso*.'

Mark frowned. '*Cinema Paradiso?*'

'Yes, it's your favourite film,' Jess said simply.

'That's really why we're here? That's the connection?'

Jess nodded.

Mark blew out a breath. 'Thank God my favourite film franchise wasn't Star Wars then.'

'Ha, bloomin' ha!' said Jess, but she was smiling.

All that walking around the antiquities had tired Mark out as, on their return to the hotel, he declared he needed a nap. Whilst he went back to the room, Jess stayed in one of the communal sitting areas. Her phone beeped. She picked it up and saw she had a WhatsApp message from Ellie, Kelsea and Lauren, a photo of them holding up a placard saying *You Can Do It! Good Luck! xxx*. It was adorned with love hearts of various sizes. Despite her nervousness, she smiled. Kelsea and Lauren had always been there for her growing up. They'd even helped her choose her holiday wardrobe for this trip, whilst Ellie and Anouska had assisted her with the wording of her proposal, what she would wear on the night, when exactly she should propose. And Ellie and Anouska had both been so supportive since her decision to propose. She couldn't have done this without them. She wondered briefly how Anouska was doing.

Now here she was in Sicily and tonight was the night. The jitters had settled. She was going to propose. She wanted to have that happy ever after, with Mark. As had always been the plan. Not with Nathan, or anyone else, but with Mark.

She could only hope she didn't mess the whole thing up.

Two hours later, she figured she had better go check Mark was still alive, since he hadn't ventured out to look for her. She found him face down in the bed, sheets entangled around his bare limbs. He grunted as she closed the door, and changed position. Actually, viewed like that he was really quite sexy, apart from the rather unfortunate expression on his face. His asleep face.

She shook him awake. 'Mark. Mark! Time to get up. You need to grab a shower before dinner.'

'Ugh?'

Articulate as ever. Her Mark. Hopefully soon her

fiancé. Soon to be her husband, all going well.

They dressed for dinner in relative silence, Mark wearing a pair of black jeans and a new shirt he must have bought himself, as she certainly didn't recall buying it. Jess smoothed down the little black dress she and the girls had chosen for tonight – they'd decided to play it safe – an LBD never failed to impress, and this one was classy but sexy at the same time. Not too short, but flared out and with a sweetheart neckline.

Mark was watching some Italian game show on TV, leaving Jess alone with her thoughts. As she fastened her silver bracelet, a birthday present from Mark the year before, and did up the clasp on her Egyptian-style necklace, which Mark had bought her for Valentine's Day a few years ago, Jess mentally prepared herself for what she was about to do.

This was it. She was really going to do this.

The stars scintillated high above them in the inky blackness whilst fairy lights draped through the manna trees that surrounded the hotel lent the evening a magical feel. Jess' nerves had abated somewhat after the previous day's conversation with Mark about Nathan. He had forgiven her, so that was good, but what if he still wasn't ready, especially given her revelation, to take that final step? Well, she said final, but this would be their first step towards a new life together.

A crescent moon cast its light upon them as the waiter showed them to their table overlooking the olive groves. The location couldn't have been more perfect. The salty smell of the sea reached Jess as she listened to the lapping of the waves. Earlier, she'd noticed the hotel's guests were mainly Italian, which would explain why there weren't any other diners at this time. Italians tended to eat much later than Brits. So she and Mark had this glorious backdrop to themselves, this incomparable treasure of a panorama of the Mediterranean Sea. There really was no finer a setting to make the perfect proposal. She just hoped she didn't muck it up, and that he said yes.

The smiling waiter placed the *caponata Messinese* in front of them and Jess kicked herself for not proposing before dinner. At least then she could have enjoyed her meal without her stomach churning with nerves and anticipation, not quite in equal measure. The tomato and aubergine dish looked delicious and the aroma had her sniffing the air like a bloodhound. But her butterflies were back. Whilst Mark oohed and aahed over how fantastic it was, Jess picked at hers, trying to coax a couple of morsels down her throat, which had become drier than a sandstorm. She gulped down a few glugs of wine. It was flowing nicely. Too well perhaps. She didn't want to be drunk by the time she proposed, so she switched to sparkling water.

'Everything was OK?' the waiter asked as he removed their empty plates.

'*Perfetto.*' Mark tried out the little Italian he knew.

'Lovely,' Jess agreed. Should she do it now? Before the mains arrived? God, this was torture. Why hadn't she asked the waiter to hold the next course? It was too late now. He was coming back.

'For the signorina, *spaccatelle* and for you, sir, the *pasta alla Norma.*' The waiter beamed. 'Would you like anything else?'

Jess wondered if he could give her courage, but gathered that wasn't on the menu. To their headshake, he replied, '*Buon appetito!*'

'I feel as if we're in a whole different world here, Jess, don't you?' Mark sat back in his chair, having a much-needed breather after demolishing half of his aubergine and tomato-based pasta with salted ricotta. 'That pasta is amazing. It makes anything I've tried back home seem like the poor cousin, or the poor cousin's poor cousin.'

'I know what you mean.' Jess sighed in ecstasy. Her pasta with sun-dried tomato and burrata cheese was to die for. 'Don't you find it too much having aubergine for both starter and main?'

'Not at all.' Mark took a sip of his wine. 'Do you think we could stay here forever and never go back? I could get used to eating like this every day.'

'I'll buy you a cookbook when we get home.'

Mark raised his eyebrows at her. 'Hey, that was out of order.'

Mark couldn't cook much. The recent dinner he'd prepared for her had flabbergasted her. It was a definite one-off.

'You're still a young dog. I'm sure we can teach you some new tricks.'

'The new tricks you can teach me, all right, but I didn't plan on those being of the culinary variety.' He winked at her.

Jess rolled her eyes, but a half-smile rested on her lips. 'Promises, promises.' Fortunately, she'd begun to feel more relaxed and that boded well for her mission.

They skipped the traditional main course as they'd eaten the pasta course and both had a sweet tooth, plus Jess was desperate to try the *cannoli*. She'd had them at a friend's wedding once and loved them, but she was sure they'd be even better here in Sicily. How could they not? And Mark fancied *cassata*. The combination of chocolate sponge, marzipan, citrus fruits and sweetened ricotta cream that the menu mentioned had won him over.

'I'm glad you'd come back here,' Jess said. 'I know you usually prefer going somewhere we haven't been, but there's something special about this place, isn't there?'

Mark took another sip of wine then said, 'Yeah, the food.' He grinned. 'But seriously, I love it here. If I love it here in February, think how good it would be if it was warm, and we could laze about, getting a tan.'

Jess had to concede that it would have been lovely to have gone bathing in the azure waters of the outdoor pool, but although the temperature was far warmer than back in the UK, she would not be braving it this trip. It would have been nice to try the spa, she mused as she tried to tune in to what Mark was saying and at the same time work out in her head how and when to propose. She would have to make her move soon as they were almost finished dessert. Talk about best-laid plans.

'–so that's why I thought this was the perfect place,' she heard Mark say. She shook herself out of her reverie to give Mark her full attention, which was when he pushed back his chair and knelt on the floor in front of her.

'Jess, will you marry me?' He held out a navy velvet box, and looked up at her, a smile playing on his lips. Then he opened it to reveal an exquisite oval-cut emerald ring. His grandmother's wedding ring. *Oh my God!*

Jess was speechless. She didn't know whether to be delighted that he'd asked her, livid that he'd ruined *her* proposal or hacked-off that she'd spent months planning to ask him and sweated, literally, all through the meal over getting the proposal right, when all along *he'd* intended to propose to *her*. In the end, she went with the former.

'Yes! Yes! Oh Mark, I love you.'

'I know, and me you. We were always meant to be together. Always. Now it's official.' He stood up, crushing her to him, his lips meeting hers. 'Mrs Featherstone-to-be, I do declare it's time for some champagne.'

Jess hoped her face mirrored the joy on Mark's, as right then she couldn't have felt more loved, more sure of his feelings for her, purely from the sincerity in his gaze. Her heart swelled, and she returned his kisses passionately and briefly wondered whether to tell him she'd been planning to ask him. She decided that would be a funny story best kept for another day.

When they broke apart, Mark said, 'You have no idea how hard this has been to keep from you. Honestly, I've been trying to ask you for weeks, walking about with the ring box in my pocket then worrying I'll lose it.'

Jess laughed. 'So why didn't you ask me before?'

Mark held his hands out. 'I don't know. It just didn't feel right, and one thing I knew for sure was, I wanted it to be perfect. Here's perfect, don't you think?'

She glanced around at the olive groves, then at the waves crashing below them on the beach. 'Pretty perfect.'

'Good, because we'll need to come back here for our anniversary.'

Jess paused. 'Is that why you asked me the other day if I'd come back here?'

Mark nodded. 'You know me, I don't like to go to the same place twice, but I thought we may want to return to the scene of the crime, so to speak.'

Jess punched him playfully on the chest. 'Hey you! That's no way to speak of our engagement.'

Mark laughed and grabbed her again in a bear hug, then rocked them from side to side.

Jess frowned. 'One other thing. You honestly planned all this by yourself and didn't breathe a word to anyone?'

'Are you kidding? No. I had to seek advice from someone who'd been there, done that. That's why I was out with Jared, and for so long. Although, to be honest, by the end of our drinking session, I'm not sure if he'd convinced me that getting married was a great idea or the exact opposite. He and Livorna have some epic fights, apparently.'

Jess bit her lip as she considered this. 'Yeah, I could see that being the case. He is very high maintenance.'

Mark's eyebrows shot up. 'He is? She's an influencer, for goodness' sake.'

'Ha! Got you going. Yes, much as I love Livorna, she's high maintenance. Anyway, he must have said something positive or we wouldn't be here now … engaged.'

Mark smiled and wound his hand round her waist. 'I like the sound of that.'

'That makes two of us,' Jess said, leaning into his embrace.

As the Prosecco flowed – it seemed rude to ask for champagne in Italy – and they excitedly began to make plans for the wedding: the guest list, the venue, the menus, the music, the location, the best man and bridesmaids, Jess couldn't help thinking, *Wait till I tell the girls. They'll never believe me.*

Chapter Thirty-four

Eight months later

'A bit more to the right,' Spencer called.

Everyone shuffled about a foot to the right and Ellie watched as the proud parents beamed with happiness and gazed down at their baby daughter, their love for her shining in their eyes.

'That's it. That's the shot.' Spencer, who considered himself a half-decent amateur photographer, had been persuaded to take the photographs at Luciana's christening. Ellie surveyed her boyfriend, who seemed to be enjoying his role. Hard to believe they had only met eight months before.

'She's gorgeous, Anouska,' she said as Anouska jiggled baby Luciana, who flashed a gummy smile, chubby little legs bicycling beneath the heavy christening gown as she tried to wriggle out of her mother's grasp.

'Here, let me,' Todd interrupted, scooping Luciana out of her mother's arms. 'It's our turn for the photos anyway. Spencer, we were photo number eight, weren't we?'

Spencer nodded.

As they stood on the lawn, which by some miracle they hadn't sunk into, despite the rains of the past week, Spencer said, 'Are you ready for your Marlon Brando moment?'

Todd chuckled.

They stood together as Spencer snapped away, taking shot after shot of the godfather and the baby who had won a place in everyone's heart. Anouska hadn't even thought twice about who should be godfather. Todd was already a member of the family in every way that mattered.

'Right, Jess, you and Mark are next,' Ellie said. Spencer had put her in charge of the running order of the photos. Well, he had handed her a list, which was virtually the same thing.

Jess and Mark posed for a photo together, then Jess settled Luciana in her arms and Spencer told them which way to stand.

'He's getting very bossy,' said Zach.

Ellie laughed. Since February, despite the distances that separated them and their various commitments, the girls and their partners had met up on several occasions and fortunately had all got on really well together.

'He is.' Ellie smiled. 'I think it could become a vocation for him.'

'Yeah, or he could set up a joint graphic design/wedding photographer business.'

'Indeed.' Changing the subject, Ellie asked, 'So, a proud moment for you, Zach?'

'Absolutely. I have to confess I didn't think I'd ever be a dad, what with Anouska working so hard all the time and never staying in one place, and me being married to the bistro, but I'm absolutely loving being Luciana's father. I'm also glad Anouska agreed to hire someone to manage the day to day so she can take her full maternity leave.'

'Me too. Shows you how much things can change from

one year to the next.'

'Too right. Talking of changes, I hear you guys are making some.'

Ellie let her champagne slide down before answering, 'Yeah, Spencer asked me to move in with him. The removal van's booked for a few days before Christmas. Then we'll look for a house next year, maybe in North Berwick.'

'Very nice. We'll definitely be visiting. And how's the new job going?'

Ellie knew she was gushing but couldn't help it. 'I love it. It's what I've always wanted and I have so much autonomy it's unbelievable. I've only been doing it six months, but already I've brought in quite a few measures that have made a big difference, or so I'm told.'

'That's great news. It has been quite a year for you.'

'It certainly has,' Ellie said, unable to prevent herself from drawing a comparison between now and this time last year. Thank goodness she had finally seen Scott for who he truly was, and thank goodness Faraway Shores Travel had decided, at her suggestion, that their new director could be Edinburgh-based after all.

Jess came over after Spencer had taken their shots; Mark had been waylaid by Todd.

'So, how are the wedding plans coming along?' Ellie asked.

'Good, thanks. Too many of them, mind you, but I think we're getting there. After much debate, we're having it in a mountain resort in Valle D'Aosta in Italy. Not too many guests. It's some trek up those mountains, but the setting of the lake at night with the Alps reflecting in it is incredible. Once I saw the pictures my brother had taken on holiday there, I knew I didn't want to get married anywhere else.'

'Sounds really cool.'

'It is. I can't wait to marry Mark there on New Year's Eve.' Her whole face lit up as she spoke.

Ellie laughed. 'Well, you did say you wanted to be married this year.'

Jess smiled. 'I like to go after what I want, and at least I got first dibs on the date of the wedding, after Mark hijacked my proposal.'

Ellie laughed. 'I still can't believe he did that. What are the chances?'

'Chances of what?' Anouska, in a classy, just above-the-knee fitted rose gold dress looked incredible for someone who'd given birth only two months before.

'Mark proposing when Jess was about to,' Zach explained. 'Right, ladies, we're being summoned again. I'll leave you three to chat.'

'Oh, remember you still have to send me the hotel details for the wedding so we can book,' Ellie told Jess, who nodded. Ellie watched Anouska, who seemed distracted by the sight of Zach holding his daughter high over his head, then bringing her down to his face and kissing her. Luciana gurgled in glee before he repeated the process.

'Anouska, are you guys going to make the wedding?'

'Wouldn't miss it. I've already asked my mum if she can take Luciana that weekend.'

Jess' forehead creased. 'Have you ever been apart from her?'

'No, but there's a first time for everything. I can't bring a screaming baby to a wedding now, can I?'

They all admitted that wasn't perhaps the best idea.

'But your mum could come to the wedding and look

after Luciana there, if you like. There's plenty of room at the hotel.'

'Are you sure?' Anouska's eyebrows scrunched together. 'I don't want my darling girl ruining your big day.'

'Whose big day?' Mark cut in.

'Ours.' Jess entwined her fingers with Mark's. 'I was just saying Luciana should come too.'

'Definitely.' Mark nodded. 'The more the merrier.'

'Actually, there's something I wanted to ask you both,' Jess said, turning to Ellie and Anouska.

'What is it?' Anouska asked, raising a finely plucked eyebrow.

'Will you two be my bridesmaids?'

Ellie flung her arms around Jess. 'Of course we will. Right, Anouska?'

'Of course. We can't say no, can we?' Anouska grinned.

'No,' the others all chorused.

'I'm not having any flower girls, though. Perhaps if Luciana was a bit older, she could have auditioned,' Jess said.

'Yes, although she might have stolen the show,' Mark put in.

'Hey!' His fiancée nudged him with her elbow.

Anouska cleared her throat. 'I also have an announcement to make.'

Jess and Ellie both wore quizzical expressions as they waited for Anouska to enlighten them. 'Zach and I are getting married next year, on the twenty-eighth of February, in Dunrobin Castle in Scotland. And naturally you're all invited.'

'Oh, Anouska, I'm so happy for you both,' Ellie exclaimed.

'A wedding in a Scottish castle. I can't wait. How romantic,' pitched in Jess.

Anouska put her arms around Jess and Ellie. 'Group hug.'

And right there, right then, Ellie knew they would be friends for life.

Todd appeared beside them, Spencer trailing behind him. 'OK, you lot, let's get a shot of the three couples together, and Luciana, of course.'

As they arranged themselves into their pairings, Todd took the camera from Spencer and clicked away. 'Just one more,' he said. 'Right, done.'

When the couples moved apart again, Ellie's eye caught Spencer's and he grinned. How she loved this man. She couldn't wait to spend the rest of her life with him. She just hoped he'd take the initiative and propose to her at some point, because she didn't think she could wait another four years to ask him!

Author's Note

Did you get your free short stories yet?

TWO UNPUBLISHED EXCLUSIVE SHORT STORIES.

Interacting with my readers is one of the most fun parts of being a writer. I'll be sending out a monthly newsletter with new release information, competitions, special offers and basically a bit about what I've been up to, writing and otherwise.

You can get the previously unseen short stories, *Mixed Messages* and *Time Is of the Essence*, FREE if you sign up to my mailing list.
www.susanbuchananauthor.com

Did you enjoy *The Leap Year Proposal*?

I'd really appreciate if you could leave a review on Amazon. It doesn't need to be much, just a couple of lines. I love reading customer reviews. Seeing what readers think of my books spurs me on to write more. Sometimes I've even written more about characters or created a series because of reader comments. Plus, reviews are SO important to authors. They help raise the profile of the author and make it more likely that the book will be visible on Amazon to more readers. Every author wants their book to be read by more people, and I am no exception!

COMING MAY 2025!

You Can't Hurry Love
A 30th birthday celebration. A sloth sanctuary in Costa Rica. A split-second decision.

When Kat MacDonald takes the trip of a lifetime to Costa Rica, she doesn't count on ditching her dead-end job, sending her uber-controlling boyfriend packing and volunteering at a sloth sanctuary.

But when she finally meets the swoon-worthy assistant manager Dexter, the chemistry between them is unmistakeable and sparks fly. Despite a rival for his affections, and her ex's inability to know when to give up, she and Dexter are drawn to each other like magnets.

Just as she's settling into life at the sanctuary and making friends, a letter arrives from back home in Scotland. A letter which could both upset her new plans and give her everything she has ever wanted. Everything except Dexter.

Kat is torn: should she stay in the tropical rainforest paradise with her beloved sloths, new friends and the delectable Dexter or pursue her lifelong dream? Or can she find a way to have it all?

A fun, escapist read full of romance, gorgeous scenery and humour, perfect for fans of Emily Henry, Beth O'Leary and Portia MacIntosh.

Have you read them all?

The Dating Game

Work, work, work. That's all Glaswegian recruitment consultant Gill does. Her friends fix her up with numerous blind dates, none suitable, until one day Gill decides enough is enough.

Seeing an ad on a bus billboard for Happy Ever After dating agency 'for the busy professional', on impulse, she signs up. Soon she has problems juggling her social life as well as her work diary.

Before long, she's experiencing laughs, lust and … could it be love? But just when things are looking up for Gill, an unexpected reunion forces her to make an impossible choice.

Will she get her happy ever after, or is she destined to be married to her job forever?

Just One Day – Winter

Thirty-eight-year-old Louisa has a loving husband, three wonderful kids, a faithful dog, a supportive family and a gorgeous house near Glasgow. What more could she want?

TIME.

Louisa would like, just once, to get to the end of her never-ending to-do list. With her husband Ronnie working offshore, she is demented trying to cope with everything on her own: the after-school clubs, the homework, the appointments … the constant disasters. And if he dismisses her workload one more time, she may well throttle him.

Juggling running her own wedding stationery business with family life is taking its toll, and the only reason Louisa is still sane is because of her best friends and her sisters.

Fed up with only talking to Ronnie about household bills and incompetent tradesmen, when a handsome stranger pays her some attention on her birthday weekend away, she is flattered, but will she give in to temptation? And will she ever get to the end of her to-do list?

Just One Day – Spring

Mum-of-three Louisa thought she only had her never-ending to-do list to worry about, but the arrival of a ghost from the recent past puts her in an untenable position. Can she navigate the difficult situation she's in without their friendship becoming common knowledge or will it cause long-term damage to her marriage?

When a family member begins to suspect there's more to her relationship with the new sous-chef than meets the eye, Louisa needs to think on her feet or she'll dig herself into a deeper hole. But the cost of keeping her secret, not only from her husband, comes at a high price, one which tugs at her conscience.

With everyday niggles already causing a further rift between Louisa and husband Ronnie, will she manage to keep her family on track whilst her life spirals out of control? And when tragedy strikes, will Ronnie step up when she needs him most?

Just One Day – Summer

List-juggling, business-owner mum-of-three Louisa is reeling after a tragedy, as well as learning how to cope after a life-changing revelation. With oil worker husband Ronnie possibly being able to move onshore, she hopes he can help her manage the burden.

But the secrets she keeps are causing her headaches and she's unsure if her ability to make good decisions has deserted her. All she seems to do is upset those around her.

With Louisa's to-do list gathering pace at an incredible speed, will she manage to provide a stable home for them all, embrace her new normal as well as rebuild their life from what's left?

And if she gets what she has always wanted, will it match up to her expectations?

Just One Day – Autumn

Pregnant Louisa is just getting back on track when life throws her another curveball. Now, it's not a case of how she'll get through her to-do lists but how she'll manage being a mum again.

No one seems to understand. How will she run her company, be partner in a new venture, look after her three kids and handle a newborn? And why does everyone think this will be easy? Except her.

All Louisa wants is to be a good mum, wife, friend, sister and daughter, and have a bit of time left for herself, but sometimes that's too big an ask. Can she find the support she needs, or will she forever be pulled in too many directions, always at the mercy of her to-do lists?

The Christmas Spirit

Natalie Hope takes over the reins of the Sugar and Spice bakery and café with the intention of injecting some Christmas spirit. Something her regulars badly need.

Newly dumped Rebecca is stuck in a job with no prospects, has lost her home and is struggling to see a way forward.

Pensioner Stanley is dreading his first Christmas alone without his beloved wife, who passed away earlier this year. How will he ever feel whole again?

Graduate Jacob is still out of work despite making hundreds of applications. Will he be forced to go against his instincts and ask his unsympathetic parents for help?

Spiky workaholic Meredith hates the jollity of family gatherings and would rather stay home with a box set and a posh ready meal. Will she finally realise what's important in life?

Natalie sprinkles a little magic to try to spread some festive cheer and restore Christmas spirit, but will she succeed?

Return of the Christmas Spirit

Christmas is just around the corner when the enigmatic Star begins working at Butterburn library, but not everyone is embracing the spirit of the season.

Arianna is anxious about her mock exams. With her father living abroad and her mother working three jobs to keep them afloat, she doesn't have much support at home.

The bank is threatening to repossess Evan's house, and he has no idea how he will get through Christmas with two children who are used to getting everything they want.

After 23 years of marriage, Patricia's husband announces he's moving out of the family home and moving in with his secretary. Patricia puts a brave face on things, but inside, she's devastated and lost.

Stressed-out Daniel is doing the work of three people in his sales job, plus looking after his kids and his sick wife. Pulled in too many different directions, he hasn't even had a chance to think about Christmas.

Can Star, the library's Good Samaritan, help set them on the path to happiness this Christmas?

A Little Christmas Spirit
CAN A SPRINKLE OF MAGIC HEAL BROKEN HEARTS THIS CHRISTMAS?

With Jacob now at the helm at the cosy Sugar and Spice café, it's the perfect opportunity for Christmas Spirit Lara to weave her magic.

Fraser is floundering in his new role as headteacher as he grapples with guilt over having to place his beloved mother in a care home, leaving him feeling lost and alone during what should be a joyful time.

Meanwhile, school janitor Paul is torn between his desire to feel needed and the pressure from his wife to retire, dimming the season's sparkle.

Valerie, overwhelmed by the demands of newborn twins, feels she's not giving her other daughter enough attention. She needs a bit of me time and for her husband to realise the responsibility for the kids falls to both of them.

And Bella, heartbroken after her husband's shocking request for a separation just a year into their marriage, longs to escape the memories of last year's perfect Christmas.

Can Lara help them rediscover joy, connection, and the true spirit of the season?

Sign of the Times

Sagittarius – Travel writer Holly heads to Tuscany to research her next book, but when she meets Dario, she knows she's in trouble. Can she resist temptation? And what do her mixed feelings mean for her future with her fiancé?

Gemini – Player Lucy likes to keep things interesting and has no qualms about being unfaithful to her long-term boyfriend. A cardiology conference to Switzerland changes Lucy, perhaps forever. Has she met her match, and is this feeling love?

Holly is the one who links the twelve signs. Are you ready to meet them all?

A tale of love, family, friendship and the lengths we go to in pursuit of our dreams.

Printed in Great Britain
by Amazon